Praise for *Winter Phoenix*

"Wildly inventive in its experiments with abecedarian form and Morse code, the collection explores the complicated legacy of English, asking us what it means for court proceedings to unfold in the language of the abuser . . . Terazawa's striking imagery draws attention to the fact that atrocity often unfolds amid beauty and asks us to consider what it means to find stunning images in times of trauma."   —Layla Benitez-James, Harriet Books (Poetry Foundation)

"In her debut, Terazawa, daughter of a Vietnamese refugee, considers the colonial and linguistic legacy of the Vietnam war in a work comprising imagined testimonies in verse."

—*Publishers Weekly*, Maya Popa

Tetra Nova tells the story of Lua Mater, an obscure Roman goddess who re-imagines herself as an assassin coming to terms with an emerging performance artist identity in the late twentieth century.

The operatic text of *Tetra Nova* begins in Saigon, where Lua Mater meets a little girl named Emi, an American of Vietnamese-Japanese descent visiting her mother's country for the first time since the war's end. As the voices of Lua and Emi blend into one dissociated narration, the stories accelerate out of sequence, mapping upon the globe a series of collective memories and traumas passed from one generation to the next.

Darting between the temples of Nagasaki, the mountains of Tucson, and an island refugee camp off the coast of Malaysia, Lua and Emi in one embodied memory travel across the English language itself to make sense of a history neither wanted. When a tiny Panda named Panda suddenly arrives, fate intervenes, and the work acts as a larger historical document, unpacking legacies of genocide and the radical modes of resistance that follow.

At the heart of this production lies a postcolonial identity in exile, and the performers must come to terms with who may or may not carry their stories forward: Emi or Lua. Part dreamscape, part investigative poetics, *Tetra Nova* sees multiple fragmenting identities traverse across time and space, the mythic and the profane, toward an understanding of humanity beyond those temple chamber doors.

ALSO BY SOPHIA TERAZAWA

Winter Phoenix

Anon

Tetra Nova

a novel

Sophia Terazawa

DEEP VELLUM PUBLISHING

DALLAS, TEXAS

Deep Vellum Publishing
3000 Commerce St., Dallas, Texas 75226
deepvellum.org · @deepvellum

Deep Vellum is a 501c3 nonprofit literary arts organization
founded in 2013 with the mission to bring
the world into conversation through literature.

Support for this publication has been provided in part by the National Endowment for the Arts, the Texas Commission on the Arts, the City of Dallas Office of Arts and Culture, the Communities Foundation of Texas, and the Addy Foundation.

ISBNs: 978-1-64605-356-8 (paperback) | 978-1-64605-368-1 (ebook)

LIBRARY OF CONGRESS CATALOGING-IN-PUBLICATION DATA
Names: Terazawa, Sophia, author.
Title: Tetra nova : a novel / Sophia Terazawa.
Description: First US edition. | Dallas, Texas : Deep Vellum Publishing,
2025.
Identifiers: LCCN 2024030281 (print) | LCCN 2024030282 (ebook) | ISBN
9781646053568 (trade paperback) | ISBN 9781646053681 (ebook)
Subjects: LCSH: Lua (Roman deity)--Fiction. | LCGFT: Magic realist fiction.
| Mythological fiction. | Psychological fiction. | Novels. | Novels.
Classification: LCC PS3620.E736 T48 2025 (print) | LCC PS3620.E736
(ebook) | DDC 813/.6--dc23/eng/20240709
LC record available at https://lccn.loc.gov/2024030281
LC ebook record available at https://lccn.loc.gov/2024030282

Front Cover Design by David Wojciechowski
Interior Layout and Typesetting by KGT

PRINTED IN CANADA

Grateful acknowledgment to the editors of the following journals in which smaller pieces of this book were published, sometimes in earlier forms: *Black Sun Lit, Fence, The Journal, The Offing, Passengers Journal, The Rumpus,* and *SAND Journal.*

for Isaac

NEAR THE TEMPLE
chamber to my heart, I wrote
a list of facts and then a list
of plums. One spoke, as if in
conversation, with the other—

1.

A calf reached for my hand.
I took its trunk in delirium,
cradling this thing like
some lost part of me had
finally returned. No, I was
mistaken.

The mother blared, at once,
soaring up on her hind legs;
her eyes shot ablaze; her
trunk stiffened into a hook,
charging like a fireball my
way.

2.

When I came to, after an
immeasurable dip across
time, I sensed the elephants
had left long ago. Under
my body, the ground had
molded into a tray.

I blinked. Shadowy trees
shifted around warping their
shapes: tamarind or copper-
pod. The back of my skull
felt magnetized though soft.
Padded.

3.

At first, I could only turn my
head a bit to the right, and
then in total concentration,
slowly, painfully, to the front
again. Heat rippled through
me.

My neck had sunk, as if
into a pothole, just below
my shoulders. I had lost
my elbows. I had no more
fingers or ankles; gone, too,
were my kneecaps.

4.

My ears then seemed to have shriveled and traveled up the sides of my face. I could still wiggle both, but alarmingly they were fixed atop my head.

It was dark. I found a way to stand upright by popping onto my buttocks. I wobbled a step or two forward, trying to recall where I was initially going.

5.

Not before too long,
looming in front of me
was the entrance to what
appeared to drop into a
cavern, square-shaped like
the kanji for 'mouth.'

From inside, perhaps
ascending a flight of stairs
with their four paper
lanterns, a dull force drew
me closer and closer until I
fell straight through.

6.

When I woke for the second
time, I felt my body had
returned to its original
container, with an ear on
either side of my face and
skin I could touch.

Yes, I said to myself. I was
Emi. I had toes to wiggle, a
backpack with crayons, and
my notebooks. It dawned on
me suddenly what this place
was.

7.

For it was here, in this temple chamber to my heart, where I was bound to meet my past and future shaped by air, water, fire, and earth.

From my backpack, I took out a red crayon and began marking the floor with kanji for 'enter,' 'hurry,' and 'exit.' Oddly, it cooled the chamber.

8.

What kept me going, guiding me forward like over any dream, was a vague 'you.' I wrote to that 'you,' even as *you* changed constantly.

For instance, you had formed, at first, in a two-dimensional box. You multiplied next into four, connected as a single unit rising from the kanji 'exit.'

9.

You were all lit from within,
a neon hue of chartreuse.
Without a face, lips, or
visible source of energy,
you hummed and droned at
varying speeds.

I was startled when you
began slipping around
each other, rotating and
making a sequence of
tetrads I recognized from an
arcade puzzle game.

10.

Your humming voice hardened afterward, forming syllables and words in noticeable English. I took out a notebook from my backpack to write.

The pages filled with your sentences, with blocks of images and sounds, thick with a kind of desperation that both bewildered and weakened me.

FROM THE BLUE NOTEBOOK

"Do not ask too many questions. Do not push for details, colors, time. Your mother owns one photograph that proves she was a refugee. Do not include it in your manuscript of insurrection. Look as closely as you can. Zoom in, much closer still. Your mother stares out from the photograph. Two hard black marble eyes and cheekbones that could cut through stone. Betray her trust. Include the photo anyway, those eyes and cheekbones that could cut through time. Betray what you once knew of trust. Somewhere nearby, a mother eats the body of her child. Somewhere nearby, a child shields the body of her mother. 'No, don't shoot.' Your mother asks if you can write it down, the truth, that is, two dark brown rings of ash. You nod. She nods. 'Okay, so write this down, my child.' Nod, again, and close your eyes to write, a sea of ash, then count from one to three, then listen as the woman speaks with little interruption."

FROM THE BLUE NOTEBOOK

"Do not push for details, pseudonyms for flowers, any span of weeks or months it took for her to either land upon or leave, eventually, that island near Malaysia. Hear yourself ask questions anyway. 'Who took this photograph and why? How did you get a copy, too? What memories insist upon deflection? But did you cry? What were you forced to do? Mama, who am I now to you?'"

FROM THE BLUE NOTEBOOK

"Do not ask about your mother's memories inside the refugee camp. Many years ago, she told you, once, she crawled out of the sea. Half-skeleton and rags. Do not ask for clarifying notes about the salt, blood, or feces caked over her skin. It caked the whole boat, too, she claims. 'But anyway,' she grins and looks away, her face shifting again to three or four or five disjointed parts. 'It does not matter anymore, the year.' It never does. 'Mama must live.' You hear her say. You answer. 'Yes, Mama, you do.'"

CITATIONS

David Duncan, the American photojournalist known for taking wartime photographs in Vietnam, once challenged the US government's intentions in my mother's country. When he stood before the Veterans Memorial in 1992, he also commented: "The Wall is a sad and intimate place." And then: "But remembering does not come easily to Americans. Maybe this is why the Wall is particularly painful for us, because it stands for something we want to forget."

David Duncan died in 2018 at the age of 102, peacefully, in the French city of Grasse, perfume capital of the world. On my mother's birthday.

CITATIONS

"Staying Vietnamese," the scholar Karin Aguilar-San Juan writes in Little Saigons, *her 2009 book, "requires a strategic and purposeful encounter not only with race and racialization but also with the past."*

I thought about this act of "staying" when I called my mother on the first day of July, the day I traveled from Tucson—stowing in my bag: books and a tiny stuffed plush I've named Panda—toward this country's southern border. "Why?" My mother asked. I heard the fear sparking beneath her voice. I answered: "Because, Mama, I need to see and write about what's happening." "Why?" She asked again. "Because, Mama, this is our history, too." I felt myself soften to jelly, taking care with every word. "But, why!" She shouted through the phone. I didn't know what else to say.

CITATIONS

My childhood was filled with all my mother's stories of escape, which were both unpredictable and permanently charred into the landscape of my brain. Beneath all this, she'd always seem to push me forward and then backward with that single one-word question: Why? Why think beyond what we can see before us as a fact? Why dream? Or why speak of the past? She'd wield most of these why's like accusations of betrayal stitched across my corneas, the child noticing the signs her mother had forgotten, worst of all, the child who then dares to write some of it down.

In Nogales, though, a wall of migrant faces stood resilient against the border's charge against them. I'd write that summer after David Duncan laid to rest beneath a field of lavender. I'd think about what memories still sought asylum with the words my mother never said. Her portrait at the refugee camp pushed me why, why, why, I needed to remember, too, and why I always felt the pull to search for her between the cracks of other borders and their current points of entry, but I did not know, rather, I did not have the language yet to tell her what I meant when I said that this was an intersecting history, and what we made of it reflects upon our past as it informs the present.

CITATIONS

The man: *"¿Cuántos días en el mar?"*
The woman: *"Tres semanas."*

The man: *"¿Y tu familia?"*
The woman: *"Mi madre adoptiva murió en el barco."*

The man: *"¿Y tu verdadera familia?"*
The woman: *"Me dijeron que había perdido a mi familia hacía mucho."*

—Hòn vọng phu (1991)

CITATIONS

I can't speak Vietnamese or Spanish, but I'm trying to learn. Through watching films, I find the subtitles sometimes carry me along.

"How many days at sea," says the man during a quiet scene in Hòn vọng phu, *a relatively unknown short film by Trần Anh Hùng in 1991. The setting is a refugee camp. Perhaps the man without a name isn't anonymous in the end. The woman, his long-lost sister. Strange, how we meet like this. Strangest creatures suffering with each other.*

The title of the couple's tragedy would be translated to "La pierre de l'attente" upon its DVD release in France eight years later, and I watch a clip of it tonight at my kitchen table in Tucson. The clip is short. Someone's added Spanish subtitles. I stop after each line to transcribe its text into Google Translate, hoping somehow to learn both languages at once, that of belonging to my mother and that of living, here, so close to what Gloria E. Anzaldúa once called "gashing a hole under the border fence" in Borderlands/La Frontera.

CITATIONS

In Hòn vọng phu, *the man eventually inquires if the woman speaks French. The woman, in response, lowers her eyes. To this, the man explains in Vietnamese, translated in the subtitle: "Para abandonar este campo, es necesario aprenderlo. To leave this camp, it is necessary to learn it." In other words, he says to earn our freedom, we must learn the language of the people who once killed our people. Here, I've come to learn that crossing through the ocean and the desert aren't so different after all.*

CITATIONS

In Voices of Vietnamese Boat People, *Binh Le (pseudonym) writes:* "You *must be wondering what happened to my mother.*"

FROM THE BLUE NOTEBOOK

"Ask about the romance. Ask if people fell in love despite the imminence of violent death. And of her nights at camp, listen as your mother answers. 'So many noises in the dark.' She giggles. Ask another question. 'Mama, how did you know that it was love?' She answers. 'Passage of time, simple as that.' Then, desire less. Desire more. Ask if people could betray the ones they loved despite all the *noises in the dark.*"

11.

Were you my spirit, I
wondered at the back of
this chamber. How long
were you at sea? Would
your response trap us in its
writing?

CITATIONS

"¿Y tu familia?"

"¿Y tu verdadera familia?"

FROM THE BLUE NOTEBOOK

"Ask about the truth. Then ask, again, about the romance. Know that one might cancel out the other. Do not ask any more questions. Count backward, three to one. Desire more. Desire less. 'And of your family?' 'You are my family.' She answers. Know that one might cancel out the other. Ask another question. 'Who am I to you now, Mama?' Watch your mother blink. 'The truth.' 'Who are you now?' 'Three weeks at sea.'"

12.

This brought me to recall
a desert winter day when
I woke up with the skin
of my naked left hip, arm,
and shoulder pressed into
morning earth.

It was overcast. Near my
feet, having just uncurled
from a ball, stood a tiny
figure I knew to be Panda.
He had then struck a curious
posture.

13.

With a Cupid's pose, the
tiny Panda held, in one paw,
a dried legume. The ground
shook open. A cold and
swift drizzle fell.

14.

I tumbled into a new
chamber with green rubber
flooring. Each wall was
covered, up to the ceiling, in
dark gymnastic mats.

Here, you were busy
regrouping your four
bodies, hissing and spitting
until you settled on a wholly
different form—

FAINT BLUE
& WINDOW
IN ASYLUM

☐   ☐   ☐   ☐

CITATIONS

No contact zone: a splintering red torch, the twisted myrtle hedge, day 23. I write this landscape thick with waiting. First, on Valentine's Day, 2017, an old woman explains the pillow that she sleeps with every night. Red branches unfurl in my mind, peeling a calendar, the pillow in her arms wrapped tightly in a large Vietnamese flag.

CITATIONS

Both entering and departing the demilitarized zone of forbidden desire, a lack of contact between two people may be punctuated by not knowing when or how one might return to the other, wherein, tucked between both flag and pillow is an army shirt belonging to the young Japanese soldier who had left the young Vietnamese woman behind in 1954, one of 600 soldiers of Japanese descent who had chosen to stay in Hanoi after another military occupation ended earlier that fall.

"This is my husband," says the now elderly Vietnamese widow, cuddling her pillow.

I think about my mother, also, cuddling her pillow named after my father, also, Japanese and left somewhere within the contact zone, and lately, how my body wraps the extra pillow in my bed at night when I start missing you, again, my sweet, blue Neptune.

CITATIONS

There are days when there are shades of reclamation closer to the flame. For instance, in the Vietnamese language, there is a word for unrequited love as a consequence of war through foreign dominance, but I don't know it yet. Suppose 1,000 years of revolution led by women would prepare us to decolonize our hearts, but, still, I push my face into a pillow named after your face alone and squish its waist as I would squish your waist with both my arms and legs.

"He spoke really good Vietnamese and often whispered Vietnamese songs," says the widow, to which the journalist from Reuters, *here, politely nods, reporting on the current state of wounds between two countries, marked by famine, brutal treatment by one people toward another, fascism leading to twenty further years of bloodshed.*

No contact zone: a state of turning from you, Neptune.

Likewise, by the time I turned 420 years of age, I knew that love was given from within but couldn't face it.

) PART CRESCENT: TELLING (

If you are here, it is because I've written this for you. The story. Not for want of telling the truth but telling you what happened. For example, when you come upon the phrase, "unannounced, the feces," think about the gun once held against your mother's head, also, her brother's head.

The war has claimed far worse than our imagination. Sister, listen closely. I start us at the edge of an inferno. The inferno stands as a metaphor for two realities.

> *ONE: After cremating Uncle Thuong during the Lunar New Year in Ann Arbor, countless testimonies poured from families he once helped into asylum.*

> *TWO: After they finished raping all the women on fishermen's boats that carried refugees, it is said the pirates set the boats on fire.*

What I see: My mother stares out toward the ocean before entering her boat. The boat may only hold one hundred bodies.

) & (

AN INFERNO. Into which we slid, pressing our fingers one by one like stalks of light against our lips. We angled slabs of flesh. Angled blue feet against the scorching of these bodies. We added. And we measured. And for extra measure, added what remained.

Afloat, piled with salt. Afloat, piled to trim the outer space, envisioning no hope.

We chose the youngest to survive us. She woke anguished and alone without her name. She carried over flames into the darkest parts of exile.

) & (

If you are here, it is because we've lived to see the flat end of a sunrise.

Do you not believe me?

Let me try again.

Red is still my mother's favorite color. As I write this, she is still alive, and as I write this, we are split. My mother is my daughter. We repeat ourselves, our wounds.

) & (

WHAT WOULD FACE HER, one decision, here, to set her bare feet dream careening through a typhoon, oared? What wrenched her out to freedom when she landed full of bones, caressing her cheek covered in salt? Would she drink from tin and eat from tin, flattened banana leaves ridden with sand? Fragments of teeth?

) & (

If you are here, it is because we were never meant to live, but listen, sister, closely. What I tell you starts from myth and pain. I stand here to remind us what was left behind. AN OCEAN into which we slid and WHAT WOULD FACE US, one decision, yes, to send our planet keeling into orbit. When you come upon a retrograde, shout this with me: "Retrograde!"

The retrograde will take us back in time. My mother is my daughter is my mother. Mother, hold my hand. I have so much to show you.

) & (

AN INFERNO. Into which we slid, our lips pressing bundles of thyme and lilac, answering such prayers with the scorching of our bodies. Leather, cotton, cashmere, fashioned dolls after our liking. We embroidered alms around the collars of an áo dài.

What would face us, that decision, leaving cities with our dead waving their scarves around a shoreline? What, I cannot for the life of me remember all their names, except, perhaps another voice haunting my voice.

What wreckage led us out of Vietnam? Hawk? Mice? Red, again, our hands.

What dawned? To leave our home for another? To fly? To crawl? Regardless, two of us would starve at sea. We laid them, what remained of their skeletons, wrapped in gauze, headfirst into the water. Then we shouted retrograde!

) & (

"RETROGRADE!"

) & (

If you are here, it is because the men have started fucking all the women on our boat. Into twelve, three, sixteen more nights we drift, reminded of these men who sleep among us. Ninety-eight tangled torsos under stars. And does it matter if we live to see the morning?

I start us at the edge of our departure. This departure stands as a metaphor for two realities.

> *ONE: I want to love despite your war. I want to know that love beyond its grief.*

> *TWO: I want to touch and feel no pain. I want to know that touch may heal us both.*

) & (

HOARSE, THE HOURS *left to wait, afloat, above the tiger's back, an ocean, churning hollyhocks like umber constellations.*

Holding out these charms, we dove into that water hopelessly in awe of what we harbored: sun-soaked apricots, skin peeling like visas, holy in their stamped, mildew-worn faceless fables. Once, I touched you. Then I left toward darkness, then a foghorn.

What evacuation makes our people braid their yellow dying toward the sun eclipsed by the moon, eclipsed by planetary maw? I reached this destination after falling toward our homeland, deep blue soil. What hand, soft and blistered reaching deeper, slower, warmer?

No one ever warned us how we'd calm ourselves to moans warbling our throats.

We left two hearts of rose quartz on the scale weighing our passage. Warrant this. What worth of us remains after we pick an ark over each other?

) & (

Unannounced, the feces.

Silence, like the Bay of Hạ Long (never looking back). Our hunger, unadorned with sea salt, straw, and incense. Smote the papers (never counting), jasmine rice uncooked, lining our nostrils. Was it sweat or bone ash? Love, our rocking tends the waters.

Heaven knows we're coming, how we capsized, stunk like honeydew and semen on this stranded, emptied boat. Falling, hands apart, we hunted for our rimes, humming nocturnes with our mouths sweet sticky closed, and haunted, we had wept.

Pry this back some more.

Last night we slipped out of a country that would bounty pre-arm us with heartbreak. No more witnesses. The open blouse, a broken sandal, precatory palms begging for rain. How parched was I to leave you for my people?

) & (

If you are here, it is because I've shifted lenses (ever since uttering "honeydew and semen"). I am speaking now to you, my love, my sweet blue Neptune.

Unannounced, the horror.

What I've seen and what I've felt.

A broken heart beating twice over. Love, this story is for you.

Shortly, I will tell a larger death than our dead marriage. Not for want of healing us but telling you what happened. For example, when you come upon the phrase, "gardenia and shrapnel," think about the soldier's grip, the soldier, blue and kind like you. I'm sorry. What we enter is another memory.

) & (

PRAY I COME HOME. Pray I bleed. The heron. 1968. The heron circled
over Huế. Pray tell me how it landed. Make it right. Six thousand villagers
just now tossed into a ditch. Praise this nightly for the song I took from you.
Praise the blessed brown mass graves. Your arm over my arm. Perfume of
tamarind, gardenia, and shrapnel, masquerading orchids loading stars. I bliss
among my dead——

) & (

If you are here, it is because we never stood a chance. Our love, one dark impasse. The ditch in which I lay six thousand roses. Down here, I cannot see you.

For example, when the Vietnamese-American filmmaker **Tiana Alexandra** speaks with a survivor in Mỹ Lai, she asks: "Why can't you look me in the eye?"

"Is it because I'm from America?"

To which the survivor slowly replies: **"Before,"**

                                        "when I told you the story . . ."

            "in front of my eyes,"

                "I see no one."

) & (

—our dead now marooned to our
legs. You touch each dimple, tendon, how you do not know the weight such
history can carry. Circa March 16th of 1968. Remember? How it's told, the
company of fire. How it's told through pictures of my faces pierced across
a country, the instant warning: never love too fully, deer-horned take each
white man as he comes.

The reverence.

The market square.

Twelve golden tipped lanterns in my commune with their tongues. Remember?

How it's told.

The tilling of my soil lush with blood commingling with breast milk, limbs, a
broken lung, believe me when I tell you how the body takes it all. The body, like
an anchor, dressed in jute and spittle, dredged up with the sirens. How they cling

to it like dreams.

On land, we found one of these sirens writhing, drunk off brandy, drenched in piss. A sailor with a horseshoe tattoo dropping his fly, the horseshoe placed where the woman's head should have been and swinging, as if from a hook, from her bent knee, a canteen.

When the horseshoe man is done, I hold the woman gently. Say: Remember?

How it's told.

The sudden whistle diving from a bird much unlike anything we've seen before. The bird, bloated with angels. Angels, tied to rope. The rope tugging ellipses down to earth. The earth withholding answers. Answer this: why move us into conquest? Rings of black hair kept as trophies. Babies made to watch and mothers made to watch. Pig sties kept with rags. The old pigs made to watch—

) & (

If you are here, it is because I stand alone against the tree.

) & (

—camouflaging jungle kept as whispers at my earlobes made to want a ravaging. An order, thigh to thigh against mahogany. A dropping of his fly. How could I want this instinct, want this ruin? Stop!

How could I stop a want kneading this tender? Led to Ha Long, once more, Ha Long. Let me swing into your khakis. Once a gook, always a gook. The reckoning. The pyre.

Give me kaolin clay porcelain saucers for my eyes. You named them dynamites. Colliding with our bones such terror and such beauty. There, my collar reaching for you, there, my mouth around your rapture, there, a sickle reaping bombs around the puddles in my spine. How it tastes, my sky retreating into flames! Remember?!

How I tasted when you loved me once a human, once worthy of tender, once no more the war I carried over wanting more than indigo and resin from my cunt embalming what serrated wanton knife dragging it gently out of exile. Don't. Don't call me pretty when her face splits from my own. What do you know about leaving her behind?

) PART CRESCENT: PANDA (

Dreamer, is it possible? We looked and wiped our faces in the glass, and last we hit the keys, an elephant fell out. Four stars of five, mysteriously green.

Panda found a hummingbird half-eaten near the bed, under the bed, above the bed. I woke and shook him. Itchy, Panda said, and then he wept.

Dearest Dreamer, hummingbirds flew through our mouths. And then Fleetwood Mac sang about going again, wanting freedom. And would you know what held us down?

My tiny Panda sat and kissed a broken mirror. My tiny Panda clung to paper. Water shattered what I had of skin calcified and trimmed with bleeding ivory. My tiny Panda screamed: "Well, who am I to keep you!" So lonely was that pall over his wake.

Sweet as cold papaya, morning rainwater drew me much closer to you, Dreamer.

Faithfully at five o'clock, defacing dovetails curled flashes in that sky like rods of flax spun silver, coupling scorpions trapped beneath a mountain. Would I drink that landslide dry, and more so, would you hold me?

Panda knows.

) NO CONTACT ZONE (

I spit them out, the thick row of Risperdal then Geodon, antipsychotics known to stop the sounds of slaughtered women screaming near my right ear then my left.

You and I are meant to meet nearly nine years from now, but at this moment, kneeling like a crab over my childhood toilet, I flush the medicine away.

The poet Bhanu Kapil writes, "Psychotic to lose something forever," and you look at me. Do I make it so obvious? The screaming, that is.

One morning, for example, I'd been sitting outside with three students waiting for our class to start. Someone mentioned seeing a bat two nights ago, and suddenly, I saw a woman with my face. She dangled over mulch. A canteen bottle dangled from one ankle, and then, I remembered turning to one student to ask if she knew much about the tree. "Not really, no," she smiled.

) & (

My friend Brandon turns to ask about how many times I've been in love, and furthermore, if I could share my first moment of unrequited love. "Well," I whisper, suddenly embarrassed for that day in 1954, my arms around a flag around an army shirt and then around a pillow. "They are primarily moments of paralysis," I admit.

"Paralysis of love"—Brandon hides the question mark—"?"—inside his hand touching the left side of his beard. I nod and look away, unable to contain an older shame then welling up inside of me.

) & (

Geodon, when taken properly, may dampen some hallucinations, notes the gentle doctor in my chart at discharge. Again, I nod, willing to promise anything as long as no one with a clipboard suddenly stops me from proper reintegration out of asylum.

I grin, holding two fingers to my lips. I place them gently on the doctor's cheek. "No, don't do that," says the doctor. "Okay," whispers my tiny Panda.

) & (

In asylum, I would fall asleep to Whitney Houston in my ears. My tiny Panda pushed one paw against my cheek and tapped his worry softly on my nose, which stirred me just awake enough to pull his tiny body closer to my chest.

"I believe . . . ," repeated Whitney Houston through the bars outside my window. Gliding in blue silk from left to right across the stage, she closed her eyes and smiled. "Teach us well."

A child wandered to the stage, and Whitney Houston paused.

) & (

NO CONTACT ZONE *sparkled beneath grey light, turning bright blue then deeper blue against its surface, just like silk or dust.*

I closed my eyes.

You wanted then to know, Neptune.

I wanted, yes, to know as well, how night was treating us like this. "Apart," my mouth wanted to add.

This morning I would listen to an audio recording of your blue and write back that it sounded like a sunrise.

Just outside asylum, I heard wind chimes dance along a sudden gust of red.

I liked, especially, the soft ones best of all.

15.

Among your voices, I could sense no center voice. It dizzied me. I entered what seemed like duplicate dreams tucked into the first.

The following nine or ten iterations would have windows in the middle of every wall. By then, your bodies had begun to shrivel.

16.

You had reorganized
into comical patterns
of tetrads without *up*
or *down* markings. A
unified cube seemed
to be most common;

I burst out laughing
although this specific
room frightened me.
There was no bed, no
chair, no extra socks;
the room was cold;

an indistinct smell—
tree bark, perhaps, or
coconut water—soon
wafted around you. I
strode to the window
facing east and there:

still, nothing to exit
from appeared. Your
four voices continued
to chant instructions.
I covered my nose.

FROM THE BLUE NOTEBOOK

"You'll seek the flat end to a sunrise. You'll push yourself onto a boat unannounced. There will be rumors of asylum. You'll leave unwell but free to work at a school, to write poetry, to rent a car, to buy with your first paycheck: shoes, hair scissors. Your second paycheck: a plane ticket west. You'll fashion dolls out of bundling thyme and lilac in thin strips of gauze."

17.

And there, crying out was
my spirit—

FROM THE BLUE NOTEBOOK

"You won't know where to put those dolls. You'll hunger unfolding like a flag, waving it in circles, crying like birds. 'Turn around,' you'll say to a face stuck on that boat. 'Turn around. Don't let anyone use your words or your books. Go.' But the sea will appear to burn most nights. You won't scream. You'll be dignified."

18.

For hours, it felt in this
chamber, I tried calming
you with art, mathematical
proofs, and absurd shadow-
tales of life on land.

You would quiet and pay
most attention to stories
about a brave and tiny
panda, told in the style of
trying to recall a dream—

FROM THE STORY "SKYRAIDER"

"The work of moving water is up to a tiny panda named Panda. He stands on the roof of a small shrine at the edge of a rice field. He looks down at the open pages of his pamphlet, a manual for flying. 'First,' it illustrates. 'Flap your arms in tight, controlled circles. Imagine for yourself a set of propellers.' The tiny Panda rotates his paws, slowly at first, forward and then backward: a commanding force of blades. 'Second, notice the year is 1965.' A Douglas A-1 Skyraider lunges overhead. This Skyraider, a single-seat bomber, can putter to higher altitudes, and though the ejection seat tends to jam in older models made from wood, wire, and turbine, notably, it's the pilot, Nguyễn Cao Kỳ, who howls like a tiger at liftoff. What compels him, the man in action, to leap from the heavens, weapons ablaze? The tiny Panda wonders about this while holding open the last page of his manual with the softest part of his foot, bare and round like his paws."

"The tiny Panda sees in a distant field: a young egret settles in the grass; its long neck bobs to the breeze almost two-directional in movement. The tiny Panda shudders at the thought of being eaten by such a bird. 'Can you imagine,' he thinks, 'flitting down a throat, such as that, coming out all skinny and hollow like a reed?' For, in his mind, the pins are stuck. The double axis, made of copper, fueled and medaled, is stitched between the polyester of limbs and body. The tiny Panda thrums. His paws spin faster than ever before. His eyes widen into flat saucers like stars rung out from the wash. They twinkle with three white dots sewn at the top of each eye, as if at any moment this stuffed animal might burst into tears. He grunts, however, like a piglet, 'Gruntgrunt.'"

FROM THE STORY "SKYRAIDER"

"'Third: Jump when you are ready.' A reenactment of our courage in a dream box requires utterance, a kind of death rattle that pushes the water out, whichever way one might fall from a vessel mid-air, and, in this way, a manual is simply made in the manner of stage directions: diagrams whistle with birds flopping from trees. At this rate, a tiny face explodes; a dark nebula, into dust. The tiny Panda is undone, and, in *that* way, uniquely, I'd meet him in 1965. He was drowning near the base of my shrine in a field of rice. I was walking on a road nearby, thinking about the nature of time combined with the nature of air. My hands were rolling up pieces of shrapnel into jagged balls of metal."

"I came across a feather before noticing the tiny Panda floundering in a pool of muddy water. He had landed face-down, squashing a lily pad. I turned the tiny Panda gently over with my foot, though he still twitched from the shock of just having been ejected from the sky at a rate that should have destroyed him. The tiny Panda appeared to have gulped in mouthfuls of an unknown substance. His round belly heaved up and down. I learned from him, much, much later, that this was his only attempt to fly."

19.

Other stories drifted
equally off-center, as
strange as they were tender
at moments. I pivoted,
however, to your reactions.

When the outlines of
your bodies slumped
to one side, a point of view
would shift. An "us" entered
the plot; you livened up.

When a shrill *O, O-O!*
began spurting out of
your bodies, I yanked
a character helplessly
across the corridor of
flashbacks.

At this, you hushed
into low tones of *o-o*
before resettling into
an "L" shape. Here,
I found my nerve to
stay put, *create doors.*

20.

What became urgent, above
all, was a total enchantment
on your part. Spoken text
had to dazzle, shock, and
unify your senses.

Narrative logic could hardly
hold you to the shadows I
cast on the chamber walls
or, at times, through my
voice. I was trapped.

21.

Across the chamber, I
danced, wailed, and crawled
on the floor, in every attempt
to keep you entertained and
set on one shape.

Descriptions of cities and
countries became erratic,
excessive. In the room, I had
only a blanket to drape over
my head.

22.

Hand puppets with dignified and stately chins would parade into my stories; these characters often had to make an exit mid-thought as if to catch a train arriving only once per lifetime; a second hand puppet simply popped into the scene, replacing its former self with movements that were almost identical, that were urgent, bobbing and easily startled or disgusted, or fainting at the sudden arrival of a ghost or nemesis; their voices equally squeaky. You would express, once, doubt by stacking up

your bodies into a single,
shaky column.

23.

I had to think quickly and
toss the event elsewhere —

FROM THE REVISED STORY "SKYRAIDER"

"The tiny Panda unpacked his suitcase. He'd brought only two items into our room: a one-piece set of pajamas and a red apple. The room was small with no definite entry point. From the corner of my eye, I noticed the tiny Panda had begun taking delicate bites from his apple. There were books in my backpack: poems by Chika Sagawa, a book on architecture by Ronald Rael, and a picture monograph from *Taschen*, the collected paintings of Marc Chagall. By that point, I was working on a book about love and combat gear. One night in his sleep, the tiny Panda kicked at the air and shouted, 'Itchy!'"

FROM THE REVISED STORY "SKYRAIDER"

BLUE (NOUN) \ BLÜ \
: An act of mediating sky, otherwise, bluer

ROSE (NOUN) \ RŌZ \
: Objects in motion;
: For instance, sweetness equals life on Earth

24.

You wiggled into the tidy shape of a letter "z" and teetered for a while. I froze holding my hands aloft with their mouths open.

I held my breath and lowered the puppets, willing you not to collapse. Eventually, you were still again, finding your balance.

I spoke a few words. You glowed beneath the surface, turning a sky blue. Staying in this shape, little by little, you rotated.

Upside-down, a dark magenta, you made a sound like someone groaning after being stretched too long. I turned to Panda.

FROM THE REVISED STORY "SKYRAIDER"

"'I faced a difficult day,' began Panda's monologue. 'A fig eater bumped into the wooden frame of our window. We dreamt of trees forgetting to breathe. In my mind, I sensed a brilliant red light, always blinking. A crop duster floated across this field of memory not too far away, made of paper. I must go there, I thought, to meet the moons of our past. The moons would ask about *you*.' Panda pointed vaguely into the setting. 'But *you* were in karaoke,' said Panda. The moons then wanted to know what was sung every night. Panda hesitated a bit before answering. 'Fleetwood Mac.' And then, after some thought: 'Céline Dion! Cher!' All of that was true."

FROM THE REVISED STORY "SKYRAIDER"

HUNGRY (VERB) \ HƏŊ-GRĒ \
: The definition of characters running to the beat of a drum

ITCHY (VERB) \ I-CHĒ \
: Not from lack of birds but their bones

FROM THE REVISED STORY "SKYRAIDER"

"'How old are we today? Well, it depends. Sometimes you have no seams, and sometimes I'm three. Together, maybe, we can add up to over 400 years old. It doesn't matter in the end. I'll make up our ages and names in situations if I have to. For example, I put on my pajamas and walked out to the streets of your mother's old city. There were bombs everywhere. I ran to hide.'"

25.

The tiny Panda shook his
head. I was dizzy again and
ever more queasy with the
odor in this chamber close
to old cooking oil.

By the end of Panda's
monologue, an awful shriek
collapsed your form at the
bottom. A window to your
right cracked.

26.

I knew, more or less, staying
in this room would knock
me out if the stories failed to
evolve to your liking. There
were no doors.

No window could fit me
through. I needed bolder
hand puppets, stronger
entrances, a longer beat to
dance against, and socks.

27.

From time to time, you took
over with commentary so
clear that I would question
who, in the end, was casting
shadows.

Perhaps together, we charted
a single story within many,
of the same voice rooted in a
four-person voice, a chorus
in one body.

28.

Whenever you spoke, I
hurried to write in my
notebooks, laying them on
the floor, on top of each
other and open at blank
pages.

Some had notes for a novel,
chapter pieces, a loose
outline, here and there. I
switched among books to
keep up with your voices.

FROM THE GREEN NOTEBOOK

"A family tree should be sketched here, ending with Tony Terazawa-Huỳnh, whose mother's name is Emi; Emi's mother is Chrysanthemum; her mother is Mai, and so forth. Everyone has four hidden names in their story: a name of myth, a name of origin, a name of sorrow, and an infinite configuration of names for a father. Do you understand? This is one record of our lives. Write it down or these names may destroy each other. Don't worry, just write. I'll speak."

Tetra Nova

a novel

Contents

Author's Disclaimer

The following manuscript, known formerly as *Cartographies of Insurrection,* is furthermore indebted to the game *Tetris* and the song "In This Shirt" by The Irrepressibles, through which the author, Kenzo "Tony" Terazawa-Huỳnh, could not arrive at the temple chamber to his mother's heart without playing them on loop.

Editorial Corrections

Multiple authors have attempted to rewrite this manuscript, which has become a collection of shadow puppets. There will be bold inconsistencies across time and setting, biographical details and costume design, laws of intermediate geometry, translator notes, citations, and overall plotlines, though every attempt has been made to fill in some of the gaps. Please forgive us.

BOOK OF WIND

Errantries

THE BROAD TREE LINES OF my mother's stories begin with her books. She was a poet before I knew her at the windows. She'd often stare directly at a spot on the glass: residue of bird droppings, water stains, shifting motes of dust outside. What I last knew of her, at the hospital where a technician called her Ms. T, affectionately, like when she taught at the university, raising me—*a sweet potato*, she would call me back then, stuck to her back during her lessons—it was her earlier books that pained my mother the most. These poems, she would explain, were about events that fractured my grandmother, Chrysanthemum, and Chrysanthemum's mother, too; my great-grandmother was named Mai, as for my mother, Emi, who was just a child during those events, in separate countries, in overlapping lines of peace and war, my mother as a writer was careful to separate memories on a family tree when necessary. Sometimes, however, I felt a terrible, totalizing fire consuming her spirit, which led her to the shadow space over and over, in a room of shapes and syllables around our ancestors. Here, I put together chapters of a life when Emi was too far from me. This was her story as much as mine.

At the hospital, I would speak to her psychiatrist, a boring but gaunt figure standing outside my mother's room most mornings, Monday through Thursday. This figure would observe, through a little window, something like a bird thrashing at the walls.

"But can I talk to her?" I remember saying in a voice set, squeezed atop a pinhead.

"When it's safe enough."

"You're saying no."

I struggled to contain my alarm. It was already February, and this was a *good* hospital I've been told. However, I could only ask questions about material moments of her daily life, like what my mother ate. Could she sleep? What was she telling you?

"Not to worry."

Even the billing clerk said that. I sat in his office weeping one Saturday. On the clerk's desk was a tissue box placed by a jar of uncapped pens. The ballpoints stuck up at different heights. The clerk was folding the month's statement into a billing envelope. When I blew my nose, no thoughts came to me.

"You must see this all the time," I said.

"It happens."

The clerk shrugged. He said I was doing my best. I did everything possible for my mother. At this word, "possible," I jolted from my seat.

"Thank you. I'm sorry. I need to go."

The billing clerk got up slowly and followed me to the lobby. He said it was great to see me, and I left without knowing if I could come back again.

My mother's notebooks, the ones she left on her kitchen table before she vanished, before someone later found her across Tucson in their backyard, on her hands and knees growling at their dogs, swirled around and around my mind. I couldn't root myself with any other image outside my mother, then known to herself as Emi, crawling on the dirt with burrs stuck in her knees.

At the library, my boss said I should take time off, but I couldn't. My mother's unfinished stories scrambled my sense of any routine. These notebooks were connected like chapters; I was convinced, perhaps if I could tidy up her work just enough, my mother would sense herself coming back when I visited, if I could just show her: "Look here, Ma, this is your novel, done!"

Every night after work, I would take out my pencils. I underlined sentences scribbled in my mother's notebooks, attempting to chart logic among their contents.

One notebook began in November. It was set in my grandmother's country, where Saigon would turn into a cloud of hot milk, bodies receding into each other for days of steam, desire, standing cocoons of sweat and cotton clinging to our legs and the softest parts of our underbellies, a family crossing a busy intersection, and the mother of this family scolding her children.

"Đi đi," my mother wrote in her mother's voice. The tone had little fear but said, "Wait. Go. Stop. Go."

Chrysanthemum had an iron grip on my mother's wrist, Emi, the eldest with short black bangs, an uneven bowl-cut, and, appropriate to any six-year-old of that hour, misery up to her knees. The girl was wobbling on a curb, willing all her organs to just plop out and die. This country is too hot, she thought, not like in Dallas where you sit in the Volvo and let a plastic dial on Papa's radio cool your brain, the oldies station 98.7 KLUV or Woody Guthrie releasing us someplace off a concrete highway to everything we might know of sound, but not like *this* sound; Emi's mother has jolted diagonally across an intersection between a window of two crossing vehicles; she screeched above the cacophony of horns and bells.

"ĐI!" Emi wrote again, punctuating the cry heavily.

My grandmother tugged the string of her family like a row of freight cars. They bumped into the backs of each other. I could see my mother freeze, just so, in her account of visiting the market long ago in 1995 as a young girl. My mother, like her mother, pulled her knee back, letting an old motorbike, a Yamaha, putter by. The child had winced. They both followed the exhaust pipe while it vanished behind a veil of dust, a shutting eye under folds of oncoming traffic. Emi could imagine this motorbike whisking her away like a tiny pink balloon into the low-hanging sky. She was not afraid of death. She was a serious child.

"Emi-chan," wrote my mother. My grandmother spoke sharply around the corners: "Pay attention!"

My mother's sister, Yoko, had been lifted to the shoulders of their Papa. Yoko's little fingers were splaying across a coarse tangle of hair. Her hands dug into a sweaty scalp, a dumpling set atop a larger dumpling.

"Yoko-chan!"

Emi was grinning. She held up a free thumb.

"Thumbs up, Yoko-chan!"

Yoko was three. She stared down at her sister condolingly. She tucked in her lips and stuck out a row of baby teeth, crooked off-colored pearls. She paused, thinking to herself.

"Okay," added my mother briefly in Yoko's voice. "Okay, she thought."

Yoko peeled a sticky hand away from Papa's forehead. She trembled and raised two fingers aloft.

"Way to go, Yoko-chan!"

"Yoko! Dum-zup!"

Yoko was pleased with herself.

My grandmother, though I never met her, seemed to regard me through the manuscript with apprehension. I had to shut the notebook. Chrysanthemum, with a round, peachlike face, large-framed glasses, and eyes grabbing everything, glimmered from the page, deep brown, golden-amber, what made her most beautiful perhaps to my mother.

Chrysanthemum was standing at a wooden cart at the market entrance of Bến Thành. Her family had knocked into each other again. Emi tottered to the side. Yoko squealed and hit the top of her Papa's head like a drum; Daichi leaned forward, chortling—*fufufu*—pretending to drop his goofy little dumpling.

Before the market's main entrance, bright flags draped over the stone extrados. Arches flanked a clock tower, offering some bit of shade. My grandmother had glanced up at that familiar clock and recalled, according to my mother's notes—"I remember being a child as I was, in Sài Gòn, yellow acacia of Tết, the men, being all my uncles, greeting each other like men deep in love, linking their elbows together and marching slowly, slowly into that street of death, the tiger lilies, the joss sticks, our shadows touching everything at once; maybe my name was Chrysanthemum, maybe not, but I was eight or nine then, it was 1966, and my father was not yet dead, set on fire, a flock of birds aflame; I can see him in this street, right here, my father is about to die in front of everyone . . ."—Chrysanthemum was shaking her head at these words, shaking a memory with them, too.

I sat up from the notebook, clutching at my chest. It was hard to breathe and look in the right direction. My mother had a portrait of her mother earlier in a different manuscript, but I couldn't find it then. Flipping back and forth among the pages, I started to have a nagging feeling that the voices between my grandmother, Chrysanthemum, and my mother, Emi, were merging with mine.

"Stay here," someone wrote.

"Stay," said Chrysanthemum, first in Vietnamese, then in sharp English.

My mother couldn't understand the errantries of this word yet. Her voice became feeble, her wrist slumping to the side. Deep imprints of my grandmother's fingers rushed to the surface of my mother's skin, tinged with blood. Emi then wondered about how, at home, Chrysanthemum would never talk to us like this, especially in bà ngoại's words, though by then, Chrysanthemum had already scurried off, by herself, into the main market hall. Her body shrank into an outline of a small, petrified girl. Yoko, noting this, began to wail.

"Mama! Ma! まー!"

※

A wooden cart sat low to the ground. An acrylic blue tarp snapped overhead. An old woman had been rooted there all day, cross-legged, minding a large basket of toys in her lap. On this cart, she had lined three rows of figurines, each one, dressed tidily in a tunic and pants. Some held up practical objects like a fishing pole or a straw conical hat. Others seemed to be dancing in place.

Across the market's open square, a clamorous flock of children in uniform played a game of tag. Behind them, squatting on the ground, a handful of teenagers were huddling around a short pink footstool. One of them reshuffled a deck of cards. A portable speaker sagged off a pile of newspapers next to them. A new wave pop song looped to the beginning. The teenagers threw their arms up at random, singing along. *Bay-beh!* Emi found herself gawking at what appeared to be a thousand wrinkles set upon a single human face.

"Yoisho, Yoko-chan," said Papa.

He was unflappable despite the weather. He crouched over the pavement, letting Yoko find her footing. She swatted at the air and then at Papa's arms. She still cried out, "まー," though Chrysanthemum had forever gone in her mind, and nothing could convince Yoko otherwise, what an awful, no-good day.

The toddler stamped her foot. The old woman chortled. She tapped her knee.

"Look, Emi."

The basket was empty.

"You know me." The old woman's lips, however, weren't moving at all. She held up a wooden object with the tips of her fingers, a miniature toy horse painted red.

"You know me," she repeated. Her voice felt strangely calm and smooth, and if Emi could think hard enough, she could simply walk away, but the voice trapped her like a summon projected on the farthest walls of her mind, thrown from behind that old woman's flickering eyes. The texture reminded Emi of snow falling across a television screen. She didn't know where to place her hands.

The woman, seeing this, explained quickly.

"And here's the way I understand each term set by our roots, comrade."

In my mother's notebook, I underlined the old woman's monologue: "Measurements of air igniting small pockets of light, light followed by voices trespassing through space, and farther, the planet Paul whizzes around our sun at 34,000 kilometers per hour. This makes one revolution every 29.4 years on Earth, the number four being a matter of degrees, not separation, and most certainly not death; four, as is the custom of our people, what's counted down until ignition, separation from most life, as we now know it, gone; four, thus, makes a commonality of war, at least what's been recorded of it so far, root erring to root, dirt divided then displaced into four bowls."

○ ○ ○ ○

The old woman had a severe, sunbaked face, which slipped like a curtain from a second face or a third; Emi couldn't figure out which voice was hers. The girl soon felt nauseous.

A bicycle, like her cousin Hiếu's, was leaning against the far side of the woman's cart. Attached to the back was a cramped wiry box filled with beige and brown-feathered chickens, every one of them, a frantic obsidian eye darting in a separate, cavernous direction.

"What you see," said the old woman nodding at the chickens.

Her voice continued to seep behind the old woman's carefully blank expression, "is a room I've created with my time on this planet, in this country. Symbols have been drawn out. Diagrams might lead from one event to the next."

Emi intuitively covered her chest with a hand. I covered my chest, turning the page.

The old woman had raised her miniature toy horse, higher, higher, and closer to the child's face.

"Don't be afraid, Emi."

There was burnt rubber mingling with the scent of salted meat. Emi caught, for a split second, two voices bickering behind her face. They shuffled in a corridor held up by the old woman's mind, two separate personalities twitching near the surface of her skin, making bubbles along the creases of her forehead; a dull echo of several doors slamming; beyond this, past and present converging into a single stream of thought.

The old woman clucked. She motioned, insisting on Emi to take the horse. "Hurry!"

Emi felt like she was going to faint. Her eyes blurred at the corners. She imagined the old woman hunched over much later, packing up her cart, already, by the age of six, I'm a monograph of stars.

✳

Emi had pulled at the hem of her shorts, wary about what bargain she was about to make or be compelled into making with the overlaying presence of two strangers in the old woman's body.

A spotted dove landed on a pipe overhead. The dove scuttled back and forth without a sound. Emi felt the splat of its dropping by her feet. She lowered her eyes. A baggy t-shirt waded around her with a cartoonish image of a bright, pink flamingo imprinted in the front. The bird posed absurdly under a coconut tree missing all of its coconuts. The old woman, according to my mother's notes, observed this. She blinked slowly, vaguely—thinking: here's our chance to escape—the old woman attempted to look as innocent and as plainly, as possible. She lowered her right arm, returning the toy to her basket.

✳

The chorus, meanwhile, in a train of red and pink stiletto heels, emerged from the market's main hall. They paused at the stereo, still slumped on a pile of newspapers, and recognized the song almost immediately. They clicked together, swinging their hips and singing off-key. It was divine to me. At the scene, I guarded my gaze, turning instead over to the teenagers passing around a soda can, shaking the marble from it, watching the marble plunk across the stool set in the middle of their game.

The stilettos were taking turns reapplying their lipsticks in front of a booth selling plastic mirrors and combs. The stilettos were adjusting their long, synthetic wigs. Gold, acrylic nails pulled up at the tube tops, smoothing out their skirts.

An offshoot of children separated from their game of tag, perhaps in a show of unionizing. The youngest pointed ferociously at her nose. I, likewise, gestured to my face, and then the old woman's face marked by my mother in her notes. Emi squinted into both of these faces skeptically.

The cart had moved a few millimeters to the right, then the left. The girl wasn't sure of her footing, and neither was I sure of myself, my work in that story.

The figurines had also rearranged themselves into several different columns. The old woman took a scallop-laced fan from inside her shirt sleeve. She tapped it on one side of her neck, an innocent gesture.

"My child," said the old woman trying her best not to appear desperate.

"Don't you remember? I'm your root."

"You're all of mine," Emi answered.

I whispered those words along with my mother, the pencil stuck in my fingers.

Emi's father, a reticent Japanese man, was crouching on the pavement at this moment. He took a photograph of the chickens. He seemed to ignore the strange, psychic drama unfolding next to the cart. Yoko, who had been pacified and oblivious by her Papa's discrete movements, chewed on her pointer finger. She reached with another hand to grip a fistful of her Papa's polo shirt. Together, they appeared frozen, meditating on a simple crate of feathers.

"Emi," said the old woman, more forcefully this time. Her crumpled lips shifted off-center. They hovered slightly beyond her face, opening and shutting too quickly a bright gossamer mask.

"Your name's not only Emi. We don't have much time . . . He found you in a tree, long, long ago."

The old woman nodded at Emi's Papa.

"Yes, I found you." The man had chimed in. He shifted his weight, kneeling from his left knee to the right. The father was impeccably dressed in shades of Easter green and khaki. He was then concentrating on a light exposure filtering through his camera.

"Emi-chan."

Emi jerked around. Her eyes nearly bulged from their sockets.

This voice couldn't be Papa's voice, she thought. He sounded too calm, like sap oozing from a tree set in the middle of my stomach, but Papa who liked to sing along with the radio, Emi kept reasoning to the old woman somehow, Papa would never hurt me, even if he wasn't Papa.

Papa took a second photo of the chickens, interrupting Emi's thoughts. She fixed her gaze on a hundred expressions compacted into one. The terrors of her name and my name were startled at the entrance to a forest.

"Emi-chan."

The girl could sense her father standing elsewhere, addressing someone else, too.

"I found you in a bamboo cutting. You were a newborn, not much bigger than my thumb. But it was Ojiisan, far away in Tokyo, who chose your name. He wrote to me, one day, a formal letter with the kanji for EMI."

"My wife, who then agreed to be your mother, wanted to give you a traditional Vietnamese name, but Ojiisan insisted. Deep inside my heart, however, I felt that you were truly KAGUYA-HIME, Deity of the Moon. Banished to Earth."

Daichi was clearing his throat. He envisioned this baby who would one day grow up to be a good son and held his Kodak camera lens away from his body, inspecting the surface for any lint. Emi inched closer to her younger sister though she could see, from the right side of her face: that Yoko was already locked in the dead center of a staring contest with one of the chickens.

"Why are these voices in my head?" My mother wrote.

"Don't be afraid." The old woman answered. Her voice had already begun to enter Emi's voice. "Go on, Daichi. Continue. We're listening."

"Iiie . . ." Daichi shook his head. "Emi, you were sent from somewhere else."

"It reminds me of a dream. You were swaddled in linen, awake. Earlier, someone had tucked you at the bottom of a wicker basket set in the middle of a clearing. After a few minutes, tanuki surrounded you. They had jumped out from behind cypress and pine."

"These clever raccoons sniffed at the wind, twitching their whiskers, fanning pairs of stubby arms from side to side. They drew bags of hot air through their cheeks, swelling up their bellies. A low hum of a drumbeat reverberated through the forest. It was night. I wasn't afraid of this dream either. It was a ritual for the name EMI."

"The creatures soon realized who you were. They widened their circle, raising their tiny legs and slamming them one by one to the ground, shaking the earth."

"'Some of us wore, I could remember,' announced the largest yōkai gesturing proudly at a hairless, spotted sac distended from his belly. 'Some of us wore,' he repeated, 'human clothing. For example, a tunic with a neat wrap, pants dyed indigo.'"

"The sacred tanuki carried on with their dancing, even after I found you and took you home to Okaasan in the waking world. If you can see them all today, Emi, you might notice a ring of claw marks on the wet, snowy grass."

"Emi," Chrysanthemum said. Her pitch was sharp. She had materialized in the third person with several bags of dragon fruit, "Hold Mama. Hand."

"Ma."

Emi didn't know what to say. Her fingers went numb. Her stomach turned over.

"Let's go. Đi." My mother's writing switched between languages in her mother's voice.

Daichi had bowed to the old woman. He returned his camera in a swift, three-point movement to his Sony bag draped over one shoulder. The old woman closed her eyes. She felt the wrinkles of her body dissolve into this gesture, merging, at last, with Emi's. "For I," wrote my mother in the notebook. "I was the old woman. My name was Lua."

✻

As the family left Bến Thành, Emi craned her neck around. The clock tower hovered there still. Its sweeping arches warbled with more doves. Only the basket remained, overturned, where an old woman had just been sitting; the figurines were nowhere to be found.

"Let's go," repeated Yoko. She squealed from her place atop Daichi's shoulders. All was set right again.

"Let's go," Chrysanthemum said to herself.

She tossed a bag of fruit into her daughter's arms, her daughter with a face like Papa's—puffy and somber on an edge of tearfulness, plucked like a cello string—"Đi! Let's go!"

The family rushed to a second market, and then a third. Low stalls of rambutan tumbled like spiders in their boxes. Mangosteens burst from their bottoms. Green papayas splayed in halves. Guava and pineapple all glittered in the sun.

Through her eyes, in the body of a child, Emi felt like a myth again, jumping and choosing its host deliberately. Muscles separated from bones and ligaments, reassembling as one breath.

Emi felt this in her writing, a slight déjà vu.

The old woman had tried to tell my mother something, but she couldn't put the pieces together. The girl had been dragged away by her wrist, south of the market in Saigon. I let myself be shuffled, too, playing the part of Chrysanthemum's eldest daughter, of rind and pulp, a system of hands separating nerve from flesh.

"Hurry. Take this." Chrysanthemum was counting out the change as she haggled with a shopkeeper.

Emi placed a smaller bag stuffed with rice cakes into the bag of dragon fruit. "Let's go." My grandmother sounded worried.

The Body Jumper

BEYOND BẾN THÀNH, I MARVELED at the mechanics of my mother's story, the bends of memory, sensation, and language older than its grammar, rules of biology, or rules of mathematics.

As Emi, she seemed to leap over the streets like a balloon. Soaring over her mother's old city, I could sense an unpredictable shift in the air. Usually, the human mind would stay put, subjective, and flat across the surface of gravel, dirt, or concrete, but we raised our arms and screamed at the drop. Emi fixed herself onto many points: the church of Huyện Sĩ, for instance.

In District 3, Emi knocked herself against the bell tower of Xá Lợi, tumbling across its pagoda, flying out with her tennis shoes intact but loose around the ankles. In District 4, plastic lanterns swayed with the gentle breeze of her passing. The girl, with her eyes and mouth firmly shut, swooped around another temple of Thiên Hậu. I was lost, amazed.

The networks of alleys, cathedrals, rooftop terraces, and electric lines were making a mosaic below her in the shape of a large, crooked heart; now *this* was certainly strange, I thought, the mosaic had begun to throb. Emi sprouted a set of wings. Her shoulders widened with a crack. The wings whirred beneath the sun. Each feather appeared tipped with emerald, titanium, and clear, tissue-thin blades. A layer of silver hair wrapped around increasingly muscular legs; a silver beard spread across the jawline growing more defined and denser by the millisecond. It wasn't a raccoon or a girl—its name was LUA, added a voice that vibrated deeply, defiantly, and dreadfully, and like you, Lua said, I've seen many things.

✳

We tumbled clumsily in a ball behind Emi's face and reached a spot in late February 1962, the concurrent events of collective memory, once again, converging like flesh over logic.

Lua, in the body of a child, my mother in the body of a child, simultaneously on the ground and simultaneously taking flight as her mother, Chrysanthemum, squinted at the shadow of a giant bird, metallic, glinting, and soaring overhead. She imagined that machine to be an angel of death, not the bomber flashing its hornet energy toward the queen.

Lua, in human form, shielded her eyes from the glare.

These three names—Chrysanthemum, Lua, Emi—overlapped into a fourth unified form, transfiguring into a spiral like Daichi had predicted in the market, in the twilit burning field. The snow would not be snow. The beast could not be a beast. The dream was not a dream. Our three faces gazed at this ash-stricken sky, for my name is LUA, repeated the voice of an old, old woman, and I've seen many things.

Kenzo

EMI BALANCES A BABY ON her hip. In her mind, she wrestles with an outline for a Cubist performance production. The script unfurls across scrolls of paper taped along three walls of a sanitized room. The room has no desk. The room has no chair. Each piece of paper holds a book. The books need to be redone.

The baby yawns. Emi says, "This is for you, Kenzo."

The *Book of Wind* opens with a floodlight on Chrysanthemum, a little girl in Saigon—Emi tracks with her finger—who rushes through Bến Thành. At the same time, a meddlesome immortal from a different cosmology, Lua, fixates herself on that body of ancestry.

Kenzo gurgles.

It's a mistake. Emi taps her finger on the line connecting Rome and Saigon. "But you have to know," she says while shifting the baby across her stomach, up to one shoulder. She tucks the pencil behind her ear. "We have a difficult series of rhythms to get down."

The baby has shrunken imperceptibly at first until it reaches the size of a nickel.

"The first rhythm weaves into a chorus of seven distinct voices. Not all are accounted for yet, but Lua's here, I'm sure."

On the floor by Emi's bed is a plastic cup of water. She rests her face against the blank space of her baby who now fusses in his sleep. She sniffs and imagines the goddess Lua closing her eyes. The mask has been etched into the outline of this opening act. I remember, she thinks, the warm breeze near the end of February 1962.

An invisible hand reached to tidy the loose ends of a child's hair. This was her mother's hair pulled back by a yellow satin sash. Her hair is tucked neatly behind her ears. Across the avenue, meters away from the Cambodian Embassy, the child, along with what remains of her large immediate family in Saigon, enters the front door of a hotel lobby. She walks across its thick carpet, into a gilded entryway of a cocktail lounge where our story of love must begin.

Chrysanthemum stares over the counter at the bartender in a white linen suit. He wears a generous smile set beneath a lean, manicured mustache. Over his elbows, he cranes his chin forward, admiring the yellow headband and thinking of his daughter, too.

"What are you doing here, little one?"

Chrysanthemum balks at this question. She's only six years old, and her father is not yet dead. What else is there to say?

There's glue in that dark, fawnlike expression. A camera is pointed at her face. She turns but doesn't blink. The motor behind her eyes doesn't move. The journalist, revealed here to be holding the camera steady, is in his twenties. He crouches on a knee. He counts with three fingers raised above his head.

Just outside, the old woman is unpacking a cart on the street and shrinks into the outline of a second child. This child walks into the same hotel, its gilded entryway with a bronze cherub at the top holding a flute, and the same bar where the first child, Chrysanthemum, notices a news camera pointed directly at her family.

In Tokyo, a nine-year-old Daichi Terazawa admires a television set in the glossy shop window above Shinjuku Station. In Saigon, simultaneously, a flock of children is crowding around the old woman's crate. The chickens are playing tag. A third or fourth journalist has crossed the intersection; there have been rumors, one says. A dozen pilots fall in rapid succession from their helicopters. The stilettos, the teenagers singing off-key near their stereo—everything has been threaded together by our script of destiny, and the girl, Chrysanthemum, blinks.

FOUR THUS MAKES THE COMMONALITY of war, what destroys a people's will to live, to bite down and bear arms, scraps of boulevards and unmarked doorways leaping toward the seats of gods. You have to know this. I've written it before, flashing in the margins of my mind, the four sides of a photograph that carve out boundaries of memory, erasing us, along with a single flash, our book of displacement.

Dates pound to mortar; roots, into a calendar of arms.

I see this, too, brushing cellophane-thin hairs across the atmosphere. Putting such moments onstage, to say the least, is a near-impossible task.

Lua has fallen into place. Six voices clash against the seventh—Emi stares at the outline of her book tacked to the wall. Each page has an element specific to its stage design; stories are woven together in a tapestry of shapes—we whisper up to the number four and stop there.

BỐN

QUATTUOR

「し」

I DO NOT SUFFER FOR THIS NUMBER. It's given order and clarity to what spared us from the conditions annihilating our people, therefore, the instance of my birth.

For example, in June 1963, four days after her seventh birthday, Chrysanthemum witnesses a monk going up in flames, of which she says little, except to say, in the ever-present tense, "We see him sit down in the street to pray."

Three years later, in the year of the Fire Horse, her father goes up in flames, at which point, Chrysanthemum learns to load the rifle with her eyes closed shut as one might root a daisy into stone—Emi's drawn a thick, blocky line between the two points on her paper—here's the circumstance of our education in Saigon, circa 1966: citizen dressed as a weapon, if not sitting down to protest.

We also learn power lies in human instinct. Human instinct is to run.

EMI sits with her back against a wall in her room. She can't see out the single window, but light passes through. Silhouettes of wildflowers trickle across the door to her bathroom. The girl stands on the outskirts of a crowd, in the street, petrified in shades of charcoal, watching someone we know publicly burn to death. You must choose, Chrysanthemum: *Do I run? Or do I pray?*

The Poet

REGARDING HIS WORK in bà ngoại's country, an American journalist Malcolm Browne wins the Pulitzer for International Reporting, of which he offers very few words except to say how the hours of June 11, 1963, would be "every bit as bad" as he expected, how the days before and after would be cruel, how the sound of our horror would flatten from wailing to chanting, how you would appear excitable, having just turned seven, perhaps in the image of Chrysanthemum, in a sensible pair of loafers crossing a street, and how, fourteen years later, in the year of the Fire Snake, Malcolm Browne would move to New York City and become a science writer for the *Times*.

Long after this move, in March 2005, Chrysanthemum's daughter Emi mulls each event over, chewing at the inside of her mouth, pinching an intake hospital tag around her wrist. It says in her *Book of Wind*, in a scene opening to Dallas, how Emi sits with a look of vacancy, repeating your name among our many entangled names. "Lua."

The nurse writes today's date on a computer, but you can't make out the numbers, and then the letters, EMI.

Chrysanthemum reaches over to shake your wrist. "Ma'am," starts the nurse.

"You, wrong!" Chrysanthemum radiates with panic. Her face splits in the middle, and suddenly, she's old. "Baby, come back!"

"No," your voice is hard.

We're taken into a room, and from that, another room. Eventually, the intake nurse will ask Emi's mother Chrysanthemum to leave for the night. Go home. Come back on Saturday. Visiting hours are between 10:30 and noon. You can sense how Emi ignores you, Lua, pushing away the rhythm of your thoughts even as we all crowd the same body. We observe this little drama between you and Emi, apprehensively from our corners, four or five yet unnamed voices collected into a chorus; how the journalist, we think feebly, could launch instinctively, no, decisively, from "bad" to Mars, and what *would* be much worse, adds Emi, our poet, than a script switching its subject matter, points of view, or narrative direction.

The poet is bareheaded, with 165 centimeters of bony muscle in jogger pants. A loose gray shirt has holes under both armpits. You watch when she approaches a block of text on a sheet of paper taped to the wall by her bed. The bed, when you blink, is replaced by a mat on the floor. The mat is replaced by a pale hospital blanket, and that's been yanked away, too.

Emi stands in an empty, stark white room. You take a step back, realizing your legs are melded with Emi's legs. We shrug, frowning a bit. It's the way things go.

You gawk where the sheet of paper had just dissolved. In its place, a padded accordion of paneling unfolds along the walls of our cell. An outline of a triangle from an aerial perspective forms underneath a sketch, in your mind, of a mask with no eyes.

Meanwhile, ten thousand and fifty-nine days ago, you might've pulled into our record a memory of NASA punting a space probe, *Voyager 2*, squealing toward the cosmos.

Let's imagine—we talk over each other fervently, inaudibly, the poet's lips moving with our words, "a cloud, a tempest, a pine"—the crisis backpedaling into our sixth or seventh voice introduced into the scene. It scratches against the decade in which President John F. Kennedy would make a statement regarding a news picture evoking "so much emotion around the world."

The poet appears to concentrate on the latter part of this quote. She pushes a finger into one of the polyester panels, making an imprint on the wall. For the past few weeks, we've been acquiescent, orderly to the point of absence. You squeeze behind us in a train of pink and sea blue forms, stacking in front of one another in cartoonish two dimensions, peeking out at random angles with googly eyes attached at the earlobes. Emi is quiet. She doesn't sigh or toss her hands in the air.

After an incident with a stuffed animal and a pencil, we'd been transferred to a smaller cell with no window and no toilet. Today, Emi glares at the camera looming above the ceiling as she squats upon a kidney-shaped container. When she wants to eat, we try rattling at the doorknob; it's our fault we're locked in here, she knows this. The city, the ward, even the minutes that pass, the seasons that drop their leaves, the blocks of identities that separate and glide apart, become but globs of dust in the vacuum. Our poet, thankfully, knows her name and date of birth. Lua, we say again. You can get out of this. But you ignore us, crossing the highway into traffic.

When Chrysanthemum visits on Saturday mornings, she weeps uncontrollably. She pushes Daichi, her husband, to say something, but Daichi doesn't know what to say.

"Emi-chan."

A map burrows deeper into the outline of what we know to be our *Book of Wind*. We try to explain her role as our writer to the parents, and then the doctors, but Emi doesn't speak. Her silence forms a solid mass at the center of our chest, above the sternum. Between each generation of this silence, we hand off a family photograph of Emi's mother and the news photograph of a burning monk intertwined with each other. We try to include them both toward the end of our book.

Baby—Emi adds, at last, to a spot on her chest where the ghost of Kenzo had just been napping—what modes of recordkeeping fling us out, if not through, the archive, if not to fault us, watching us fall to our knees? People run across an intersection in Saigon. They drop everything. They press their palms together. Chrysanthemum stands there deliberating in her mind, whether we should run, whether we should stay on this curb and pray; if Malcolm Browne, the journalist from America, would call these events "every bit as bad," how can we set the standard for our *Book of Wind* without a single unified voice?

The fluorescent light flickers on and off, on and off. Emi is with us again, alone, in her room with no furniture, no paper, facing the audience.

I bloom with a stone, she tells herself—and we listen. The larger crane arrives to pluck out its feathers. We stand in the marsh of Emi's imagination. Snow-white plumes drift into mud and clay. A red hornet dives above the jungle and plunges, squealing like a water droplet lifted from a hot iron plate. The hornet has been shot; its legs are singed a golden yellow.

In arriving here, at the scene change, multiple tones of our language are limited by present and present circular tenses. We find ourselves waiting for you, Lua, the record cosmic keeper of steel and fire, so help us. Emi can't render this production into one coherent draft. Our setting, the dates, and plot points switch all over the place. "For now," my mother says in her writing, "I'm only four. I've seen many things."

Sometime between 1964 and 1973—for, as we know by now, the years of our calendar don't stay in one place—Chrysanthemum falls in love. She tells her daughter this, unprompted, as she sips a cup of lukewarm tea. The boy . . . begins Chrysanthemum without any context. The boy comes from a nearby village. He cannot read. He cannot write. But he can sing.

Beautifully like a bird, Emi's told, like the moon beating wildly at a summer harvest, spreading its silver-tipped beams over a lolling rice field. Chrysanthemum stops to find the right word, the right connected speech in her English: like an *air raid.*

Beneath the conjunction of her sentences, into the swoon of a memory she never wanted to keep but passed on to Emi regardless, Chrysanthemum's voice begins to turn. She rounds a corner, switching languages, switching pronouns, and grammatical conventions, a tightening in her throat.

The boy has nothing, narrates my mother, her mother, Chrysanthemum. He arrives this morning in Saigon.

She speaks in the constant present tense, without quotation marks, a story pulled from thin air, beneath a sash of hyacinth perfume. A window has been locked between this memory and a memory of leaving her heart behind, in the glass pushing at a swell, in the vestibule of our book fracturing into multiple parts.

We're sitting in Dallas, sometime after 1995 but before 2259. In simple terms, I was born as Emi or Kenzo in the ribcage of a country, not that of my own. We place ourselves as children and mothers in a kitchen; as a writer and a narrator, we make scenes from horror in the presence of ghosts. I'm fourteen, no, fifteen, six . . .

Chrysanthemum cuts in: Emi, listen. I think he wants to come inside.

I see my mother writing at the kitchen table, closing her eyes. She exhales, and in my mind, the story opens to a backlit doorway in Saigon. I see the doorway and the boy, his bare arms deep in the color of July; he, who would have been my first grandfather if it weren't for the war, in the premise of dislocation, he, who would have been guiding us now, here, out from the tunnels, into the mines, over perfume rivers and derivatives for dirt, air, finally, as we continue to count before ignition, the number four, the number three, the number two, the eight or nine countries bombing us out, speaking in circles of liberation or autonomy.

We sit quietly around the kitchen table like a stack of tangerines in the shape of a pyramid.

A rice farmer, Chrysanthemum keeps going. She ignores the shift in attention and perspective, recalling now the voice of her dead father. A rice farmer has been killed, says her father in a gentle but deep tone, and this—she waves in the direction of a skeletal boy groveling at our feet— this is his son. We must take him in and treat him like our own.

Chrysanthemum stops her story, or her father's story, unable to pick the two apart, to continue, it seems. She presses the tip of her finger into the corner of her eye, fighting back a contradiction she can't seem to reveal. Once more, she's crying.

The boy is given a good pair of shoes and a new family name. Although for our record, the boy's first name shall remain, as it does today, unknown.

Instead, we hear President Charles de Gaulle say in 1964, "The shock caused in the south by withdrawing our troops and administration would expose the country to new perils."

"It was a matter of believing if she could find a sense of cohesion to self-govern . . ." To see, I add in the wings interrupting, becomes an act within its present moment, stark as daylight set against the backdrop of a theater. According to the past, we have no proper way to say it all except to blend the tenses. What *happens*? What *happened* next? What ripples from the shock of withdrawal, in the present or the future?

The boy now shares a room with my young grandmother. Naturally, they fall in love and keep this love a secret. When my grandmother later flees her country, she is doomed to never see the boy again. It should be noted that they had planned to elope in secret, but the boy was never told what happened to Chrysanthemum, that she was forced to flee, also in secret from Saigon, with the clothes on her back; that she, along with little brother, Hau, were first to leave the backdoor open; they were told to *run,* and she, along with Hau, would run until they reached the sharp edge of a river's mouth. Imagine, we say, some tempest rhythm forming in her lungs.

"He writes LOVE poems," interjects Chrysanthemum abruptly, giggling. Even here, my grandmother refers to everyone, including herself, in a distant third person. Time collapses. There is no yesterday or tomorrow in that narrative. After Chrysanthemum escapes, the boy allegedly dedicates every line to an impossible future with the girl my grandmother used to be. "He learns to write and read when Mama is GONE."

As both her daughter and scribe, Emi attempts to fill in some of the wide blanks my grandmother leaves behind. The boy *wrote* poems and composed long, dramatic letters in Chrysanthemum's absence. Allegedly, the aunties who stayed behind would burn these letters, letters my grandmother only learned about in rumors, after a few aunties made it to America, decades later, bearing more than scars.

Emi's notebooks carry additional memories of Chrysanthemum conjuring such stories about loss, fatality, and heartbreak, along with solemn claims of the boy's inevitable descent into madness. Perhaps my grandmother wanted to caution some nightshade blooming in Emi's chest. Perhaps Emi understood more about this boy than Chrysanthemum could admit.

One story stands out clearly to me now. Chrysanthemum swoons on her birthing table at the Dallas Presbyterian Hospital. At approximately 10 p.m., as if by a divine summon, the boy appears directly to her right, by her side. He looks down at the baby in Chrysanthemum's arms. Chrysanthemum is asleep, and Emi, the newborn, stares up at the boy, who stares down at her, and Emi, the newborn, appears healthy, quiet, swaddled in a thick milky blanket; at this, the boy begins to weep.

Here's a point of some contention: did he or did he not exist?

In one version of this story, my Japanese grandfather, a young man then, approaches the boy, who hovers pale and sniveling next to my grandmother's bed. The ghost is invisible from the waist down, with imperceptible legs like a root forbidden to return home. My grandfather rests a hand on the boy's shoulder. He's not a jealous man, but Daichi hears himself say, "Please, can you leave us. It's enough."

Another version feels more accurate.

The ghost looks down at Emi, and Emi looks up at the ghost. Then they both smile.

There are rumors of a village, and from that village not far from the boy's birthplace, my first and hidden grandfather, of loving days going by, of someone leaving in the middle of the afternoon to join the enemy. Phạm Hổ, the poet, would write about it in 1950. In my mother's notebooks, she would also refer to a collective "we" singing the poet's lyrics in dark overdrawn eyebrows, our costumes glittering onstage, and Emi would regard this chorus carefully.

The performance has to be perfect, she would think. Saigon is about to burn. My mother, she would say, is going to load a rifle. The year is 1963, 1975, or 1973, interchangeably. Chrysanthemum sprints barefoot across her city at the pace of a galloping heart. There are loudspeakers almost everywhere but we can't see or afford them just yet; they play a familiar anthem scattered with the sound of an American Christmas.

Emi sees her now, Lua, dressed in the body of a teenager, running toward her enemy.

In Saigon, there's a banyan tree, twisting its long wrinkled neck to the music of destruction, ruffling yellow leaves against the crack of gunfire, mortar upon steel and flesh. Finally, according to the press, in one of these years, the US has been dropping—in the present imperfect tense—17,000 pounds of bombs over the city of Đà Nẵng.

It's all the same in the voice of an old woman. I look up, have mercy. I hold closer to your face a miniature toy horse painted red, balanced between my index finger and thumb. You can call me bà ngoại, I hear myself explain, but you hesitate before taking the horse. Your mother, who might turn seventeen, begins to scream, and according to our record, she understands the aftershock, a "new peril" that pushes a nation to the edge if not the edge of her own body.

She runs, as she has always learned to run, between the whiplash of a bomb and its crater, beneath a curtain of bullets pelting her city like a water bucket slashed with fire, the motorized commas of a rotating aircraft lifting us, once more, a third of the way to paradise before dropping us to the ground. We leave behind that ghost of a boy who waves obscurely at the sky. According to Chrysanthemum, we'll all spend a lifetime trapped in exile, mistrusting the very rhythm of our hearts. "I met him," clarified the poet Phạm Hổ. "I met him. I shot him."

In Emi's mind, Chrysanthemum was once a girl who loved a boy who would one day become our enemy, but love would be the end of us, she'd later tell us. Indeed, the boy my grandmother used to love would open his mouth into a scream before whatever took his heart would also take his name, I imagine, in our city of devotions.

Chrysanthemum drops to a knee. She aims her rifle at a straw-covered board. It's been propped on a stick at the far end of a dusty field behind what used to be her high school.

My grandmother would later claim that the target was a simple wooden board, not a man. Here, however, Emi chooses to write about a board, not the neck exposed to the sun.

Another question begins to form in my mind. What's the difference between hate and straw? How do we recreate our truth to access a different truth, the multiplication of a body and distance through genocide, betrayal, and martyrdom, the boy who would have been my first grandfather, before that, an ancestry of straw or grass stuffed into the shape of a wild, teary-eyed raccoon; he's already dead in my grandmother's version of history—how do we document in a language turning her grieving face away from the rest of us?

"Shoot." I hear the boy say. He's older now. His jaw is clenching; he's handsome. "Just shoot me. I've made my peace, comrade."

"Did you kill him?" Emi asks immediately without thinking.

Chrysanthemum glares at her daughter in the kitchen, peeling the rest of a tangerine. "Why Emi say that? Mama never SAY that."

Or, was it all a lie, the fragmenting of collected memories coming together onstage?

Who have you killed? Who have I killed, comrade? Who are we both, truly, in three or four voices of a chorus coming together? Lua, tell me, how does your understanding of our planet bring you to war, what compels us to obliterate the people we love when we have no other choice?

My grandmother gasps. She wrinkles her nose, standing up from the table. The chair grates across the floor onstage; it echoes into the audience. "Someone STINK."

In the shower later offstage, at home, I hold my head under hot, running water. Who are you to me, Lua, I try to ask. And why can't you leave us alone?

For now, the journalist Malcolm Browne, exhausted by the tragedy of it all, travels north and notes simply in his records, "Hanoi remains a beautiful and bustling city."

1945

THERE'S WIND. The wind reaches speeds up to 1,800 kilometers per hour. The wind is raging, round and round, our planet Paul. Now we must be vigilant. Lean into the glass. The glass becomes our portal. Go ahead, Lua. I'll read you the rest.

Our reading guide: At the opera house in Hanoi, at the end of Tràng Tiền Street, a young economics student in his third year at the university bolts down a hot stretch of pavement. He's panting, softly out of breath. He's afraid. You can see that. It's very clear. Fresh droplets of blood have dribbled down his white collared shirt and appear now as bright acacia blossoms. One sleeve has been torn at the shoulder.

The man's name is Tan Huỳnh. In two days, his father will be summarily executed by his best friend behind an unmarked Japanese convoy truck, but that is not a matter of importance, comrade. What matters is this man you're about to meet might pass, from one generation to the next, a mission that you must also complete upon this stupid, stupid planet. So, Lua, pay attention.

It always starts like this, at the rally. A man becomes his singular witness to the present moment of a war declared by his father's people. He conjures up a sensation of *Now, Now, Now*, gasping from each filament of scenes before a world that does nothing, and even that which multiplies to ten, and if not so, hundreds and hundreds of testimonies splattered across time, moving collectively forward, a tide of angry, famished men as they march collectively onward, and, arriving at last to the front doorsteps of a grand opera house in northern Vietnam, these men go completely silent.

You take my photograph on that street and then a photograph of the men standing tight-lipped in their square. One by one, each man begins to raise his fist.

The date is August 19, 1945. A reporter stands in front of the opera house in Hanoi. He's holding a reading guide and notes, in pencil, this building was first modeled after the Palais Garnier in Paris, a neoclassical reflection of its colonial master's ambition in 1901, but today, he also scribbles, the building stands for so much more. Would the people burn it down?

He turns a page and underlines the same date with two lines. August 19, 1945. A people's revolution or the people's insurrection, terms depending on which side of history one might choose to stand upon. Here, the text trails off. What difference does a language make? On the street, Lua meets this reporter who repeats: Look. The man holds up his identification card, repeating, I'm American. From America. *M. Browne.*

Lua nods and turns her back to the crowd of men, standing behind her, each one of them raising a clenched fist, like a heavy sea of lanterns, in the air. Take my photograph, she gestures to the reporter. The man obliges.

There's no record of this photograph today, and one might further argue, perhaps, that no record of a reporter by the name of *M. Browne* in Hanoi existed in 1945. But you have to trust me, comrade. She was there, and I was there, too, for I was that man named Malcolm, and this is my story.

A university student runs across the street. He's bleeding from one ear. He's afraid. I can see that. This is clear, as well, to everyone he passes. My connections at the Pentagon have also informed me something tremendous is about to happen to his country. My job is to stay out of it. But here you are, Lua, asking me to take your photograph.

✳

At the hospital, a man dressed in baby blue scrubs stops to take my temperature. It's around day-break, and the night technicians have just changed their shifts. Morning, says the psychiatric technician. Who are we speaking with today?

I tap the camera resting against my chest.

There's wind. The wind reaches speeds of up to 1,800 kilometers per hour. Your name is Lua. My name is Malcolm. When our eyes meet, a convergence of selves. Atop your head sits a five-point crown in the shape of a large, golden starfish. Queen of Mercy. I hear the men chanting—Freedom! Freedom!—so let the glass dissolve. We all come back to our surface, gasping, dried, and pulverized, made suddenly awake. You duck into a slipstream of time, and then another, and then, once again, here we are zooming through our portal of selves. Who can keep up?

The technician replies, hm. With delicacy, he rolls the blood pressure machine closer to our bedside.

The August Revolution, I insist, or what at least has been known to the Western world as something less than documented, does not end. An overlap of scenes. Fin.

In this film of bodies, fronds combust at their tips, curling into smoke. Lungs expand. Bare legs march, crisscrossing the reel; cheekbones, made too stark in black and white, triumphant beneath the sun; and the film, rendered silent in our city of selves. Patterns of storm clouds accumulate, thin into tiny wispy spirals, speeding up, then reversing, freezing again. We all start over in our film of liberation. A toad is squatting on its leaf.

A larger toad, nearby, pierced by a dart.

Are we here, or are we there, in our city of coups? In Hanoi? Or after Hanoi? It doesn't matter anymore. Give thanks to this universe if not our ancestors, may they have mercy on our souls.

Note: the planet Paul's core produces energy at approximately 12,000 degrees Kelvin. A hurricane might slow near the surface of this planet but don't count on it, my friend, for as I attempt to tell you my name, a sense of identity slips over. Read this carefully. Not slowly. I mean, backward. Freeze then reverse. And if we are wont to reach into the chest of Paul—don't worry, I'll go first—if we are wont to reach into that beating chest of Paul and place one hand upon this burning core of hydrogen, rock, and magma, shall we sooner understand the breaking of his heart? So, yes, back to the question of love, what you have heard is true. My name is Lua, and yes, as you suspect, comrade, the former wife of Paul.

```
Secondary case note: Speaking with a morning technician,
the  patient  Emi  reveals  another  identity,  Malcolm
Browne, a relatively known American reporter stationed
in Vietnam during the war. Defining a traumatic event
is still unclear. Patient, noncombative.
```

We've met again in late December 2015, and by now, you're a performance artist. I'd seen some of your work online, but most of what I've learned about your live gigs has been documented in small, local features. In Tucson, for instance, I read that you once pressed a large knife to your throat. In

Ljubljana, two years before that, a group of men had volunteered to come on stage and hold each of your wrists as you attempted to run off the edge of the stage into the audience.

I regretted it almost immediately, stated one of the volunteers to a journalist from Serbia. Saša, another audience member, agreed with an affirmative shake of the head: She warned us, but I wasn't sure if that was literal or not.

At the coffee shop in southern California, you swirl a finger in a water cup. The last time we met, I say, we were both in Saigon. You'd been with your mother. Do you remember that? You were five or six years old, and I had offered you a little toy horse. But now you've grown into yourself, Emi. Look, here you are, taking a sip out of your large mug of cappuccino. Your face is still young, though some wrinkles have formed around your eyelids. My free hand glides over the notebook in my lap, and the left holds a black ballpoint pen.

Though I might be Kenzo or someone playing Kenzo preparing to play his mother, Emi, I've taken a few more notes about myself in the third person: Her name is Emi. She is also Lua, as I've come to understand, a performance artist who blurs the line between identity and time. In case of displacement or memory loss, please return to Emi's parental figures near San Diego. The address is included below.

The brain is so wondrously weak, pushing its way down the human spine, the network of hunger. You tap your fingers against the cup. Your fingernails have been cut to a short, practical length. I put my braid in a bun. My name is Lua. My name is also Emi. I'm a multitude of selves switching at any point in the conversation.

Our table is nailed to the ground. Rust and salt edge its little clawed feet in an orange circle. A very good table. Good for Lua. You often speak in the third person, too, I've noticed.

The coffee shop is a four-minute walk from the beach, and we'll go there after you finish telling me the story of Tan Huỳnh, a university student whose father was executed, in 1945, by his best friend at the back of an unmarked convoy truck.

I open my notebook and scribble—Hanoi was a bustling place, narrated Lua—and the story has begun to come together like a pointillist impression of subconscious memories melding into one, attempting a portrait of collective history. Still, and perhaps to this end, you choose to speak interchangeably among all points of view.

Lua has just arrived from the planet called Paul. The year is 1945. Lua is sad and doesn't know what to do with her new body. First, she travels to northern Vietnam, where she meets a reporter from America. She forgets his name now, but the reporter claims that what is about to happen on this day will be known as the August Revolution.

There's a plastic hanging pot twirling above us at the café. Next, your mind falls upon the notebook in your lap. It's a very good table, you hear yourself repeating. The cappuccino is churning a tiny truck, inside out, in your stomach.

Together, we're working on a reading guide, tentatively titled, *Book of Wind,* and you become that marvelous pothos plant twirling in its plot, I mean pot, overhead. Tell me, Lua. Where should we begin?

My fifteen eyeballs pulse, I hear you thinking.

You scan your body for the eyeballs. You point to one with a heavy eyelid, just below the sternum. This is a strange body, I agree. These eyeballs ripple awake, one by one, along with the pair along your left clavicle bone, and circling up around your pelvis and hips; strapped to the back of your shoulder blades are also a set of wings tucked into your shirt. Continues your voice: I'm upside down and right side up.

You close your notebook and face the sun, each eyeball swiveling wildly in its socket.

✳

There's a film camera in one of my eyes. I love the light here, in southern California.

At the coffee shop, a man is pacing back and forth on the patio. He holds a silver box up to his mouth and is working on, what humans of his planet call in the latter part of this twenty-first century, what most of them refer to affectionately as a *podcast.*

Once more, the man repeats into his handheld device: once more, it's like . . . jumping out of a plane without your parachute.

The podcast button blinks—*Live, Live, Live!*—while the man goes on and on to explain these centrifugal forces snapping the planet Paul into action; and, at the sound of my former husband's name, my head springs from the bottom of my coffee mug to meet the eyes of a nervous, tiny Panda.

The tiny Panda twitches his ears. His eyes are black and embroidered with large white circles to represent dewy eyes, tears on the verge of falling. Staring up at us from the edge of our table, he turns to gaze at me, and I imagine that he blinks, just about to burst into uncontrollable weeping; yet, his eyes are huge, much too huge, holding all that thread which never leaves the surface of his face.

The tiny Panda, I notice, is about seven inches tall. He wears a one-piece set of brown pajamas fastened up at the collar by a small safety pin. Over his heart, on the left side of his outfit, a large round sticker peels up and frays at the bottom. It reads: I VOTED EARLY.

The tiny Panda looks as if he's about to dissolve in a cup. Where did you come from, I ask this brave and tiny Panda. And why are you here? The tiny Panda shrugs and waddles across the table.

I paraphrase the following from memory: first, explains the physicist in his podcast, the planet Paul's sixth moon, Enceladus, named after a giant in Greek mythology, who once presided over earthquakes and volcanoes, completes one rotation around my former husband every 32.9 hours. It's been thus hypothesized that Enceladus (the moon) gave the planet Paul plasma, if not whiplash, plasma that would heat and stretch under Paul's magnetic field until it grew *so strong* that the tail flicked out, banishing me to Earth.

I'll go no further. Blood pumps hot like petrol in whole gallons from my face. My kidney somersaults. The tiny Panda has returned to his heightened tiny senses, shuddering at the shoulders and pulling out a lima bean from his tiny pajama pouch. He hiccups before hopping into my lap, burying himself, headfirst, in the bottom of my shirt. Meanwhile, the human physicist continues to jabber, on and on, about the mathematical, centrifugal breakdown of my marriage.

Here, I block out all of the rest. I push my forehead into the collar of my shirt and whisper down to the tiny Panda, who, by now, has teetered toward the edge of a nap. Panda, let's go home. Okay, nods the brave and tiny Panda, closing both his watery black eyes.

The tiny Panda pushes the felt tip of his tiny paw into my belly button, yawns, and falls, at once, to sleep. My belly button opens, pulling us toward the rings of the planet Paul. The portal opens. The portal is an inverse of flesh, polyester, and time.

Comrade, please forgive me. If it's not so clear by now, it seems I've lost the reading guide and tossed it right out the window, I mean, into our glass oblivion. The portal is a sundried tomato. Yes, follow me.

We're approaching my former husband, the planet Paul, once again, undone. I bare my teeth and chomp. I'm older, turned into a human, worn by gravity and time. The tiny Panda cries and kicks his tiny legs. I hold his tiny paw. Comrade, be careful. Blink twice and you'll miss everything.

Look! I hear myself shout into the glass of Lua. The portal starts to shift. Hold tight, my tiny Panda! We're coming home. I hear a voice by the American writer, Susan Sontag: "They hastened to emphasize—almost as if it would be bad taste not to—that the full horror of America's war on Vietnam couldn't be seen anywhere in the North."

In moments of great distress, regression may be triggered when the human subject dreams most clearly of a wound, in my case, banishment. I dream the ink runs out. I dream of shouting at my students at the university in Tucson, where I've tucked myself on Earth, for now, as a teacher, as both their priestess and their Jigglypuff. They call me both, interchangeably, as a mandate from my syllabus.

Two centuries of dust and rock, thus, begins the slides of my PowerPoint. An architect, a young, earnest freshman named Andrew, gawks at the back of the classroom; each "lecture," in my mind, is a long durational performance that I practice every semester at the university. We're getting quite good at it, the students and the priestess. Eventually, I may ask them to call me Ms. T or Fräulein Maria. It all makes sense to me in the end.

And is this me, a ghost? Or the presence of Cher in the presence of a ghost? And if I were to tap my ghost-bone knuckles on this whiteboard, would our curse of banishment be over? Would I gasp, wide-eyed and face up, floating through paradise, most gently down the Mekong? Would the children, as they often are quick to gather like pure light beams in discovery, descend around the muddy banks? Would they sprint and holler? Would they call me River?

At the Library of Congress, there's a map dated back to the year 1942. I imagine running my fingers down the parchment fabric of that map. The map is traced by a single moss-green brush-stroke. Upon closer inspection, this river Mekong holds small dragonflies and lazy whirlpools in her arms. There are markings, too, for future sites of conquest in my mother's country. For example, Sontag comments in her records, a book that she later titles, *Trip to Hanoi*, "Each plane that's shot down is methodically taken apart."

My arms stretch out and wiggle. The currency of wind indicates what remains after cartography. And herein lies a buffalo; herein lies the reeds, bloated shells, and shrapnel in the reeds; barrels are filled with ore and bodies of mice; herein, bodies drift into mangroves, turned up on their bellies. Tiny phantoms crowd, furthermore, along the riverbanks of my past, my mother's past.

They wave, and children jump from shore to shore of Mother Mekong, a perfumed river of blood and rubies. "Chị, sister!" They shout, "We miss you! Come home!"

At once, I wake in exile, weeping and drowning in my bed. The tiny Panda, fast asleep, rolls over on my chest. It's a nightmare, I tell you. Let's keep it all together, comrade, for you must know the price we pay in fleeing those we love. Thích Quảng Đức is burning. Malcolm Browne is watching, and of watching, his president repeats, "No news picture in history has generated so much emotion around the world as that one." And with this *generation of emotion*, I fall year by year in orbit, faster and faster around a plane of dust that I can never leave in this life or the next.

When we last saw each other, the planet Paul called me selfish. Perhaps he was right. Perhaps one day he'll start to understand exactly why I had to leave him. "But at that moment," David Halberstam of the *New York Times* writes, "I looked into the center of the circle and saw a man burning himself to death. I was to see that sight again, but once was enough."

Bluegill

ABOARD THE US SUBMARINE docked near the waterfront, Frederick Nolting Jr., ambassador to South Vietnam, poses for a photograph. The date is April 4, 1962. Beneath his beige suit and tie, the man feels a swamp of thick heat enter the fabric of his undershirt soaking a layer of fuzz across his skin. He reaches up to scratch at a growing itch behind one of his ears but misses it entirely. He can't seem to track the itch with his finger, leaping behind the scalp, and soon becomes annoyed.

A group of young sailors ducks their heads to scuttle by. Nolting squints and follows them with his eyes, turning his wide-set face and pair of bovine shoulders in a series of jolts, not knowing where to look next. His arms shutter up to one side at the elbows like a symphony orchestra conductor's bringing in the cellos first, the bass second, and finally, a bassoon, French horn, tuba—stoic, shifting forward in their chairs—at the back, a percussionist standing before her cue, stunned to find the last pages of her sheet music entirely missing, and the symphony goes quiet in Nolting's mind. Saigon Harbor, too, appears to be holding its breath.

In the water, a child bobs for empty beer bottles. I recognize her as some descendant of mine, but Nolting, who doesn't look into the water, begins to soften into thin vertical ripples from the waist up, a distortion of perspective I wipe from my eyes and gulp at the air, turning to vanish with a flurry, kicking down its hot, murky surface. I see the child's legs before this, my bare brown legs and knobby knees. I see the child puff her cheeks, the child in a pair of green drawstring shorts diving for bottles at the bottom of a seaport. Across our pier, my older brother scurries up a palm tree for a better view of the black submarine. All morning, a large crowd has been gathering along the waterfront. Someone eventually brings a handcart with steamed pork rice buns, offering them at generous discounts. One of the spectators is curious. Will they shoot a gun? Or cannon?

"Don't be stupid," replies his friend.

"This is for show. It's expensive to do something like that. Look, a camera, behind us."

The two men glance over their shoulders, prompting their neighbors to look, followed by a whole network of what makes a crowd compelled to turn from the back, starting as two, then four, then ten, pivoting, careening to look, look, there it is! The journalist, with his white face obscured by the instrument, raises a free hand to make that circular curt motion from his wrist, but this particular section of the crowd, all men of black eyebrows and coffee-stained lips parted in various stages of grimace, wonderment, absentminded waiting, continue to stare without shame at this ever-present American. Malcolm Browne sighs and sidesteps to the left, closer to the boy still climbing a tree overlooking the harbor.

Nolting has developed a migraine. The marching band at the pier moves to a second formation, much to Nolting's dread. To his right, stands Ngô Đình Diệm, the current acting president of South Vietnam, who greets, standing at ease before him, Lieutenant Commander James H. Barry of our USS *Bluegill*. Both men start speaking to each other in French.

The English translator assigned on this day to Frederick Nolting Jr. has tucked himself modestly off-frame. I think of such moments as a collection of stage actors: three make a triangle (four, a war) fixed with interchangeable devices like grammar, speech, or metaphor. One cannot move without the other's explicit permission, and they all smile vaguely at each other.

Whoever takes *this* photograph, I imagine, counts from one to four. *BỐN, QUATTUOR, SHI*. A tremor rises from under my feet, a deep and agonizing groan. The machine careens to one side. I feel my blood, at once, drain from its skull and right myself against the railing. Comrade, help me. In a minute, I'll remember one of my names, but on the USS *Bluegill*, I take off a white sailor's hat before handing you a cigarette. You nod and put a hand on my shoulder. We're wearing identical uniforms, freshly laundered, crisp, and billowing out at the ankles. I think of my mother, bless her heart, in Boston, sitting at the radio and thinking, that's my boy, my sweet boy, Carl.

Looking back on everything now, I didn't know who I was trying to be, really, a shifter easily jumping from one body to the other. Some were more difficult to inhabit. The Americans especially made me dizzy, and I found the photograph of Diệm unsettling, impossible to place among a sea of images not meant for reproduction, except for this conversation among diplomats aboard a submarine.

Diệm's mouth parts into a modest but open grin. He gazes somewhere, off, toward the water of his country, a hand nestled inside the captain's hand like a sun-dried tamarind embraced in a series of half-shadows, in the pale grip of a moon. In our year of linen and mortar, I think, as well, of people huddled around their stoves. A blue open room with fish and oil and garlic sizzling in a wide, discolored wok, a family taking turns at the meat, shredding it with their chopsticks; to the north and farther inland, another family slicing at stalks of jute in the field. These are all my families, or all my descendants, as well, but to make a horrible story short, I steady myself again on the railing, unable to make sense of place or the single photograph or half my names.

You drop a sheet of paper on my desk at the Library of Congress. You scratch at the scabs on your face and think of an anvil, a river belly-up among remains. I see cuts along the waters of your mind, Lua. Can you read my mind, too, the newsreel and archival records speaking out of turn which reminds me of another name, Emi; it must be my name. The ghost is an enemy now, I hear you start to say.

According to the *Times* in 1962, a goodwill diplomacy tour would lead to a "favorable breakthrough" in South Vietnam. Adds Nolting, "Yes, but it will be difficult."

Shortly after this, Ngô Đình Diệm is taken hostage and killed by his captors. I want to stop and vomit. How can this be documented in a timeless span of the photograph? The saber cracks into a singular shot. I fold our rhetoric in two. What remains behind is an essence of sage, turmeric, and red star anise. This is my mother's home, and this is a text made within the confines of time.

On December 21, 1963, one month after Diệm's assassination, the US secretary of defense Robert McNamara would write to his new president regarding the "neutralization" of Vietnam, the clacking of keys against its gills, and, in Syria, sometime before AD 100, I recall that the goddess Atargatis once killed her lover before jumping into a lake of mirrors. A boy's heart sinks to the bottom of this lake, only to be picked at by the mud-scraping fish, and this is our planet in June. My name is Lua.

Lua, for the time being, somersaults into a hundred million directions, and I ask the impossible question over and over again: Did she ever meet that boy, Chrysanthemum's lover and enemy, at the bottom of a lake?

In history, I turn into a bull that bolts around a ring, turning over the ceramic displays and glass, only to be lost midair, breathing in and breathing out, dazed as the fish shot right out of the water. I also read that McGeorge "Mac" Bundy would draft a memorandum in October of 1963, which he would then deliver promptly to the US secretary of state, the secretary of defense, and the chairman of the Joint Chiefs of Staff.

The memorandum admits, regarding the war of which, later, General Maxwell Taylor, former commander of the 101st Airborne Division of the US Army, will also admit, "There are no heroes." And, indeed, there are no heroes in our history of wind, in place of discussion, the document continues without logic from steps A to B. Here, Bundy reveals the president's plan to quietly withdraw one thousand troops by the end of this year, 1964, and a hand strikes its record below the hold of ships. Perhaps this could be, too, an extension of what happens on the USS *Bluegill* before someone is killed, and the crowd goes all quiet again. Regarding, here, the subjective shift between mythic points of view, I give you a splintering of selves after an AK-47. Sing! You twist your mouth into a grin. I dig a fingernail into the eyeballs of my clavicle. A dog begins to bark. I tell you in the distance, Lua, that Caliban is cursing us, the "red plague" indeed for ridding us, "for learning" us a language!

Nothing scares us anymore, not even my loneliness, for this is a texture, deep blue, and twilight, mostly sweet around the edges, numberless, and suspended by logic I can never understand, or the winding and rewinding of stories once belonging to a banished goddess flung into the waters from the planet called Paul.

Lua, also, to the thought of uttering what remains of minutes hurtling through space, I'd rather die all over again; to be a ghost, an utterance of textures, opening and closing a window on the sixth floor of what was once called the Texas School Book Depository, out of which, allegedly, a man once shot and killed a US president.

You open the window. You shout into the street: Lua, look up!

The ghost inserts a light bulb into her mouth. The light bulb flashes red. Near the window, there's a plague inside my mouth. I think perhaps I'm that ghost, ridding us of terrible, terrible languages.

The ghost is gazing down from the window. Lua shudders. Come home, says the ghost. No, she answers. Lua has no fixed subjectivity pinned to one body, only a memory. For instance, in 1966, three years after the president had been assassinated, I may watch Chrysanthemum, hold a blood-soaked ribbon to her cheek. There, in Saigon, she makes a vow to herself, in the presence of ghosts, to survive whatever violence sparked her father's body in the backseat of a van, inside a scorched belly of the insurrection she never wanted.

This day would have been warm, unusually so even for winter in a southern city. Then, the man, who would have been Chrysanthemum's father if he hadn't been set on fire, turns into a tall pillar of ash, which takes, according to his wife, Mai, less than thirty minutes. Before this, Tan had most likely stopped for coffee before Lua, a relatively unknown goddess from the Roman pantheon of war deities, and in our minds, as well, the *former* wife of a planet called Paul, came crashing like a rocket upon Earth, past into a present, reversed.

"Two thousand years ago," Kennedy once announced, "the proudest boast was 'civis Romanus sum' (I am a Roman citizen)."

Does it matter when or how Mai knew that her people would be killed, or who ordered each citizen's death? And does it matter: who would make Chrysanthemum watch it all, who pulled her by the hand and hissed for her to flee? A voice: One day you might remember this, my child. Now run!

The little girl—later in exile, Chrysanthemum as a little girl splitting into ten separate parts—splits her body into three or four disjointed identities with separate names for each. They ripple to a clattering of hooves, replacing bullet holes for eyes; and Lua, having just then landed in a field of hyacinth nearby, sits up, blinks twice, and glancing at her toes, cries out. Where did they go?!

The little girl, not too far away, runs barefoot down a dusty road behind that field. She outstretches both her arms, appearing as though to launch, at that moment, and out of deep azure across those wings, one tiny Panda falls from the sky.

The tiny Panda lands face down on a lily pad and will wake in fourteen days, according to unofficial records. Lua yawns. Her mouth, in the shape of a small circular clock, is followed by the ticking sound of a spiral locust cloud tumbling out. But, anyway, comrade, this story isn't, really, about her.

It's easier to say that Chrysanthemum fled her country by the instinct of her feet. It's much easier to note, as well, how she vowed to never run again when she arrived in midwinter as a refugee in Ann Arbor, Michigan. This year, to her, is still unknown to the archive. When did she leave? When did she arrive? But what do we know as semantics? First, a local church gave the young Chrysanthemum a clean pair of blue jeans and a checkered woolen coat. The woolen coat had red squares and an inner lining made of polyester, bright red as cherries from the can. She would have clutched each item of clothing around her bones. She would have spoken her first two words in the English language, what she learned on this island off Malaysia—another story for later—*thank you.*

Yes, I hear it now, her voice cracking to Michigan's winter. *Thank you. Thank you, yes, my name is whatever you want.* It's easier to say, as a consequence, I've started running through this country as my mother's checkered red ghost, arriving first in Dallas, as a newborn, Emi, and then later, very much elsewhere, as the fifteen-eyeballed body jumper Lua Mater.

Exactly how our bodies came to turn from one into another is not, here, a matter of relevance. Comrade, all you need to know is that we've learned to run, yelping, and grinning through a nation that would rather look away, only, it must be noted, through their cities, both unarmed and disarmed, through their Western sense of individual, planetary time progressing forward, evenly and calmly as though, claiming innocence through a singularity of logic, linearity, and easy winds, *alone.* One more explanation: fight or flight.

In Luc Besson's science-fiction action film *The Fifth Element,* Leeloo says, "I don't know love. I was built to protect, not to love, so there is no use for me other than this." She means: to protect human life above all else despite the end of life as we know it. Leeloo, the tired warrior of our future, is most certain of this fact: *I don't know love.*

Leeloo's orange hair flutters across the screen. Her eyes are green or icy blue. We can't tell from her scene whether they flicker with tears or gaze up toward the open sky above us. In the film, even those colors start to blur, for us, in a multitude of hearts of mythic despair. I know her, I think. I know that look, looking up at the heavens, might signify a calling.

It's now the year 2263. A great monstrosity of rock and magma simply called Great Evil lunges greedily toward Earth. The planet shivers as the shadow of Great Evil looms. Annihilation of all life, as we now know it, nears. Scientists, resolved before the face of doom, have started counting down: *Ten, nine,*

eight . . .

Leeloo suddenly collapses. Her collapsing body is then swept up into the thick, rippling arms of Korben Dallas, played by the actor Bruce Willis. Korben is the archetype brute-cute but emotionally unavailable white dude. Leeloo's also white, played by the actress-model Milla Jovovich, but I digress.

To save us from extinction, we must all sprint into the temple, all together now: Korben on sabbatical from his taxi-driving days, the graying priest Vito Cornelius, the priest's boyish apprentice David with a nervous bowl cut on his head, our mean-supreme intergalactic talk-show queen Ruby Rhod, played by the eternal Chris Tucker, finally, the plucky companion to our banished Roman goddess Lua, a brave and tiny Panda, played by the tiny panda named Panda, gripping in one tiny paw, his tiny Panda tool, a pointy stick covered with dried banana leaves and pink chewing gum.

We place four stones around the temple's inner chamber. These sacred stones, for those who don't know, so help us all, carry each essence of life divine to save our planet: Air,

water,

fire,

earth.

Leeloo, wake up.

"WAKE UP! It's time for you to work now!" Korben shouts at Leeloo in the chamber. Leeloo, now jittery with exhaustion after an entire sequence of fighting for her life, snaps awake and gasps in the open arms of Korben Dallas. She can barely keep her eyes open, in focus, for the final scene.

The director yells, "Cut!" Orange light pierces my cranium. Orange blossoms are on fire, once more. Wake up! I hear the man now shouting, and I'm gasping cinematically in sync with a girl named Lua, I mean, Leeloo, blinking in and out of consciousness. Emi, wake up! My father's hitting me across the face again. It's the year 1993, and I'm 404 years old. I'm quite tall for my age, but that's not very important to know. What's more important to know is that I've been speaking with my father's four cruel Shinto gods at once: *Izanami,*

Susanoo,

Fūjin,

Kōjin.

The six of us are trapped inside my father's empty closet in our family home in Dallas. We're trapped in the closet, next to all my father's clothes, which are folded neatly in two separate rows inside his open suitcase. He had discovered me lying here, earlier today, as someone else's ghost, unfolding all his clothes and laying them in a circle around my body, perhaps the child of a ghost my exiled Vietnamese mother has been raising. In her singing, she produces something unnamable. Wake up! My stern Japanese father shouts again. Look at what you did, Emi! Pay attention! His hand coils back above his head.

A tiny Panda waddles through the door and into the open closet. Upon seeing my father, the tiny Panda runs toward him and begins hitting at the legs with both his tiny paws. My father, however, doesn't notice the tiny Panda, but he stands to leave at once, the look on his face a plastic sheen cast over everything.

The tiny Panda falls to my feet and weeps uncontrollably. With a quiet clicking from the back of my throat, I fall, at once . . . Lua, wake up, whispers the tiny Panda's voice, the voice of a small child. Emi opens both her eyes. A tiny Panda is leaning over her face, my face. He's clinging to his tiny Panda tool, which is gripped between his tiny paws as if in prayer in front of him, and it looks like he's about to cry again.

Indeed, in times of great distress, regression may be triggered when the human subject dreams most clearly of a wound, and my father, who fears the holy rapture of his daughter, must leave this story untouched. I ask you now, comrade, what holy drama, in the absence of time and dominant narratives of conquest, must we behold inside our hands? In other words, why did you have to hit me, papa?

Leeloo's sobbing. She has given up all hope for Man. She heaves, "What's the use of saving Life when you see what you do with it?" She means: This hurts, the imperial legacy of Man's mistreatment of life, turning toward genocide, mass destruction, and war. In response, Korben Dallas strains beneath Leeloo's dying weight and stutters: *Leeloo, you're right,*

you're right

you're right, but there are—

there are some things—

        very nice things worth saving,

                some beautiful things—

           beautiful things—Korben stops to think.

           Like love? Leeloo asks.

"How did the Enemy love you," asks the poet, Agha Shahid Ali, "with earth? air? and fire?"

Sunflower, I don't know. The whiplash is my mother, her mouth, our voices. I speak through her, in the voice of Lua, wife of plague, for she is speaking through me, too.

We're standing in Tucson at the corner of Court Avenue and Telles. The date is still unknown, if not irrelevant, for the archive. Lua's arms spread apart and tremble. Her fifteen eyeballs freeze in one rotation, bulging. They dilate ink and onyx pearls from their lids. She counts from one to four. She calls upon the weapons laid before her by the men kowtowing with supplications after two millennia of wars: to conquer, to triumph, to bayonet, a rifle, M1918A2's, and the grim-lipped wheels of a Howitzer, a Starlifter, and F-4 Phantoms falling from the sky, all crackling with ore and flint and jute. Her wrath bolts out of places we can't see. She fractures what she knows of place and setting and who belongs inside that place.

She roars past another mountain, an impasse at the speed of two, three, four billion light-years every hour, wrath, roaring inside a bell jar at the bottom of an ocean. What. The human body filled with magma cannot hold her plates. Lua feels her body as it shifts into a scream, I scream, SIX MILLION dead throats of my mother's people screaming, blood ash falling from the sky. And does it matter if these memories of war took place solely in Vietnam or the wintery golden farce of a Saturnalia in Rome, against the hands of time?

A girl is running naked down the road as if inside another gruesome hologram. Her brown skin is cracking open to fire and napalm rain; and, here, she's running like a fireball, SMACK, into Lua's wide-open arms. Lua stops to scoop up the little girl, who's fallen to her feet. I turn around, holding this little girl in my arms, running forward, allegedly, to my saviors. The tiny Panda hiccups and scampers right behind us.

Fight or flight! I shout. This is not my body, and most certainly, this is not my voice, for I am Lua, wife of plague, shouting through the quadrants of another city into which I'll never place myself, or ourselves, the rolling of the eyes into each history of nouns, watching our every move, so Lua runs, too, for I am Lua in the corners of Tucson like every other city where we find ourselves running into the Dusty Monk Pub, o'er Alameda, toward Old Pima's County Courthouse, and the girl is strapped against my chest, another girl named Lua; in running, Lua morphs into one giant fuzzy sphinx moth with this single mission: light whatever darkness in her heart before she slams into its flame, and in running, Lua can barely tell who smiles more, Jigglypuff or gods, humans passing by, humans remaining on earth without their gods.

Civis Romanus sum, repeats the US president in 1963, may the god of all things winged be swift and merciful. She dons her five-point crown, beautiful starfish queen, bedazzled, draped in Gucci. She shouts her highest-high note, supreme in the language of bees: BJÖRK, what are you doing to me, LADY? Lua, or a mythic version of my selves, demands that you make a choice: to WATCH ME RUN, for as I write through multiplicity of what is possible or not, my name becomes whoever is reading this, yours.

We meet a tiny Panda who stands at the edge of a large temple chamber in this vast space of his noble, tiny Panda mind. The goddess shouts, once more. She clenches in one hand her tiny Panda's paw, which grips in his other paw, a tiny Panda tool. WATCH ME RUN. She swings up to the planet Paul. I am Lua, wife of plague.

"The whole world is dressed in light," writes the poet Xuân Quỳnh. "Bitterness turns into poetry."

Fact: American soldiers have slaughtered my mother's people. Memory's an engine looking back upon itself. My mother walks across a beach named Tamarack in southern California. I'm sitting on the sand minding her purse and shoes and three full jugs of drinking water. "Just in case," she says.

My mother's singing loudly, out of key. My mother sings a folk song in the style of Vietnamese diva supreme, Khánh Ly. My mother's padding barefoot down the hairline of a cold Pacific Ocean in winter, singing out her sorrow. I watch her turn into the spiritual essence of a chickpea with arms, waddling toward the water before jumping and then scampering on two brown legs back to shore. The chickpea bursts out into a squeal, *hee hee, hee hee,* every time the ocean waves reach up to nip and tumble at her heels. I laugh, *hee hee,* along with my mother. I sit and watch her *just in case.*

I'm squeezing both my knees into the tight shape of a red rubber ball. A brighter red rubber dart soars up from this, toward the sky. It pierces another toad in my mind, and suddenly I'm rolling down the sand through dirt, and gravel, suddenly in flight. My fuzzy moth eyes open. My wings are set on fire. I'm screaming. No, we can't turn back. My tiny Panda faints.

The portal starts to open, and I face it, this planet of another home, my *former* husband, the planet Paul, in what seems to be an end of infinity, Paul, the beloved. Come home, he says. I answer, no, and close my eyes against a portal counting down: ●●,

●●,

●●, and swing into it,

running.

Wife of Plague

LISTEN. In the hour of a hyacinth, love is measured by its colors. We shift forward in our seats thinking about this sentiment as the operatic portion of our performance begins. The commanding diva, at eighty-two, wears jelly slip-on heels and ribbed nylon socks pulled past her ankles. The frills are studded with what appears to be diamonds. The diva steps daintily into a soft magenta spotlight. We all gasp.

A mild tingling at the base of our spines bolts up like thousands of optical fibers branching toward the reaches of our fingertips. It takes every bit of mental composure, a series of three sharp inhales through the nostrils, to keep from squealing in ecstasy.

The diva turns her palms away from each side of a perfectly round waist, arms suspended in a strict butterfly pose, repeating that familiar line:

"In the hour of our hyacinth, love is measured by its colors: cream, lavender, pink . . . *This* is easy enough to do." She's paused for some effect.

"We just need to count."

The diva then turns, ever so slowly to her left, our cue to get ready. Into the microphone, she starts to hum an old, old melody. Our eyelids soon become heavy, but we remember, humming along from our places scattered throughout the audience.

A second overhead light swims back and forth over the diva's puffy face moving toward the center of an equally circular body covered now by a mask secured around the top of her head behind sharp catlike ears. The mask is bejeweled all over but has no clear markings for a nose, eyes, or mouth. This creates an illusion of blossoms.

"I couldn't compromise," says the diva toward the end, bowing low at the waist.

Long after she leaves the stage, when we awake, we hurry to keep waving little paper fans high above our heads. Glancing into the theater from a balcony, in a private box near the front of the hall, we might appear to anyone as a room shimmering with moths. The echo of the diva in heels fades away, clomping faintly offstage. We hear her giggle, "Jiggly!" and notice a mustache painted upon every one of our faces.

Before this, in the opening act, the diva had appeared as somebody else.

"My name was Lua," she said. She was taller, tough at the shoulders. Her voice was low, husky; her eyes, otherwise completely black, flashed with hints of cyan.

"I had a pear in one hand, a pomegranate in the other. I couldn't make up my mind."

She seemed to be talking to herself, unaware of the audience. We fanned each other anyway with folded sheets of paper, nodding along. The diva's words went off script but regardless produced an effect of bewilderment and a lush atmosphere intended by, according to a small notation in the playbill, one of the seven original librettists.

Our diva wore a skintight suit of crinkled aluminum. Its texture matched a silver-bedazzled microphone that a stagehand expertly switched out between the two halves of her monologue.

"A wooden brush dipped into jars of milk," she said. "I had the face of a deer. It was *my* canvas. Every color seeped onto a bright, suspended screen." She spoke into a plastic hairbrush.

At that instant, coincidentally, a wrinkled king-size bed sheet unfurled from the top of the stage. It fell inches behind the diva with a flapping thump. A projector bulb flashed on a corresponding scene. The diva jumped forward a bit but pretended not to notice. Her voice continued feebly:

"Now, when I think of this image, a cloud of ink in milk . . ."

Her voice failed, by merciful timing, with the microphone and nearly every light in the theater, except for the exit signs, cutting off.

We sat in the dark for a moment collecting our breath. The air conditioning unit in the ceiling kicked on for what seemed like a full minute. Somebody else knocked a knee against the back of my chair, passing down the row into the aisle.

Most of the audience would trickle out eventually. Only a handful of us remained by what would have been an end to the overture. The seats cocooned around our bodies. I, for one, was still enchanted, closing my eyes and leaning back, imagining *that* particular jar of milk mentioned by the diva earlier splashed on the screen. I imagined the diva, too, long ago in her youth behind a Yamaha grand piano. Her tiny legs protruded out from underneath her body. The tip of each foot hardly extended off the edge of her bench. She weighed twelve pounds. From head to toe, the diva was less than twenty inches tall.

The room was pleasant, sunlit by an elegant, two-story window with a cheery view of a rose garden. Inside, to the left, dark Victorian drapery flanked a wide bookshelf. In the middle, a door had been propped open. Sensing a presence, the diva startled for a second time, glanced down, across the carpet, up to the camera, both ears twitching atop her head.

By the next act, our diva's conflict became more transparent. The projector, having turned back on, was the only source of light for now on the stage. It crackled as the diva spoke with an individual no one could see, though we all assumed, with the steady angle in which our diva nodded past the empty sections, the target of her monologue sat somewhere toward the back of the hall. An imprint of a human hand intertwined with another in slow, stop motion on the sheet billowing behind her.

"What I hope to explain," began the diva. Her silhouette shrank against the film. She took on a skinnier and deflated outline; her costume had changed. In the shadow of her body, we saw hips, the skeleton quivering under blue hospital scrubs.

"What I hope to explain," the diva said again, "is a reason I'll never come back home to you, the planet Paul, the temple shrine to Paul, the trimmed castle windows with a seated version of you, on every sill, the planet Paul in khaki or brown trousers, laced-up shoes, staring at the landing, a stone parapet beyond."

We craned around in our chairs trying to locate the face of such an unfortunate, hated man. He was nowhere to be found. We shrugged. Our cheekbones stiffened with layers of perspiration and bronzing powder.

The diva had suddenly fainted. Two paramedics rushed across the stage, at the ready, rolling her body onto a stretcher and then lifting it carefully before scuttling off.

I had gone to the premier by myself. With three hours to spare before the *Book of Wind*, I wandered the lobby, admiring up and down its main stairwell a series of photographs mounted along the walls. They ranged from joyful ovations during curtain calls to more private instances behind the wings, blurred and consecrated.

Near the top of the stairs, an ambiguous shot from a stage rehearsal of *The Magic Flute* caught my eye. In this photograph, Papageno, the bird catcher, brought close to one ear a miniature silver bell; I could almost hear it tinkling.

Past the landing, near the restrooms, a digital screen was tucked into a wall. It played a silent montage of clips from a classic film set in Ho Chi Minh City. A thin xích lô driver leaned his body to one side as if creaking on stiff invisible axes. He tilted slowly back to the center, pushing himself up on two pedals, weaving the trishaw into an alleyway. His face appeared calm. Set beneath his hairline was a grim outline of sorrow. The driver wore rubbery sandals splitting apart at the heels.

Minutes passed. The xích lô creaked into a smaller, shaded corridor. The back of the bicycle, linked to an empty carriage, made the whole thing appear like a horse in the field stripped of its days. Toward the end of the alley, there was a candlelit entryway into a home. Somebody waited there, thinking about how best one might approach a ghost such as this.

The xích lô driver parked his vehicle outside. He sipped briefly from an empty plastic bottle. With the other hand, he waved in vague, elliptical gestures, dusting off his bicycle seat. The ghost turned and quickly vanished into the wall with a single wordless step.

I left the theater after seeing this clip. A two-minute jaunt around the block would clear my lungs. The cool winter sun felt forgiving against my scalp. The film looped, again and again, eerily familiar in my mind. It dawned on me suddenly. The ghost had been played by the young actor, Tony Leung. The alley stretched to my left and right, the open door through which an American soldier passed beneath the awning into a narrow corridor, brushing his shoulder against mine. The planet Paul was that American, blond. He wore rubbery boots. I was parched. We turned and locked eyes.

When the deity first met the planet Paul, she was a student at the temple of Saturn in Rome. One day, near the forum of Capitoline Hill, the planet Paul himself appeared in search of a new consort. Lua, who had happened to come around the corner at this moment, passing the god's altar with a tray of citrus, sliced and sprinkled with salt, pretended not to notice him. She moved quickly and kept her face down before setting her tray on the flat surface of a musical instrument case.

The planet Paul was intrigued. No one ever ignored him, especially in *his* temple. Struck by the deity's bare feet covered with unidentifiable blood, the planet Paul said, "Yes, that one."

Lua turned and regarded him.

The next day, an oracle instituted their marriage certificate. At first, Lua conceded. She did express, after all, to some extent, an interest in the planet's charms, confident in the ways he seemed to know exactly what he wanted, not an ounce of cowardice in his movements. It helped too that Lua studied the planet for years before ever meeting him in person. She recalled in a textbook about Saturn that the planet's work circled a season; he took on a name, Paul, sowed a course of time among mortals and the universe alike.

Everyone knew however of stories passed around regarding that beautiful and calculating nature. The planet Paul, like his temple, stored mountains of gold and silver by his heart; would there be room for love—hot, stupid love—was a matter of rhetorical debate. In any case, the planet Paul took on forms of valor, the only thing he knew of himself. Among humans, he became mighty, true; he had a strong, military brow and a devastating treelike nose. When Lua gazed upon that face, hours before their wedding, she shuddered.

"I don't want it," the deity thought to her surprise, but it was much too late.

Millennia passed. By the end of 1994, next to the Mekong in South Vietnam, the deity found herself observing a hyacinth floating across the river. Its tangled green roots and leaves sheltered a few toads underneath. Lua picked at the ripe orange flesh of papaya cracked open against her thigh. On the opposite bank, her immortal husband would wait, in the meantime inspecting a new Sony camera in his hands. No one could escape him. The deity sighed mournfully. Her body shrank into the outline of a perfect pink circle.

A young Tony Leung crosses the street to Bến Thành Market in Saigon. He appears exhausted, worn by gravity, language, and space; *pater et mater,* as they say. Magnolia leaves and blossoms curl around his face.

In the opera house to the north, on the main stage, we watch a scene during intermission that reminds us of him. It cuts to a spark followed by a glass soda bottle tossed into an open window. A panicked middle-aged man rushes out, hiding his face on the avenue. The film against a bed sheet is black and white. The man is on fire.

In the final clip, a mother and child carry plastic bags filled with fruit. Behind the pair, the child's younger sibling wears an expression of mock astonishment. The toddler sits atop the papa's shoulders and slaps around the papa's head. Papa leans back, laughing, pretending to drop the silly, little dumpling. The audience titters.

In Trần Anh Hùng's film *Xích lô*, we're introduced to a boy known simply as Cyclo. Before the climax, Cyclo visits an unnamed rifleman who sits at the far end of a dim, cheerless apartment.

The rifleman barely looks up when Cyclo enters. We see the man cleaning and polishing an AK-47.

"Have you heard her songs?" He says to our guest.

Cyclo shakes his head. No, the actor doesn't speak much Vietnamese.

"Listen," says the rifleman. "Basic notes."

The scene pans down, over to a busy street outside the apartment window. The rifleman has a gentle voice. "Here's her song:

o oo ooooooooooooo

ooooooooo oo oo."

In 1933, when the xích lô was introduced to our cities, the French occupiers became giddy with the new commodity. Human bodies replaced horses. No engines required upkeep. The locals however regarded this machine as bestial, especially in Hanoi, as the melding of legs and wheels became more difficult to distinguish one from the other. Any passenger could plop in the front without ever needing to look behind him, to the driver leaning like a bag of bones over handlebars. Every ride became more and more discreet. Eventually, they were all driven by ghosts. Sometimes, the wealthier merchants brought their families to the xích lô, posing in front of it for a portrait.

At the Grand Opera House, rows of xích lô waited on the curb. I kept thinking of the film during intermission, in one clip especially, of the obscured man running out of his home into the street. He had been set on fire. Why did the man cover his face?

I wondered, instinctively, raising my palm and turning it over. I couldn't recognize the smallest finger. The nail was too short. The joint toward the top bent at strange dips in the skin. I wiggled this hand. It felt heavy with spirits: a squat-nosed phantom of brick, for instance, ghosts of shrapnel and paint, the ghost of ruby squatting at the market with scales of rice and trinkets painted all different colors of the rainbow.

It was necessary to mind these visions; they always got away from me and dipped into paragraphs I lost with the *Book of Wind*. I shook my head, suddenly speaking to my mother on the phone. Tomorrow was indeed my wedding day. She was desperate.

"But," she said, "He cannot sing."

"Yes," I said. "I love him."

"But . . ." My mother's voice became tiny. She was right in the end.

During the overture, I reenacted this moment of realization. The planet Paul carried no music in his heart. I looked from the audience to the back of the hall. Onstage, I pulled at my nose, prodding at the loose folds around my skin. A particular jar of milk stood on the kitchen counter that morning I packed my bags, trying to leave. The brush had been left there, bleeding ink into clouds of cool, white liquid. I stared into the audience once more. The film flashed over my body. Someone had fastened a full-length mask around my face. Behind it, I could weep freely. My lungs puffed up, and here was my song:

Lua

IN 1945, PHOTOGRAPHS of Sông Cửu Long took on a different sheen. Green became muddy, almost silver. Palm fronds and toads along with a damselfly gliding over its surface cast strange reflections on the water. I didn't know her yet, but Lua existed on that river as an iteration of every voice combined—Chrysanthemum with the last of nine dragons, a Trưng sister before battle, and the husbands to one of them praying at the altar of our ancestors. The story was simple. For centuries, we learned how to swim, jumping from the outer banks with all of our clothes still on, kicking up silt, or compressing our chests before we could reach the bottom. We farmed little studs of iron from loosened beds, pulling up the remnants of a thousand-year war for another. An old xích lô groaned upside down. Its front wheels separated, drifting toward a slate-gray delta. Perhaps monsoon would take the rest. As a water hyacinth, I had many hopes.

Jellyfish Dance

I. The Tanuki

IN THE FIFTH YEAR of Keichō, toward the end of its winter season, I found myself in a thick indigo-dyed tunic reaching past my knees. The tunic had the bones of recent enemies stitched along its back in a rippling lizard scale pattern. Gripped in my left paw was a heavy mallet. I stood upright on two feet sealed in the tanned hide of another animal, caked in layers of mud.

When at last I spotted my father in the woods, I charged in his direction. The great tanuki, Hirotaka Terazawa, was no longer for me to fear. His eyes turned in surprise but with a flicker of the air pockets around me, he caught that critical moment before I could strike.

"Katataka!"

His terrible voice boomed, throwing me back into the pine, and I recalled with a flash of lightning, with my skull banging on hard, unforgiving dirt, how once I was a pup; the smell of blossoms repulsed me. This triggered, in my far vision, a stack of oranges on the altar followed by a disturbing scene on a dusty road in my third inner mind: a human wedding procession, its bride in concealment from evil under the bright red parasol. She raised her powdered face to catch my gaze. For a half-second, we stared into each other's eyes. The bride screamed first. At home, in my den, I hid this realization of waking in a strong clay pot. Outside, the youngest pups still crawled on all fours.

The final vision consisted of another human ritual we dutifully reenacted every night. With our dancing and drumming, wild grass pressed in concentric rings on the billowy Shiroishi plain. The circles flickered and rippled out beneath our feet. Maps were also drawn on the ground. My father interpreted them and explained how to be killed while running was considered the highest honor in our clan. Then, I didn't believe him, but now I do.

During the rebellion, for instance, many of us died. Tanuki turned against tanuki. My father was prideful, sending nearly everyone he knew and loved to certain sorrow. He couldn't be stopped, even by my mother, unsheathed in the field of our ancestors, stabbing at the topsoil six or seven times until the god beneath it woke in a fury.

What happened next, I don't remember, but the earth swallowed up my mother.

As the records later showed, my father would lead our clan to near senseless extinction. One spring, after millennia of dying, purple wisteria bloomed around Karatsu's fortress in our bay of Saga. A tiny stuffed animal stood against the shore-facing wall. The animal carried an oversized head on nonexistent shoulders connected directly to thimble-sized paws. It appeared dressed in simple footman's garments with the blank expression of stars twirling at a close distance. The face blinked; it was a panda. The panda's head, after a minute, drooped in its helmet against a tall bamboo guarding stick.

Panda woke himself up with a painful hiccup.

"Anyway," he thought, "I see no point in kneeling like a fool before some ghost who watches but does nothing."

II. The Scholar

Centuries later, in 1922, the classical scholar B. B. Rose would frequently get up from his desk in Wales and drift toward an adjacent window with a dazed expression on his face. He liked teaching at the university which was near the coast and often, in the garden, he paced or wrote letters to his mother. She would have liked the gardenias best, he imagined, and sometimes he included a sketch of the rich evergreen outside the gate to his apartment building. Under a slab of granite, he kept these letters, stamped in a large paper envelope with no mailing address.

B. B. lived on the third floor in a spacious flat that received overtures of moonlight two or three nights a month. The main charms he believed, however, were the black cherry paneling for walls and a writing desk made of oak. B. B. had a sensitive nose. He could appreciate every note of timber waxed and mingling in its salt-damp climate, but when the scholar slipped into melancholy, which he often did, such flavors held him rigid to the bed.

One day, pulling himself across the room, in his pajamas, B. B. decided to try something new. He reached a panel by the bookshelf. At chest level, he mentally measured the severe impression of a human fist retracting slowly from the wood. B. B. leaned forward. He paused and pushed his tongue through a pair of chapped lips, sliding it flat, dry along the wainscoting trim.

By June, B. B. had been losing more sleep over his thesis. The research involved a rather obscure Roman goddess, Lua Mater. There was not much else to find in the archive, yet, speculating on the root "lues" meaning "plague," or the honorific "Luo" for "purge," a pestilence of touch, the scholar soon felt some frightful truth that was my name approaching. From a corner of B. B.'s room, something invisible flapped and knocked a flame clean off its candle. The wax dripped and hardened into a wide copper sconce nailed above the mantel of a fireplace he rarely used. The scholar, superstitious since early childhood, went to the cabinet near his washbasin for a thimble of syrup. After some gulps, he shuddered and went straight to bed. There, he had a nightmare. He perceived himself at a short but misty distance from outside the window. His face appeared cottony white, puffed out at the cheeks; it was seamless with the texture of synthetic wool; its round surface was punctuated with the watery eyes of a stuffed animal staring over the windowsill. Through a perspective pivoting back into the room, B. B. could see how this creature was, in actuality, a tiny stuffed panda wearing a set of pajamas uncannily similar to his. The tiny panda waddled across the room returning to his desk. With a sigh, he plopped next to the inkwell, pushed his tiny paws together, and peered down at the notepad.

"No records," he thought, "existed of a sacrifice made to Lua, except for a blade from a defeated enemy brought to her feet."

The night stretched on. Panda kept thinking of the pyres.

The tiny Panda also recalled the scholar Titus Livius in 27 BC working on a manuscript for *Ab Urbe Condita*. In Book XLV, Livy had hastened to illustrate how piles of confiscated weapons were set ablaze at the altar of Saturn's consort. Panda couldn't stop himself; he giggled. Livy was hunched over the manuscript like a late cicada emerging from a corn husk. He worked diligently for weeks at a time, barely sleeping or eating, and often swatted at one of his ears without ever scratching it. One night, the scholar cast a glance at the lunar eclipse by the upper frame of an open doorway across his room. He contemplated the image of Lua beyond a past inaccessible, even to him. The goddess blew puffs of air on the back of the scholar's neck. With his other hand, Livy slapped at this space, too.

The tiny Panda had settled unnoticeably on the scholar's right shoulder. His tiny face craned to peer over the book, attempting to parse out rows of illegible text. Something startled the tiny Panda. He spun around. There was a candle suspended, in midair, burning brighter than ever.

III. The Dancer

Leaving New Guinea, upon his release from imprisonment in 1946, Mister O was shaken by the inconceivability of war. A day could easily pivot to daybreak cracking at the horizon with an inkblot over and over until one bolted up in his cot, covered and panting in layers of greasy, cold sweat. As cellmate number seven, I felt in my heart some obligation to narrate what could or could not be accounted for; after all, most of us were dead.

I existed on this line between consciousness and movement not afforded to me while I was twenty-four and still alive. As a ghost, I could observe Mister O's survival as a simple event linking our bodies to the profane, collected incarnation of humanity through his survival alone. For instance, when he was drafted nine years ago into the army, Mister O had been a trained dancer from Hokkaidō. This knowledge of the dancer's past stopped at any bearings around who I was, a gymnasium folding up in the middle like a collapsible table; in that image, arriving at a sprawling field of unspeakable horror, I couldn't remember my home, my first name, or any mode of existence beyond that simple age of death, twenty-four, of who I felt myself to be, of what the peninsula south of the Pacific would bring us to become, phantoms with no essential facts of our existence; yet, as I watched Mister O wake from his fitful sleep in our prison cell, his fingers curled up like he was about to dance. When he sat up, he would stare blankly at all seven of our bodies strewn across the floor. No one else would survive the night.

It was only logical, perhaps in retrospect, how Mister O had been the sole pacifist in our squad. Seiichi Matsumae, an undeniably handsome and respected lance corporal, carried a deep affection for Mister O, perhaps for this reason alone. I couldn't remember feeling my limbs or human attachments by that point. Who sent us to fight? I couldn't tell.

Occasionally, in the jungle around our base, still hot with fear and magmatic tremor, Mister O would dig himself into a foxhole, waiting for the marsh to fill with water and for dusk to settle in our bones. No one bothered to retrieve these when we first learned of our emperor's surrender. Our spirits stayed put. We wanted to go home. Yes, it was clear then, after the Australians, at last, captured us and threw us into a cell, who could keep that solid form against Mister O remaining tethered to a bridge between one plane of existence and the next.

Aboard a ship returning us to Japan, I watched Mister O regard the water with much dread. In an hour, he had witnessed our bodies fold into skeletons and plunk without ceremony into the ocean. Seiichi had been the first to go. Mister O cried openly, steadying himself against the railing. At forty, he seemed, at last, to split the stem of his spirit from our spirits too. A cloud of jellyfish bobbed to the surface and surrounded each of our corpses before taking them under. The dancer's breathing quickened beneath his uniform. I saw the rising and falling of the jellyfish with the fabric of his shirt. Mister O's fingertips vibrated. His face evolved, taking on a sallow corner in both cheekbones. I had a strange thought they would never fill out again.

Later in Tokyo, Mister O returned to his craft. We would watch from the audience in a mirage of projections set up vertically in three- to four-foot glassy panels. Mister O choreographed a solo piece around this memory at sea. His arms and legs twitched in the air as though every one of us, through the sinking of our bodies, had become electrified onstage.

Toward the end of his later recitals, it was reported that an American, Susan Sontag, was so moved by the Butoh dancing that she rushed toward the stage. A tiny Panda stood at the end of it, tearfully holding up his tiny Panda stick in a defensive fighting posture. He didn't know what else to do.

IV. The Dance

BUT LOVE CAN lead us to this solid point—we're thinking from our seats in the audience and carefully add—love, on film, a green mantis careening across its horizontal plane of glass; below that, an oceanic movement of a piano accompanies an obscured diver clutching at a harpoon. The scene cuts to a series of blown-up footage zooming onto grainy blood vessels pulsing with black and white cells like the jammed canals of a dream under its microscope, both luminous and symmetrical in rhythm.

Onstage, our diva raises an arm in a universal gesture of grief. The film projects over her body and casts a shadow of the camphor tree onscreen behind her. The diva sweeps the back of her hand, from left to right, over downcast eyelids. The diva is gentle. She wears a black wig sprinkled with clumps of ash and bright paper lilies. Her eyebrows have been thickly painted on. Talcum powder covers her face like a bride, including the mouth, its lips creaking open in a slow grimace. The hidden teeth give an illusion of decay.

At one point during her solo performance, Mister O stops moving entirely. A sharp crack echoes downstage. I wake to the shock, in the audience, of my name being shouted by the river. My vision splinters, refracting with hundreds of cicadas and then pixels, adjusting to the stark physicality of twilight around me. A tiny Panda has taken shape on the mud-blasted ground. He flails a tiny paw toward my stomach. His eyes widen in a panic; I'm bleeding, I can see that. Through a bullet-sized rip in my uniform, through what appears to be its darkened fabric growing a second belly button by the moment, black oil begins to pour out. I feel no pain. I count about six or seven voices rushing across the bank and realize that the field of sorrow has been rerouted in collective memory, plucked from the audience in 1946 to a river in South Vietnam, though I've lost already any bearings over the fact of my bodies, of what I used to be, of who I've come to be by 1978.

"Chrysanthemum," says one of the voices stopping to address another.

The voices sift around a curtain of mangroves into the sieve of history. I've forgotten, again, how to move my legs and all of my arms.

"Chrysanthemum."

I'm raising my head, attempting to answer her, but Chrysanthemum's name comes out too gently, too lovingly. "Shoot. I've made my peace."

V. Hà Nội

IN THE CITY of her enemies, my mother recounts a group of villagers, toward the south, who tried to escape by the river.

She says, "Hold baby like this."

My mother gestures with a closed fist across her chest, and I offer a tiny stuffed animal to replace that. She takes the thing without looking.

"Hold like this," my mother says a second time.

A mirage opens on either side of her shoulders like jasmine petals. I imagine variations of my mother, Chrysanthemum, sitting at a kitchen table in Tucson. She's told me a story about running to the river from another village; everyone there carries a stuffed animal, a tiny puffy-faced panda, in the cradle of her arms folded tightly across the chest. The night is closing in, and along with it, an unspoken dread of bayonets.

We're squatting on plastic stools by the curb in front of a restaurant in Hanoi. This simultaneously overlaps with a booth at a breakfast chain restaurant in Frisco, Texas. By the time we visit her father's grave in a village near Saigon after 1992, her minds make a hexagon. Her mind is old. In overlapping cities, on the table between us, I observe my mother ripping a paper napkin into terribly distinct pieces.

Soon, in every story, the mother who looks like my mother will act out a choice, in her memory, no one should be ever forced to make, but here they do, ahead of logic, running with a century of moss and stone. She collapses on the dark embankment. Chrysanthemum has torn the tiny body away from her body. She pushes the stuffed panda face down into the water until the thing stops kicking.

"Mama," I try to say, but she doesn't answer.

"Go!" The stage echoes with her voice set far, far away in three different places at once.

VI. *The Mausoleum*

AT THE MAUSOLEUM, we shuffle to the central chamber in a winding line; hours before this, we've wrapped around the building, then through it, in a series of concentric, spiraling blocks.

We now stop when we're told to stop. The socks in our sneakers remain damp from waiting outside in the rain. No one can sit down. There are signs posted everywhere. No sitting. No smoking. No spitting or chewing gum. No photographs. The hall throbs with mosquitoes. The metal standing fan slaps at the marble-thick air.

My mother feels lightheaded. She grips my arm with both hands and leans against me. No, she thinks we shouldn't turn back. Deep inside this place is a resting home for Uncle Hồ. He waits for us.

"He," my mother says in a high-pitched whisper.

Her eyes are trailing to the ceiling, to the people behind us, to the uniformed guards carrying automatic rifles propped at every post; the afternoon enfolds us, unbearably so.

"He," she says again. "Wait for us."

The dead man waits for us.

"Emi," she says.

I worry my mother is going to faint. "What should I do? Do you want a story, ma?"

"Okay."

"In the fifth year of Keichō," I begin.

My father in Japan blossoms in a vision. He sifts through piles of documents at a kitchen table in Tokyo. There's a polite triple knock at the door.

"Excuse us, sir."

"Please," my father says.

The representative bows and touches the rim of a crisp curator's hat. In this gesture, my father notices the golden insignia of the national museum: four-pointed leaves embroidered on the wristband of a white silk glove. My father nods, stepping aside into the entryway shaded by an old pine tree outside the window. The museum representative and three shorter assistants bow uniformly a second time before taking off their shoes.

The event is swift and efficient. In a single afternoon, they remove my father's ancestral sword and package the armor with its helmet. My father points to a cascading bouquet of a thousand paper cranes in the second room across the hall.

"That was my mother." He starts to explain.

The representative is polite. "We cannot take it, sir."

My father understands.

"Emi," says my mother. In Hanoi, we've inched around the final corner in the mausoleum. A waft of air-conditioning billows through its hall from an opening and closing door to the inner chamber. I sense my mother perk up, her energy restored.

"Almost there!"

"Yes." I'm glad. A sign by the door has a stern image of a camera crossed out in blue packaging tape. "Should we keep going?"

"Okay," says my mother. She looks up at me, smiling, gripping my arm until parts of it go numb.

"Okay." I'm thinking carefully. The story is difficult to narrate in English.

"It was winter. We were animals but wore shirts that came down to our knees." I quickly add up our memories. "Did papa ever tell you about the mythic raccoons, the dancing tanuki?"

My mother's eyes are fixed on the doorway a few meters in front of us. She shakes her head. I feel the rhythm of her thoughts shifting like a piece of stone, a voice meeting her voice from that dry coolness of its central room, as are we, the banished millions around the world waiting for our exile to drain from this nightmare, and may some peace within our spirits be greeted with peace, and may we meet the future as we walk into our past embalmed at the limits of our sorrow, and may this sorrow bathe our feet on the shores of a delta, and may this exit receive our spirits for we have wept as we have reckoned with our bodies too many times before, and may this sorrow, at last, be lifted; may we finally go home.

VII. The Brave and Tiny Assistant

OF VLADIMIR LENIN'S EMBALMMENT, the Russian scientist Yuri Denisov-Nikolsky had reportedly admitted how those who did this work were stricken with a violent tremor in their hands. On the morning of September 2, 1969, I recognized a familiar sensation to this phenomenon in a way perhaps my compatriots could not. We stared into the watery chest of Uncle Hồ in his final hour. When he finally passed, I felt myself pass too. My paws shook uncontrollably. I held the double string to his ancestors like a rising braid of incense, and when our courage remained, alone, we brought Uncle Hồ to the secret location in the north.

The quiet doctor from Moscow, along with his team, took a separate route according to the map my father provided before meeting us by the entrance to a cave. I cannot say more about this event, or much about my journey to Hanoi, but felt some peculiar history of cloth and saline braid into a complicated knot. It was my mission to understand, therefore, what could or could not be filed into a box or documented on paper.

"Panda," said the doctor. His greeting felt firm but sweet like mangoes.

I stuck out my paw. He crouched on both of his heels and looked me square in the eyes, like an equal. With his right hand, which I observed to be smooth and fair, not a blemish to be found, the doctor would grip my paw between his thumb and pointer finger. He shook it. The tremors stopped. I was pleased. One by one, I would meet the other members of his embalming team. I quickly forgot their names. We were ushered into the cave. Our work soon began.

Inside, the doctor measured Uncle Hồ's dimensions with a silver-edged tape. He would ask me to hold a few numbers in my tiny Panda brain, but I felt ashamed in knowing this could just as easily slip into the puddle of forgetting.

"Can you do it for us?"

I nodded anyway.

The cavernous wall behind me was cold and slippery. I magnetized, shaking all over again. My new surgical gown was draped in a pool of fabric around my feet. In my right paw, I held up a scalpel, focused on my breath, and desperately tried to keep the thing from dropping to the ground. Now I had to be vigilant.

One of the assistants would unwrap a second roll of gauze. I watched our Uncle's caretakers go to the corner and light more incense. They gave thanks to the spirits who wandered outside among the rubber trees and the foxholes too, and the crimson blankets of blood-sucking insects and other noisy creatures dancing all around our death, or the basilisks, may they take pity on our souls.

I don't recall why, but something else compelled me to dance on a fresh stump outside our cave when I left for a break during the procedure. My eyes flashed over the trees beyond the highlands. The heat of the afternoon turned prismatic and fractured over mountains at painful distances. I saw Lua on a flash of green, coral. Her legs disappeared into the thickets. Her neck fell back. She fainted.

In fracturing, it felt as if my body and her body combined with the bodies of light, splitting into millions in the throes of gravity or revolution. I met the pace of her presence with my heart and galloped at what seemed like 34,000 kilometers per hour around the sun. I was molting, burping, teething, once more, sparking into flames. Meanwhile, the goddess dropped to her knees. I was confused about where I was and shouted at a helium cloud speckled with ice.

"Lua, WAKE UP!"

But Lua, who was far, far away, couldn't hear me. She cried, turning her face from the face of a crying planet looming an arm's length away. The planet had eyes that looked vaguely like the eyes of another tiny Panda, like me.

Lua pushed this face, it was my face, pushing our grief into something small. Was this me, a ghost, some old deity clipping shifts in time or personalities, but nothing more; the collected rings on a hill or in space, were they both reduced to dust, each moon no better than a firing squad? I couldn't bear it anymore!

VIII. Karaoke Night

THERE'S A SONG Lua likes to perform at the karaoke bar attached to the Best Western on Stone Avenue in Tucson. Every Thursday in 2019, she modifies a rendition of "Un-Break My Heart" by the diva Toni Braxton.

Meanwhile, B. B. Rose stands vacantly at a pharmacy in Wales. He points at a spot on the shelf behind the counter.

"Can I help you," says the pharmacist.

It's impossible to flee from history, let alone keep our subjectivities in order. The tanuki, with their inner and outer rings and their tunics on the plains and their sighs and their dancing, scrape another century into my heart. The cosmos carries this hard energy in every tangle of its reach. Stars burst every second. The supermassive black hole burps up a million stars for the day. At 9 a.m. in any time zone across the great Earth, our Milky Way clocks in and spits out seven for the year. We still applaud this effort just the same. In 1993, another diva, Mariah Carey, would be singing "Without You" live from Madison Square Garden, Mister O once again crying stardust from her eyes, oh, the drama of it all.

"But O, the bold tosser of trees," recites the poet, Horace, gazing at the sky, "Enceladus rules the wind, rushing against Minerva's deafening ægis."

Minerva's ægis, bleating across our skulls, Horace blinks and looks away.

The tiny Panda presses his tiny face into the center of a hyacinth, and it activates a portal; at that moment, *Voyager 2*, out in space, murmurs to the makers of our universe thrown into this vast and bottled ocean. What else could I say without my name, my many names, how I observed, with the soundtrack of human bodies pulling us easily from one life to the next, how each planet could bear us as Lua alone? Cue: Mariah Carey.

Downbeat: "I can't live . . ."

I'm dressed in fire, running into the wind. Let this exit be too quick if not surrender.

Jump to CITATION I: POETICS OF LINEAGE.

BOOK OF WATER

Black Stream Water

ON THE FIRST of April, they hurry toward the Victoria Hotel on Trần Hưng Đạo. Shadows on foot alongside the grave foreboding walls of military quarters now crowding the districts of Chợ Lớn, an assassin who wears low on one wrist, with its buckle turned out, the green Omega Seamaster watch. Half-past three. Dropped off earlier than planned but no matter, thinks the assassin, I'll finish our job myself.

A small birdlike cry rises across the market center, and the assassin makes a tight fist before pressing the watch to one side of a hard-set face otherwise obscured by night. The air hangs low and damp. No sound behind the glass. Our assassin removes the watch and drops it in one swift motion over a curb. Cast over the shoulder, two eyes like steel drums black as tar, without a marker for age or markers of nationality, fear, doubt, but the single cloth tied at both ends of a flagpole stuck indiscreetly in the ground, making the blood-red line on the corner of a colonial teahouse near the riverfront, veils tossed from a footbridge to the current below; these signs have all been noted; six men sit up in their truck, lighting a cigarette and passing it around the cargo bed in a pale, terrible silence; the assassin quickly approaching the Victoria Hotel is not particularly handsome. Greasy black hair clipped in short uneven patches, as though someone earlier had hastened from the far end of a light bulb in the basement of an abandoned dance hall, "This is our only way."

"I conclude . . ."

"Hush," interrupts the woman's voice, our sister. In this nightmare, the assassin pulls at the scarf obscuring a set of lips moving incoherently underneath, love is just the end of us. I carry seven ways of being; you, a flash of light. The gate to our destiny will open in but a few hours. By dawn, one of us will already be dead, very much so, and I will still be Lua. The rusted hinges of this gate embedded in Lua's mind begin to creak as the gate opens, along with this, notices the assassin, a trilling of cicadas in a high-stalked field north of our father's village, a hoof of a bewildered stag taking its first tentative step over that threshold of time, and this, on our planet, is the year 1966.

Like most students at the university, in a time of war, studying poetry in translation, the assassin ruminates on elements of fate, what happens or does not happen if the assignment involves anyone else but you, the planet Paul, the soldier known as Paul, but death as we know it, thinks Lua as she pivots around the final corner marked by a lamppost, will be my own doing, my power in these hands that guide a knife into your chest.

"His name is irrelevant," instructed the sister who had cut Lua's hair earlier that night. "Find the officers, and you will find him. The third floor with the other Americans, go."

The assassin, who we know to be Lua, wears a pair of khaki trousers and an olive green coat that appears to have been lifted from a dead man's body moments ago, my dead body, in fact; I simply follow Lua like a fool documenting every thought, gesture, for who knows what reason, except in that moment, glancing up toward the third floor as we approach the hotel, the assassin reveals a patch of cocoa yellow skin, just like my skin when I was once alive, where the lover's kiss reminded me of joy a few times and the surface up and down those notions of days, evenings; here, in the room by a harbor where all my worries dissolved; my younger sister, long gone now, and the submarines we both witnessed every day from the pier, the ones that went under in a rush with their striped American flags all about and their sailors tossing the bottles overboard for my sister to catch; everywhere, these ghosts pace in confusion, and I'm just one of them. The voices pass in the chime of a dainty clock on my bedside table, the clock of mahogany, the expensive kind carved with the image of a warbler peeking over its branches; a window, thrown open, and you, suddenly atop this wretched body about to slaughter it like a pig.

The assassin laughs a little and pushes the silly ghost from her mind, thinking, the planet Paul, the jasmine musk of a city blown through my hair, my home, the waterfront, once more, running your fingers all over everything good, salted with a haze of tenderness and desire, all mine, all mine. You remember wanting to learn Vietnamese so you could understand my heart and the ways I cared for life before I hated you; beyond this was rage, I recall, a deep nothingness for humanity, and the planet Paul, you, who simpers across a wide sunlit room on that morning of January 15, 1966. You inhabit the young body of a junior officer. You jump across the foot of a bed. Here's a stone, you grin, the planet Paul, I found it during one of those patrols in the woods just east of here with my buddies . . . Lua, who hasn't yet learned of her next assignment, brings the stone to her lips, warming it beneath her breath, have mercy, I say, for you are all but a fool with the heart of a human.

The ghost drifts from room to room muttering to himself. This is my voice, the ghost of every man Lua destroyed in her run from the planet Paul. I'm reduced to a third-person singular, talking about myself in circles. In rooms with these memories, but especially in this one, Lua takes her glasses off to steal a glance at her target. He's fallen asleep. The white shirt clings to his chest. The scent of eucalyptus surfaces in memory. They drive up a knoll together. I see the planet Paul grip the steering wheel and think only of drowning. The image shifts back down to earth. Each day blurs into a single hour, elements of ore and magma.

Lua touches her face, quieting her mind, pushing me out again. She leaves the army truck idling in front of the concrete barricade at the hotel, years after a soldier's alleged murder. She stops at the teashop and stares into a portrait of the great-grandmother framed at one end of the room. The portrait moves, a reflection of each voice speaking back to her, for I am here in your body, says Chrysanthemum, the third daughter of Mai Thị Huỳnh of our eminent southern skies. The young

Chrysanthemum smiles, tossing behind her shoulders, the smooth black hair that she washed for the occasion of Tết; there are glints in her eyes, like warm pieces of gold. A clock above the countertop freezes, and the young Chrysanthemum leaves the teashop. February, a thundering cloud. The boy from her childhood, the one who used to fish with his bare, skinny arms stuck up to the elbows in the sand as dark as his face, attempts in this instant to cross the street on a rickety cyclo.

"Chrysanthemum," he laughs at the girl. "I'd like to give you a ribbon. It's made of silk."

Chrysanthemum shakes her head, Mama would disapprove, but I don't know why. I'm only twelve. Papa isn't here anymore. He might tell us what is right and what is wrong, but I don't think this is right, says Chrysanthemum. Here, the boy smiles, continuing to smile though he wants to weep in a puddle of shame.

Lua watches the little drama from behind her window at the teashop. One day, she plans to approach the girl Chrysanthemum and will become Chrysanthemum, in the body of my mother; one who will continue to be an assassin, the other, her memories of love. I whisper this plot into a rotary phone at the bar in downtown Saigon. Voices at another end crackle like a prism over fields of grammar. Look, I say, rock, sheets of paper, and Chrysanthemum's future daughter will be named Emi. My name will be Emi, remember that, Lua. In the bottle of time, I also report that two hundred American officers, in 1966, were asleep in that ten-story building on Trần Hưng Đạo. Only three were killed in the blast, one of them, allegedly, a planet named Paul disguised as a soldier. I did this because I had to, ma. I hope you understand.

Chrysanthemum rests her hand on the phone before walking out of the bar. Her eyes narrow in the morning light. She walks toward her family's house and passes a sandy-haired dog panting on the sidewalk; the underbelly is distended with thirst or grief, maybe a little bit of both. Good dog, she observes while shuddering and repeating to herself, because I had to, because I had to, ma . . . In the tangles of her mind, the rupture roots its way in a thousand directions. The woman's name is Chrysanthemum, though she's now accompanied by the voice of Lua, two bodies merged into one, the separate corners of a world, after all, one of us must write to the dead, and it's not easy to keep each narrative in order. First, you loved me. Then you required softness, my black, unbraided hair, bodies I could stay in for longer periods of life. My name was Lua, wife of plague. The planet Paul tried to kiss me as most humans did when I was Chrysanthemum and then Emi. He took every shape he could to find me. It was awful. In that nightmare, I stand over the bathroom sink, ringing out my underwear in cold, cold water, continues Lua's voice: It was simple, the story marching forward without much logic to my name. The body converged into mine, and bitterness fell upon the feral, open tongue, and *now* you want to kiss me?

The planet Paul shakes his head.

Look, a tiny panda named Panda sits to offer his humble assistance. He knows I struggle to write a confession, so I tell the tiny Panda, just wait, the book will come, and we will call it the *Book of Water*.

Outside the room is another looking glass, and from that looking glass, I dart into a timescale overlooking a house on Earth. The desert rooftop and palo verde freeze into diagonal images of Tucson in the late twenty-first century, a sheath resting atop another, grids of oceans and sanitary stations, green pods stretching out in rows farther and farther past the pollen of hours, a range of mountains moving against the golden prismatic sun; the sun is fake.

Here, on the dusty windowsill, the tiny Panda works to reduce his tiny Panda fears, such as the image of a spider tangled up in the web of its enemies. From a narrow ledge of consciousness, the tiny Panda drops a silver coin. We listen as the coin pings and echoes, accelerating at a speed just fast enough to kill him at the bottom, where he stands inexplicably at the bottom, the tiny Panda who, looking up at the window's ledge, starts to weep from fright and dreadful confusion. He stands at the bottom of this black crystal lake, looking around just long enough before gesturing with his tiny paws that he'd very much like this dream to end—and, looking up, midsentence, I notice you, the planet Paul, are once more looking at me through the window.

I start to wonder if you ever knew what you did to the people I loved and what you did with each heart inside your hand. Why did I trust you, Paul?—the pen stops; I notice the paper has been covered in a line drawn portrait of stars and delta minnows jumping from the pulp. I hear the tiny Panda grunt like a tiny piglet as he climbs up the window's ledge. He sits with a tiny huff and pants heavily despite his best efforts to calm down. We've arrived at a timescale with long subjunctive sentences that include the words "if" and "if-then not." The audio weeps. What's wrong? I ask the tiny Panda, but he sits there pulling out a thin white thread from a corner of one of his eyes. He reaches down with the other paw to scratch at his tiny butt.

"Itchy," whispers the tiny Panda.

Earlier in Tucson, he found a hummingbird half-eaten by my bed. I remember wondering if this tiny Panda called for it in our sleep, but that would be an omen, and the tiny Panda didn't like such things. I knew this about him, and there were no hummingbirds in a timescale away from the planet Paul, so why did you come, after all? In the weeks of dreaming, tiny hummingbirds appeared to me everywhere I went. There were hummingbirds in trees, a hummingbird egg in the toilets, and everything painted a hummingbird teal. You came over one day and ran a dirty fingertip on the surface of my stove. I let you stay the night in my spare bedroom even though your wife was calling and calling again from Wisconsin. This was a hummingbird you saw perched above the railing in my empty closet.

What becomes impossible to love beyond all this, and what of love after the wars I never wanted? Worse, the planet Paul, this timescale eventually betrayed us, a conquered and conquering soul has no other end but the impasse splitting the parts of me and you. This is a memory of faces in the language of clarity mashed against the speed of apathy. What stood for other names if not my name, too? In other words, how was my body, human or not, Vietnamese or not, turned into something else you could easily love before leaving this Earth? These questions bubbled out of me, and you slowly moved into the morning, away from my kitchen. You entered the living room. I could see that you wanted to go home, back to your planet, the planet Paul, and your eyes were like bright crystal shards tossed into a lake of melancholia.

The tiny Panda followed you. He pushed at the fabric of your pant leg with his paws. Get out, he seemed to say while grunting furiously. You pleaded to the brave and tiny Panda, yes, I'm sorry.

To this, I answered, no, what's in the truth of your liberating force? Did you come for me, a balm?

I dream for you: A role.

My role: Interpreter, and the scenes that unfold in the present tense. You press a cloth against a woman's face. You say: I'm going to ask this one more time. Who are you? What's your name?

You pause to look at me, the interpreter. I look away and stare across the bunkers, at the trees, and the year is, once again, 1966.

These trees dance in pairs like replicas of gods, mammalian, walking rubber trees, the image I'm bound to carry for the rest of my life, separate from flesh on Earth, and images that trickle in my mind roam around each room like a single leaf, and every night your face hides under moss and dirt becoming overgrowth and waste. You want to know what it's like for me as a human body on Earth. You arrive and pick any one of them, coincidentally, a soldier, but your face is that of death, as it has always been, such as, on the seventeenth of February 1859, when the French Admiral Charles Rigault de Genouilly first motioned to the silver buckle on his belt, marching his troops into the citadel. I recognized an evil then, your face among a thousand white faces, dragging my daughters, screaming, from their homes. Or, further back, in AD 248, my Lady Triệu, who, at the age of twenty-three, mounted her battle elephant a final time and raised her sword, aiming it square between your green, hazel eyes.

"I only care to ride the breeze," she shouted, "step over the waves and slaughter each shark of the wide Eastern waters!"

It was then a deep leather drum resounded with the howling beyond another corner of this world in my mind; it was then, inside this mind of Chrysanthemum, my mother, and beyond that, her mother, we moved further back to the year AD 43, where you stood gaping in the middle of a swamp in Vietnam, where my sisters Trưng Trắc and Trưng Nhị charged at you, where my sisters led each army of ten thousand, eighty thousand women, all including their mothers and the mothers of their mothers through rivers of blood; it was then my Lady Triệu who flew out the sky, across two hundred years, to "save our people from drowning." She smiled, as I now smile, thinking of my poet-queen.

Out here, in 1966, the jungle clicks to life snapping branch to branch, insects and bright red birds pushing the heat around in smaller circles with their wings, I've noticed, sharp as knives, as though to slice the water droplets from thin air.

You're losing patience, I can tell. Perspiration gathers at your neck, soaking through the camel-colored khaki of your collar, and I see you, soldier, rolling up your sleeves. You ask: Who are you? What's your name?

I look at her, the woman who sits like a stone strapped to your chair. You glare at me, the translator who fails to translate properly; I'm Lua in the body of a translator. Here, beneath a watchful gaze of history, I know that you hope to be done with a theater of madness, clearing out our throats like warm sap that leaks from the waistline of trees. The irony, I murmur crouching down onto a knee. The woman turns her head. Her hair is loose. She wears a blindfold. I soften my voice with each word's translation. I start to plead, comrade, just tell these men your name.

Between my ears is a symphony of nightshade and amber.

Soldier, I turn back to you, the planet Paul masquerading in the body of a soldier.

She's so tired. Can't you see?

I open up my mouth into a terrible grin, stretching a row of teeth into the curtain of beads, but you look at the pamphlet in your hands, playing your role much too well. What can I do now? The ghost refuses to say her name.

The tent is not so big. The woman refuses to say her name. It's obvious for me, the interpreter, and obvious for her, my sister, the magnitude with which our tongues must work inside another way of telling this war in a way that makes sense, demanding more language. To talk with clarity, to speak with clarity, out here, perhaps, we aren't so different after all. What's my name? You never even asked. How many modes have you attempted to extract pieces of information from my body, yes, I'm in that chair, and what else did your country test within the limits of a question? By any means necessary? There, a setting is placed within the origins of reasoning, and you, of men who watch cruelly, test out the bark between English, French, a misplaced glory, glory; the woman with a face similar to mine was just found in a forest clutching at a beat-up transistor radio. Your men had dragged her through the overgrowth into the open tent. The water now snakes down her chest and darkens the fabric of her blouse, an unspeakable ocean. Comrade, please, I beg. I'm reaching for the woman's hand tied behind her back, the woman's hand like mine inside a nightmare of my own. *Say anything. And I will tell them. Anything.*

"What did you say?" The planet Paul snaps.

"I tell her my name. If she knows my name, she will trust us."

Trust us, regarding such events of a late October day in 1966, John Sorell, the journalist from Melbourne, witnessed a similar incident of torture at Núi Đất, an Australian military base less than ninety kilometers away from the city of Saigon, the city of my mother's birth. He says of this later, "This girl was on the edge of fainting."

"I felt nauseous," adds the second interpreter, a former SAS Sergeant named Jason Barham.

"She was distraught. This was after the commander asked me to tell her in her language that they would cut off her fingers, stick [redacted] up her parts, and do to her almost anything else that caused unbearable pain, what you could imagine, sir." At this point, the sergeant stops to pinch the skin between his eyes, a bridge quaking from this life to the next, a bridge comprised almost entirely of bone and sinew soaring through the torrents, threatening to take away whatever words remain after a flood, and this was a Western, English-language version of our nightmare, bleeding out of years into the history that simply could not be a matter of straightforward narration.

You're very quiet, soldier, fingering at the loops holding up your belt in the waistband of your pants, and I split into two people and two languages, interpreter and the body of Lua, these present-day memories waiting for speech. I wait for the man, as well, Jason Barham. I wait for him to continue telling his side of the story, but instead, he gazes, as we now imagine, to his left at Gabriel Carpay, the press photographer, who, at this critical moment of testimony, stares into the blank camera roll and says absolutely nothing. *Mama, please.* I hear myself begin to weep imploring the woman in the chair. *Just tell these men your name.*

In this nightmare, love is just the end of us. You press a calloused tip of your finger through the woman's hair, through her arms, but, still, she does not speak. She refuses to speak. The wretched trees of Núi Đất start to moan. Out here, I wonder, if the photographs of torture were never taken, would the torture have existed? Out here, I also wonder, how many women did your men imagine, *close to fainting* in their monstrous arms, drowning, photographed or not?

"Yes," scoffs the Australian Prime Minister Peter Gorton to his Parliament in 1968, denying any proof of harm inside that tent, "a little wet, I agree."

✳

In this nightmare, we step over the wild grass and through some threshold of a mouth keeping her name separate from mine. I know this, having written it before, my face, an *orifice* of water, another crater for your bombs. Meanwhile, up north, a college student by the name of Dương Thu Hương turns twenty and flees into the jungle. She immediately joins a volunteer brigade of forty women. They hide in tunnels. They sing and wash their clothes. Many years later in exile, in 1991, the student-soldier would write, "We discovered six naked corpses. Women. Their breasts and [redacted] had been cut off and scattered around the grass where we found them."

I crouch, pressing my hands into wet grass, soaking a droplet through my palms, and in this nightmare, I begin to feel a body sweep into the stream; my lips reciting Dương Thu Hương's words closely translated by Phan Huy Đường and Nina McPherson, "We buried them." Yes, we buried them, sister. In that nightmare, I look up and notice you are looking at me, too. "Where did you go," you ask, the planet Paul, the gravel in your timid voice becoming another box of time; we return to my house in Tucson.

"Who are you now? Who am I, now, to you?"

Who am I? I look at you and smile.

What does history require of subjectivity?

What left me to fight against your sense of individuality and self-belonging to a single narration? Who am *I* to you? The bitter sieve, perhaps, a piece of glass turning up, around and around in that nightmare of poetry, where am I, if not Lua, the gatherer of weapons? In this nightmare, I'm also sibylline and the guardian to one brave and tiny panda I've named Panda, and my trillion faces multiply above the ground. I loosen bedrock from the poisoned earth; drop by drop, a flood must come.

※

Today is written in the word of time. The date, again, is deemed to be irrelevant, but if you need to know by now, my love, in June we stand for water. I see you dart from door to door. In Tucson I stand in the present tense, holding a book titled, *The Lover,* while you stand there pale in the face at my doorstep.

Who are you now, you ask, do we live in Vietnam in . . . 1966 or the year AD 248? Elsewhere, in this old timekeeping body of mine, who am I to you? I ask these questions again.

You don't know; of course, you don't. You shake your head. You want to kiss me, and this makes me want to scream. The book falls to a grassy patch in the desert and opens to a page. There's no date, only the subject of resistance. Please, the planet Paul. If you allow me, I'll explain. The French writer Marguerite Duras has been living in the south of Vietnam. The date is April 4, 1914. At the age of fifteen and a half, she boards a ferry, which crosses the Mekong. Here, she marvels at the whiteness of her skin against the river's mud, and I spit back her words, "The story of my day does not exist," and regarding her future nonwhite lover she adds, "He's looking at me. I'm used to the people of this country looking at me."

A radio crackles against my cheek. The book, *The Lover,* withers into ash. Why am I reading Duras? I want to know that love is possible within the context of my skin. What parts of me exist, entirely of my own? What currents do they shift to, in what forms and voices and . . . More importantly, who am *I* to *you*?

You place this empty cup on my kitchen countertop. I hear the ceramic clack against the marble. Outside, mountains bloom into the violent midday sun. Are we in Tucson? You repeat. I shut my eyes; you step forward and touch my face; startled, I lower my fangs, sharpened by millennia at sea, and hiss.

Who are you now?

You stumble back and whisper, Emi, it's me; wincing, it's only me, the planet Paul. The grass becomes linoleum. A kitchen floor becomes, in uttering some name I cannot answer in this life or the next, a place for water without mercy, but I ask you now, the planet or the soldier named Paul, how much hatred do you know, and in what ways has your inheritance of war knotted inside these years holding onto a stone?

Be gone. My tiny Panda nods and flails his tiny paws. You back away across my living room, toward the front door of the house. Be! Gone!

Okay Panda, you hurry. May you please tell Emi, if she comes back, that I care about her and—you wave the arm weakly toward my direction—I'll try again tomorrow.

No. The tiny Panda shudders. Go. A. Way! He runs to grab his tiny Panda tool which has been tucked carefully for this moment behind the kitchen stove. He scampers forward. You stumble out the front door into your pickup truck. The engine turns over. I imagine the tent flap, with a thick leathery snap, shutting over my eyes. Let me try again. I write this *Book of Water* for a tiny Panda and the ghost, but for you, the planet Paul, another way out the temple chamber of my heart where I'd like to kill you if I could. In February 2018, the poet Khaled Mattawa reads new poetry in Tucson; the poet Susan Briante introduces us after his reading where I hear someone tap a bright blue knuckle on the glass window behind us.

I kneel before his feet, to take the hand into my own, and I cry, it's an honor, comrade, to meet you at a time like this, on a planet . . . I'm grateful, and my million faces multiply.

Mattawa, the poet, smiles. He straightens his stack of papers on the table. The ashen margins of a circle fold around his words and Vietnam, and then, later, when you come back, you're quiet as my body shakes at night. You're holding a grenade pin. I'm in the dark, alone in an empty house, the water roiling toward the edges of my bed.

Later, I share a slice of cake with more poets and Mattawa at a coffee shop near the campus, where he, in turn, takes my hand before choosing the next words carefully, "Love becomes a site for revolution."

After this, I glance into the palm lines of history, the planet Paul, smooth and Western in its wide-eyed carelessness, absent of a consequence, true consequence. In this nightmare, memory is trampled by your skin against my skin's displacement, an ocean into tongue; I'm writing in the best ways possible using the colonizer's language in a colonizer's sense of wonder, linearity, and place, logic, passing right through the stream, sinking in every reason toward a book of diction alone. In other words, Trần Dạ Từ writes in the poem "Love Tokens," translated by Linh Dinh, "I'll give you a savage war." The speaker is facing a beloved who has the name, perhaps clear subjectivity, though of lesser importance to whatever scatters across a page, the rolls of wire, the car bomb which never explodes on a crowded street, and teargas for "the modern epoch."

Then, "That's our love, take it, don't ask."

In this nightmare, I follow you into a forest. Eyes securely stapled to my forehead. Where are we? A hornbill answers. She bobs on a branch somewhere above our heads in the canopy. In Washington Square Park, I recall, my tiny Panda unzipping himself from inside my backpack, which swings over my left shoulder and slips past my elbow. We've been walking for hours. The day is my last day in New York, and I want to enjoy the people.

You're on my mind, the planet Paul. The forest turns into another, the dancing troupe in a square removing their green parkas, dipping down their toned legs, and bowing one by one.

I hold my hand against my face, the cool breath meets bone; a tiny Panda pokes his head over the top of my unzipped backpack, followed by his tiny paw. The tiny Panda feels around for the air and wind. Where do you take us? My tiny Panda seems to ask with blinking eyes.

You'll see, I say.

The tiny Panda hops with a nod to the concrete in a quiet thump and scampers ahead. He reaches a tiny clearing, which I follow in my mind. The tiny Panda pauses before sticking out a pink nub at the end of his tiny tongue, and out that tiny mouth, the tiny Panda sniffs at mist up to his knees. He turns around immediately, reporting how this mist tastes like something licked then pumped out of an AK-47, splayed like supine starfish over gray stone, and now we're back in Vietnam. Sticky, adds the tiny Panda for clarity. He punctuates a setting with his tiny paw and seems quite pleased with himself for helping to establish this time jump in our *Book of Water*.

Farther away, perhaps inside some vast echo of the tiny Panda's brain, there's a cliff upon which starfish nap in clusters near each other. I sense the urge to wick each belly, taste the salt, and that is how my tongue, splintered into many intellects and bodies, tries to tether subject-verb agreement to geographies of movement, the image being noun and logic, point A to point B, in other words, impossible to name without any sense of rationality except for how the woman, who looks just like me, was discovered, blindfolded, and dragged through the jungle by men with faces like yours.

Therefore, I write using a slant, the confession of your death real and unreal as the naming of what's been loved despite its brutality; that is, the following attempts to re-enact a space between soldier and trophy. In simple terms, it was noted that for centuries of war, soldiers like you would drag, people like me, grinning from our homes to do what can't be named, and at this point, Paul, I must ask if you intend to kill me, too.

Emi, you sigh.

No, I answer. Keep going, soldier.

In this nightmare, I follow the sound of your feet walking in front of me. If you leave me here in the jungle, will I take the blindfold off myself? Will I untie these hands myself? How can I, without so much as one good switchblade, bayonet, or ice pick to my name, defend myself? Bear left. The red birds soar into asphalt, open faces smash into the fog, or do I have this backward? I step forward and stop to look around. Then, you follow. The blindfolded woman is quiet as a stone. Fog gives way to red fern, golden cypress, creeping juniper, and toads. Toad psalms thrum, unseen to our failing sense of touch, though everywhere we turn, our faces twist aghast. Toads, from what we hear, are chanting in unison, inciting a terror in my mind, taking up rhythm through my lungs. Bold, deep-gutted toads bellowing through the broad-shouldered leaves, click-clacking long as fingers, olive green; watchful leaves which flay about and hum; slim forsaken leaves waving apathetic arms.

We do not speak. We cannot speak, for I don't know your name. Rhythms swell and then drop like heavy stones into our bellies. Here, it crouches, a rhythm made unspeakably loud, and here, I begin to name myself in much clearer terms; you should know exactly where I move and where *you* move in time next to this body, if not my tongue.

We are now the unnamed woman, a banished wife, and gatherer of swords, a woman, *made* to love and women, giving *you* a car bomb, a car bomb standing on the street and reaching up with four fingers extended calmly to the sky. I repeat after the poet Trần Dạ Từ, "exploding on the crowded street." The women who overlap centuries of voices with a century of landscape, tea plantations, Perfume Rivers, tunnels, bridges, and tombs, made to prelude; herein lays the forest of our hearts and herein writes a passage. "For this purpose," adds Jean-Paul Sartre, "the calculated extermination of the Vietnamese people was only meant to make them surrender," to surrender what, and in this nightmare, we walk, crouching into, dare I say it, love. You do not stop to look back. This cannot be done. Such are rules of combat: Lead by instinct, know precisely where *your* freedom lies, and young man, take as much as you see fit. Standards like this have been set before you first found me in a jungle which did nothing to defend my cold brown body, muttering away like a ghost into the radio, and now this is *your* jungle sheltering *your* rotting heart, still, the toads croak in prayer.

In this nightmare, the thick air smells like pine and mildew huddled where the ribcage drips, rotting day by day, luridly lush green on the crown of a monster, soft and shifting all over, cool beneath our feet, tender, holding vigil. There are birds we cannot see and cannot dare to name. We hear them warble above the toads like mournful bamboo flutes. We find, as well, young blossoms clustered near our path, their faces turning yellow in the fog and all that horror. Gero Gero, cry the toads.

Somewhere nearby, pebbles plunk in a shallow stream.

Gero Gero. Only fools would answer.

In this nightmare, you reach for my hand, which pulls me forward. I cry, and you pull me faster, faster through the trees. I hear myself cry again. You groan, and suddenly we've stopped. Roaring, before us, is the waterfall. Flanked on either side are thickets of sugar palm and bush that look like wax myrtle, magnolia in bloom. You grip my hand and march us through. I press my thumb into your wrist. Let me go, I think, and you release me. We stand now, panting, completely dry before the gaping mouth of paradise. "Thus, we cometh," gasps the poet C. D. Wright standing near the back corner of my mind, "we cometh to judge the light" which pales this place, "not the dark hall it obscures." You stoop down to pick up a stone.

In this light, I see your face and the ridge of your brow bones where a skull bows into wheat, cattails, and stars; your face reflects lakes, the good life in the US, a lake I lapped inside some province of memory too much before, of whom I kept my love or the reckoning . . . You turn the stone over in your palm. I think about what haunts us both, the carriage of reality, the blasted face no quicker turning than to ask for alms. To this effect, the filmmaker Trần Anh Hùng commented, "My goal was not to agitate the audience but to condition them with a certain kind of melody and way of breathing. Now, however, I have this urge to shake you to your bones."

If my goal is simply to make a rhythm with a book, where should I sleep with you, on moss, or bark? The forest moves around in twenty different directions, changing partners, but we must rest in the narrative repeating itself. Should we march or keep beneath the terror of phosphorescence, your hand nestling my hand, or flesh, something animistic, pumping water through our bodies? In this nightmare, we force inside ourselves a word that remains hidden from shame and a soiled tongue; to rush over the scalp, to roll over and die, as your men wanted us to die millions of times before, remember? Your hands crawl around my waist. Your thighs press against mine where it aches, and, here, the gap between us whimpers, too stunned to call this love, welded to each other at an edge of despair, too close to slipping off. To where, at what point of stopping, how much far-ther does it stretch, into what warmth, against what touch? Might there be an open field of grass tomorrow when we reach the other side unscathed, will there be a barricade, and will there be kindness or tenderness? I fall. The woman falls headfirst into a veil of mist. The last thing I see of her is a black cloth knotted around her head, which is also the back of my head, two ribbons flut-tering, gone.

Errantries [2]

THIS IS HOW I reshape that word *mist* into *sương mù, la brume,* a drop of fog, and the six illnesses reducing us to tears: you meet me at the cinema in Chợ Lớn, a translation smacks us in the face; you lean forward kissing my cheek. The woman onscreen blindfolds herself with a black piece of cloth. She stumbles, backpedaling from the space off a crag as if being pulled up by the strings of a puppeteer. Her hands have also been, inexplicably, tied behind her back, each event a clean reversal. Your name is Paul, the planet Paul, though I've called you many other things.

A second film begins. "I'll start, okay?" a soft voice announces.

From the corner of my eye, I see the shadows of your profile to my right, your silent jaw clenching then unclenching, a thickset brow staring up at the movie screen. The speaker is illuminated like a morning Vermeer, bowing her head over a tattered pocket-sized book. Your hair is orange and white, thrown about in a messy sweep, the streak of blue running through it. The velvet-cushioned seats in our cinema hall have begun to creak sporadically, and the air smells of musk, tobacco, and tamarind paste. I see the chest under your lapels, the old captain's uniform, rising and falling; your hand, the hand of a pale, oversized planet, clutching at one of your knees. You look like CAPTAIN AMERICA.

Mùi, who is played by the actress Trần Nữ Yên Khê, has just asked if she can start, okay. Her husband off-frame doesn't reply, but Mùi recites the translated poem anyway. "The spring water," her voice lilting up and down, "glimmers delicately when disturbed."

Khuyến enters briefly into focus before cutting away. He has princely eyes and princely shaped ears, a shy but full nose. He adores his wife very much. His mouth tips over. In the kitchen you tug at my waist, a memory perhaps incanted by the interlude of marital harmony. I drop my foot to feel the cinema's carpet under my shoe. I count to the number four in English, grounding myself. The cinema is half-empty. You've disappeared and it's 1951.

Included here is a sketch from our wedding day. You had sent a rather fussy invitation, hours before, to your mother and your father, separately, to Terra and Caelus, earth and sky. I cried in a dirty bathroom stall at the courthouse in Rome. No one came, naturally. When I looked at the mirror across this stall, ashamed of myself and the situation you put us in, there was a face suspended over mine. She opened a pair of black titanium eyes. I wasn't afraid. The ruby-diamond teeth gleamed with caps of silver—something borrowed, as they say.

I made a vow to this face, that one day I would kill you, would set about to kill you, the planet Paul.

A secret has been kept here ever since *L'Odeur de la papaya verte.* When I return to the film by Trần Anh Hùng, I think about the intention of his final scene, the one about spring water; I think about the language of the second audience, in a realm of ancestors and the dead, the unintended critics, a word for mist occupying our minds at great moments of inconvenience: by the fireplace, in your home, on the planet Paul, at the market down the piazza in 42 BC, before the pickup counter at the butcher's, at a shop of dialectics, an old woman reaching up to pull the toys off her shelf, the costumed figurines arranged in a peculiar obtuse triangle, the frames which shake every term of colonial meaning, metaphor, zymology, literature, away from any logical course of production, if any production at all, the mechanics of a Westernized plot for the Westernized audience, the sensations of history turning to mist, *la brume, sương mù,* the cinematography of Trần Anh Hùng which allows for such image-to-image transference, what evokes in that essence of Mùi reciting in her careful Vietnamese, a verse, translated, regarding the cold pool and its basic reflections, what ripples but stays its course forever and ever, what eventually becomes a single run-on sentence, and toward its end, I'm gasping.

Mùi is quoting from the 1906 novel, Natsume Sōseki's *Kusamakura*. I recognize the curvature of her mouth moving around with quiet pleasure, a form of literacy and sound and rhythm taking the shape of a cherry tree twisting behind a thin veil of smoke. Mùi has become an association of my lived time on Earth, how I've learned to speak like a human, and how I've learned to move more like a human, memories given by Chrysanthemum, as well, as the one photographed at fifteen in Saigon, at the airport, where she now stands waving at her older brother who boards a plane.

Chrysanthemum stops to laugh at this sentence.

I move in a zigzag, trying to reedit the story to her liking. "But what do you think about our book so far?"

She answers, "Is it about love?"

"Of course, Mama."

"Good." Pause. "Who is Paul?"

Chrysanthemum watches as her sister runs a small ivory comb through her hair. The sister is humming to herself. She believes that no one from the house will return for the next hour or two, her primary master at the opera with his fiancée. From an open doorway to the servant's quarters, Mùi's room, Chrysanthemum feels a cold sweat of the fourth obscure illness coming on, a terrible thumping in her throat, the hand's five fingers shooting out from behind to grab the back of her shirt and twisting its orange fabric in a tight, damp circle while her body goes faint, careening forward, the phantom keeps us from falling into the scene onscreen and forgetting our names entirely; at the cinema in Chợ Lớn, I hold onto both armrests with all my might, Mùi has not been disturbed, thank heavens.

Chrysanthemum is always placing herself squarely, unabashedly, in the movies we watch together; it's her way of relating to the world. She sits on a low stool by a burner in Mùi's kitchen. The boundaries of her mind and the projection machine are blurring into one. She catches her breath. She transfers, image-to-image, into the thought around Mùi's heart and the texture of it, what might change us both through the irrevocable acts of love, a girl who creeps into the bedroom of her master's wing while he's away with the fiancée at the opera; she opens a small drawer to his bedside table. This is wrong, thinks the girl.

"What's in the drawer," asks my mother, interrupting. She's turned to poke me in the ribs. A man behind us has started to cough.

"A drawing of Mùi, several sketches of her face—"

"That's nice of him."

A young Khuyến takes his seat at the grand piano. The new servant girl Mùi has emerged with a modest tray of coffee and rice cakes. Khuyến ignores her. He has always ignored her. He shifts around the pages of his sheet music on the shelf. For a long beat, he gazes toward the far end of his sitting room, deep in contemplation. There's a portrait of his mother adorned with pearls, a gold and jade bracelet on both wrists placed delicately, neatly, in her lap. One of her hands appears to be cradling a music box or a closed paper fan ("I don't understand," announces Chrysanthemum laughing from her seat next to me in the theater). The painting sits in our parlor long after her death in this decade between 1951 and 1961, in what feels like an extended morning of the bourgeois household yet untouched by rain or spring, the faintest corner of a canvas turning up with the murmur of fighter jets flying overhead. Khuyến inhales through his nostrils. He wears a charcoal gray cashmere sweater and, under that, a white linen shirt. He leans over to press the keys in D minor. Mùi stares at the back of the man's head. I don't know where to start, she thinks.

The fiancée has snuck in with a gift. She places it on the marble foyer table and runs a manicured finger through a bowl of decorative water, disturbing the lotus that floats there. She has brought a new vase wrapped with expensive paper. "Is she pretty," chimes my mother.

"Yes, wearing a blue dress."

"That's nice, very nice."

The servant girl Mùi watches as her master and the fiancée avoid each other like two strokes of brushes cutting in and out of the frame. Against her chest, she hugs the empty silver tray, biting her lip. She drops it just as you leave the hall, shaking your head in confusion, "Where's the plot."

Stay here, I whisper to Mùi from my row in the dark. Stay here, with this story of music with no last name.

At the end of our film's closing credits, the piano has come to a total stop. The lights flare on. In the lobby, I find myself leaning against a wide carpeted column, rushing a few notes into my pocket logbook. Turning another page, I sketch the water hyacinth in the top left margin. It reminds me of another film by Trần Anh Hùng, set in the future and starring someone who looks vaguely like Tan Huỳnh, Chrysanthemum's dead father, played by the young actor Tony Leung, who has left a café, Chez Kew, at the exact moment I leave the theater in Chợ Lớn. We smile at each other, meeting in the street and linking arms. We return to Chez Kew and find a table outside. Later, you might ask me if we ever went to bed together, what a bizarre and stupid question—I want to kill you, Paul.

Chrysanthemum stands on one side of the tarmac in Saigon. She waves at her older brother who now boards a plane in 1971. He wears a three-piece suit. He turns a final time to wave at the country of sorrow. There are three directions we can go from here: present, future, and past. The epicenter has no form. I have no other forms to use, to make legible, what I came here to explain. Tan, who looks like the swaggering version of Tony Leung, takes out a box of American cigarettes from the front pocket of his shirt. He taps the box against his palm, loosening a cigarette, which he offers out of sheer politeness. I wave a hand in front of my face. This signals the waiter. The waiter stops by with two bottles of seltzer water. I'm expecting you, too, the planet Paul, to reappear whenever you feel like it, for that's how you are—fickle, stingy, mercenary, blue—I hold the logbook open on our table. Tan squints and leans back with the cigarette, contemplating this situation. You're there, Paul, as a simple sketch on the page. Here's the wedding, I say to Tan, and here's my face, all misery, volcanic ash, and gold. Just now, I've told him of the tortures in Núi Đất but chose to leave out minor details, here and there, like whether or not my mother, Chrysanthemum, knew any of the girls personally. She knew one of them. She was her friend. This is true. I divide our language into three more parts, into the corner which vanishes, counting first in English, backward, from present to past:

3.

I have no Vietnamese name.

2.

So I make one up.

This: belonging to my grandfather, Tan Huỳnh.

This: belonging to Chrysanthemum, the daughter of Tan Huỳnh and Mai Thị Huỳnh of our great southern skies. As the interpreter for all three, I realize my role has been rendered nearly futile. The woman, who's just been blindfolded onscreen in the previous film, refuses to speak. My job, as her brother, is to keep that woman alive; so I tell the soldiers anything.

"She wants water. She's asking for water."

There's a photograph, too, but I won't include such evidence in my *Book of Water*. Furthermore, the word for *country* is *nước*. Another word for *water* is *nước*. Perhaps our captive is begging for both, but I refuse to tell you this, soldier.

"Making it into a formula," writes the novelist Sōseki. "An artist is someone who works in the triangle," the shape which remains after all angles have been removed in our human zone for reason, the basic senses of sight, touch, and smell, arriving at the "four-cornered world," and then "a figure flitting through the shadows."

The dialogue—you, the planet Paul; Chrysanthemum, my mother; her sister, Mùi—work in the infinite loop of illnesses, I point to the least deadly one of them. In this theater, I take a seat in the center row. You walk in by yourself, the planet Paul, so sure of himself.

1.

The planet Paul: "You love me, say you love me."

Tan: a tangled forest, stirring.

Chrysanthemum closes our book and shakes her head in mild confusion. "Who's Paul?"

"I'll explain it differently. Ma, are you ready?"

"Okay."

The pregnant woman Mùi, in the film *Mùi đu đủ xanh*, continues reading in her careful, even lilt. Her left hand has drifted up to rest on her pregnant belly. In the final scene, we're confronted by hints of upheaval in South Vietnam, or the political that collides with the philosophy of beauty; Mùi, the servant girl, has replaced the object of Khuyến's desire. She sits in a high-backed wicker chair surrounded by fruit and lush, green flora, like the queen on a throne. The most violent act we've perhaps witnessed before this, after a hundred minutes, has been the burning of an ant or the single slap across a face, the shards of a broken vase that Khuyến calmly and deliberately cleans up, by himself, in the dark.

Before she marries this man, her master, Mùi flees to a corner of her kitchen. She's terrified of Khuyến's gaze. He is finally looking at her; finally, after all these years. The human concept of marriage crumbles before us. Don't you understand, Paul? You're next to the piano. You try to press the black keys but no sound comes out. An engagement ring has been returned in the middle of the night. The sapphire clatters to a tile on the floor. I sit in the hall and wonder what my mother would have done if her brother had never left the country.

Of its debut in English, *The Scent of the Green Papaya*, the *Times* will later report in 1993, after a New York Film Festival screening, that the romanticism has been "misplaced" though "well outweighed by the film's haunting visual loveliness." The servant girl Mùi has fallen, allegedly, in love with a stranger after ten years of living apathetically together.

In this house, we end with Mùi. I move to another seat in the audience. Huddled together in the first row is an English-speaking man next to his English-speaking wife; I can't make out much of what they're saying but hear the whispers, "A Vietnam as yet unscarred." I hold the newspaper clipping of the critic's review the next morning and fling it to the table in a rage.

At Chez Kew: you, me, and Tony Leung.

Behind that, there's a testimony of Scott Camil, a veteran of the US First Marine Division. He has just now explained that a woman would beg for water while being tortured by his men. I don't know where I am anymore. The floor slips underneath me. I'm in the theater of madness, but not really. My sister sits at the foot of my bed. She's reading from a book of poetry. She pats my hand and says it's going to be okay. On the stage is a veteran. He has started to weep. Anyway, a hurricane never dreams.

In 1961, by the age of twenty, Mùi has become pregnant with her master's first child. In this scene, she cups a melon-sized mound poking through her tunic. "Strong waves," she reads, "in a rocky swell."

Her husband Khuyến looks away. I am one without the other, the camera and hospital, the dissonance of strings and silk, áo dai, pregnant, looking at you, soldier, always looking at you. Breathing in: a harmony of voices rising like a bell over water.

"Cherry trees," adds Mùi.

Yes, the cherry trees. I agree.

Mùi is now at rest, eyes closed, on her bed at the hospital behind a crimson veil. The cadence persists here: trees "that spread in every direction and curl up."

Mùi is awake. She recites from her place at the foot of a benevolent statue. At the corner of an old opera house in the north, one by one, a crowd of men raises each fist. Mùi: "swaying and twisting with rhythms of the water."

At this moment of recognition—she looks exactly like my mother, Chrysanthemum—I begin to tremble in the audience with the sixth and final illness. A melody shifts places, twinkling in the rafters. "It's interesting," she says. "The changing trees keep the shape of a tree."

Sideshows

I. The Golden Lion

IT HAD THE RHYTHM of laughter in my cardigan pocket, the weight of a box filled with hard candy rattling about in flavors of strawberry, grape, cherry, and sour apple—sugar crystals coated with wild, wild color. I felt it when I crossed our hotel room. You sat to one side of the tall Palladian window staring over traffic. A cool Monday morning in Venice after Hadrian's party, you were flattened, you would say with little tentative waves of your hand by the temple to your face.

The radiator went quiet. I fished for the cardboard box in my pocket and threw it at the wall by your head. You ignored this; your foot was propped sturdily on the radiator; the candy burst from the box and scattered everywhere along a cold hardwood floor.

I stooped to pinch the crystals one by one into the cup of my blue palm, meanwhile, cursing you under my breath.

Com'era, dov'era.

No, the world didn't burn you. Instead, you seemed to be bored, staring at the line of frozen horses down the piazza of St. Mark's.

The colors of your eyes oscillated from green to wolf-silver in their reflection through the glass. "Some verses," you commanded in that low, pious breath, the hems of your trousers rolled up to your calves.

Before I could stop myself, I straightened my shoulders back as my hands flowed over with candy, arms bent at the elbows, neck exposed like a stained marble fountain, and this tongue of mine running on engine steam far, far away.

I recited your favorite scene from Bergman's film, *Persona,* the one with a book about the incomprehensibility of human fear, the nurse holding it open on the picnic table outside, casting a sideways but monochrome glance at her patient.

When I punctuated the quote toward its end, we left for another film festival.

I hated you for knowing supposedly everyone from this half of the continent. Aboard a ferry at the dock of the Lido, you introduced me to a row of critics and their spouses who nibbled, to my dismay, on the corners of egg mayo sandwiches.

The strangest part was not the bread cut into triangles or the sanded teeth of your smile; I smiled too as your dutiful, overdressed Lua with frills up to my chin, tugging at the glove past my wrist, hiding that blue, blue sky.

II. Apple, Mimi, Io

AT THE PARTY, Hadrian is winking at Antinous who hurries to gather the animals for a portrait. Apple and Mimi are nowhere to be found. The dog has leapt over the meat bowl, licking it empty.

I'm sorting the brushes by size on a sheet of paper dusted in thin layers of eye shadow. Hadrian is holding a set of martini glasses aloft, two in each hand, dressed head to toe in drag. I'm thinking we have our roles to play, and you're about to ruin everything.

From outside the open window, across a piazza of Tibur, there's a faint scuffle quickly followed by a shattering of bottles, the clomping of hooves on wet cobblestone in a careless villa night. I can hear you ascend three flights of stairs to our apartment. Antinous has taken a cue from Hadrian.

"Oh, Mimi."

Hadrian nods. I lift my face to say something brave but catch your glare in the entryway.

You're the planet Paul in ugly army boots, acting like someone who's never had to be anyone else before. You remind us all of Napoleon, a footman without a name or death certificate, the Count of Monte St. Croix, three mice to Rhodôpis on her way through Egypt, Disney Junior himself, and the planet Paul, once again, arriving at a party uninvited.

You walk into the foyer, glancing a moment too long at the vanity mirror propped near the candy bowl. You have the face of an American superhero, bronze, and square-jawed in dark aviator sunglasses.

Hadrian glowers at you from across the room.

A double click of the tongue and Io, the dog, might tear into your throat, but Io loves everyone.

Antinous is screeching suddenly, "No!" and tosses a cold drink in your face.

"Why is HE here?!"

My husband, why can't you let me go? It's enough that we've entered the realm of angels. Still, you track me down like a talisman, my friends say. And I'm sorry for you in those brief moments of disgrace, the legendary planet Paul reduced to a dimension of flesh and a tightrope swaying between mortality and worship.

Enter Isaac with Mimi on one shoulder.

Isaac: in a pair of platform heels.

You: dripping in iced cognac, standing there, wiping your hairless blond face with the back of your hand.

Isaac floats by with a second bowl of candy, a chocolate bar, and bundles of licorice, brushing you aside.

"Excuse *me*."

Isaac is also wearing a bright laurel crown, dazzling in Sundance gold, and a feather-trim duster coat that sweeps a luxurious marble floor. No one will look at you for the rest of the evening. Good riddance, Paul. There's the door.

III. The Trần Nữ Yên Khê Fan Club

By autumn, her film *Xích lô* would win the Golden Lion at the Venice Film Festival. Someone had nervously tapped on the back of my chair at the closing credits. I leaped to my feet when the lights came on and cheered like a squirrel. I couldn't help myself. There was something in the final act shifting a language for music in my mind. The planet Paul was also there, halfway down the aisle toward an exit, pleading for me to stop; I could feel it in his tone.

"Sit down, Lua. You're embarrassing us."

But I wouldn't, I refused. I needed something to say to the director. *Nothing* could stop me. There I went pumping Uncle Hùng's hand up and down, up and down again. His wife, the actress, stood nearby, politely smiling.

Two rows of critics—I felt them shifting in their seats—sucked in their pineapple lips. They stood after a few seconds, muttering to each other in French or English, clutching at their coats, shuffling out the hall in scandalized pairs. I whirled and felt under my breasts. The plague indeed spread into Saigon after 1995. A girl with her young mother waded through a market. The mother appeared uncannily like Trần Nữ Yên Khê but with spectacles that made her eyes look blocky and tired. I wanted to shout at her, "Chrysanthemum!" But my voice belonged to time, an ancient unspeakable grievance.

Night Chorus

THE TECHNICIAN Franklin Cárdenas swings back and forth in a swivel chair behind the nurses' station. His body careens dangerously to one side, threatening to break the chair. His shoulders are built like a Ducati. "V-rum v-rum." The back of his tongue purrs. His lips are bristled in a mustache and beard stretching gleefully at this private sound effect. It smells like raw onions. Diesel.

On a low counter set behind the station's main wall, Franklin reshuffles a deck of cards. His hands are large and pensive, our Franklin of El Barrio Hollywood stops to count under his breath— "One. Two. Three. Four."—all in English, the Aces face up.

"I don't see how she's ever leaving here." The technician adds, "Our Circus Arizona."

He imagines the new patient, Emi, wandering down the corridor in a pair of loose intake socks, the cone of a spotlight traveling overhead.

The father visits every Saturday, Franklin has noted. The father stays in a room in the Best Western near the airport. The father has flown in from Texas. All the nurses know him well by the third or fourth week, his head shaking and tired, teary-eyed.

"Poor guy," Franklin says to the stack of cards to his left, facedown.

"Daichi waits in the hall whenever I leave my shift." He says, "V-rum v-rum."

A jump cut catches the muted expression on Emi's face.

"Darlene is signing him in."

On the sticky note pad above the card game, Franklin pauses to scribble pieces of additional details of that circus engine in his mind.

"He's calm," writes Franklin. Below this, in a list of carefully plotted circles, he adds, "Princess of the moon" and wonders about Darlene, some karmic debt, I don't know. Franklin shudders. He glances at the clock behind the shatterproof casing drilled into the wall above the nurses' station. It's exactly 3:33 a.m. Franklin, though not superstitious by nature, has decided to restart the game of Solitaire anyway.

His girlfriend is probably asleep by now. He imagines the top of her head illuminated by the box television across their La-Z-Boy chair. She's curled under a blanket by now. Maybe they could get a dog. He comes to this realization gradually, just like the dog in the story the patient rattled off earlier onstage in the courtyard. It's always the same characters looking back at the face in a mirror or looking at a pit bull mix named Io or someone named Paul, the planet Paul.

"I like it. I like her stories. I don't know why, but I do."

The technician Franklin stares at the three Jacks spread before him. "But when I listen to Emi in the courtyard, even when she's turning them all around, I never know who exactly speaks, but I don't pause to ask what makes sense or not."

"It's the way she puts us into the scene," he's said to one of the Jacks.

Jack is apathetic. Franklin keeps going. "Holding me there inside the random places and calling us all kinds of names like Malcolm Browne, Lua Mater, or Tony Leung, and yesterday, I was Captain America! Would you look at that!"

Chuckling: "She knows her films, though. It's like Emi lives in all of them at the same time. It's why she drifts around so much. It's never Emi, never *just* Emi. It's Emi plus Lua, or Emi plus the mom named Chrysanthemum or President John F. Kennedy, or Lua as someone else before Emi, or Lua wandering inside Emi as a child, or Lua sitting in the movie theater of central Saigon or Hanoi, or maybe somewhere else."

"There's a tiny Panda involved too, hey, man . . ."—the janitor has shuffled by, buzzing himself out.

"Hey!" The janitor nods.

Franklin looks back at his notes. "She's not that unbuckled," he says. "But what do I know?" Franklin leans over the card game to meditate on another row of numbers laid out in front of him. He doesn't feel that old. His girlfriend is almost thirty-four. They first met in Nogales, long ago, down a road from their college where they both met in a class about an intersection between Plato and calisthenics.

They would move to Tucson, after one of them graduated, for Marguerite's uncle. They have stayed here together ever since. The plot was simple. His sweet and rational Marguerite, gray-eyed and soaping up the handwoven rugs at the carpet shop six days a week. It's a slow life. Slow, but good—Franklin tells Marguerite that realization when she comes home from work one afternoon, and he also tells her of the new patients at Sonora. Marguerite listens and asks a question or two, here and there, nothing too specific. She's not one to gossip.

Emi has her back turned to the doorway when Franklin rolls in with the medicine cart and blood-pressure machine. Emi's roommate is still asleep, planked under a cocktail of tranquilizers and a kind of sadness that keeps you up for days in the red hatchback Volvo until your eldest, the six-year-old with pigtails and a trembling bottom lip, finds some reserve of courage to take a plush iguana from the bed, down the stairs, into the driveway, and reaching up to knock on your side of a back window, will start to ask, "Mommy, mommy, where's daddy?"

"Morning!" Franklin says. He's lifting a skinny arm into the thick measuring cuff. Emi watches this. She continues her story: "Khuyến?"

Emi blinks at the roommate who doesn't reply. The roommate drools a little on the pillow. Emi looks at Franklin and repeats her question.

❋

Franklin turns a card in his mind and sees the King of Hearts. "I'll come back with your pencils after breakfast."

"And Panda?"

"Yeah, hold on."

The shift ends with dawn and Franklin checking out for the weekend. On his long drive home, he can't get this image of a tiny ridiculous Panda dancing on the windowsill at Sonora, shaking its little hips and little arms, a pair of watery eyes staring up at you as you leave with a pinprick hole boring through your fragile heart; Franklin stumbles out the room, into the hall, gripping a handle to the blood-pressure machine. His nose is stuffed up. He struggles to breathe. He wants to cry but stops himself from crying.

At the gas station on Speedway, he sits, idling the engine, and runs the back of his hand across one side of his face.

False Starting Points

IN THE PATIENT'S NOTEBOOK, Franklin instantly recognized his handwriting.

"How else could we avoid it," he thought and lowered his eyes. With a careful thumb, he leafed to the next page. The sentences were all cramped together. Punctuation marks landed heavily on lines often ripped into little holes across the paper. Even though it appeared to be Emi's journal, Franklin shook the thought of taking this thing from her room and leaving the hospital with her work. "It's her work," he thinks.

"Captain," the note had said. "If it's indeed you . . ."

Franklin read a paragraph in his handwriting that continued to meld Emi's response with his:

CAPTAIN, if it's indeed you, we have some questions. But first, strange, you write to me directly. Why? I've asked my publicist to contact your publicist, along with the Pentagon, but the closest we got was a photo of Panda who stood in front of a vending machine at the Sydney Opera House. Panda stared at a bag of potato chips, and this led to my next question: Were you working in the US or Switzerland? I ask because, according to the New York Times in 1967, Geneva rejected a proposal to host the Russell International War Crimes Tribunal regarding my mother's country, Vietnam. Simply put, it would make America look bad, and that's where you come in, Captain. I've seen your films,

a few of your stage performances live, interviews on camera . . . To answer your
first letter, no, I'm not angry.

Franklin paused at the next words. "Does it get easier," he read, "to love?"

"Or be in love?"

I imagine you're sure of what's good and bad. Perhaps later we can talk about
fate. But for now, I'm curious: Have you heard of the film Persona? *Perhaps.*
Perhaps. You're an actor. It's the obvious question, but I don't want to assume.
I first saw Bergman's Autumn Sonata *at an empty theater in Kolkata many*
years ago with one of my exes. I haven't truly loved since then, or, on the flip
side, I've loved too much. Persona *was recommended by another friend in*
Ljubljana. A novelist who went on long walks with me almost every day of
my residency in 2019, pushing the stroller of his baby up a hill in Tivoli Park,
the leaves wet with rain . . . Anyway, I've wanted to talk about this film with
someone else. If you have thoughts, I want to hear them.

Chris, I mean, Cap'n, here's a line to a poem that I like: "Tu sarai innocente
sì: ma l'alba ha un tiro a segno più forte," which translates, "You may be
innocent yes: but the dawn is better at target shooting."

That's Amelia Rosselli, translated from the Italian by Lucia Re and Paul

Vangelisti, in a collection dated sometime between 1960 and 1961, titled Variazioni (Variations). I fall giddy with Rosselli's work, the careful "innocent yes" without a comma piercing the frame. It brings me back to Persona. Elisabet Vogler, played by the actress Liv Ullman, is in the hospital after a nervous breakdown. She's horrified by images of Vietnam on her television. When I first saw this onscreen, the event that involves burning (details of which I won't go into here) and Elisabet's reaction, I admit I was a little mad at my friend. He didn't warn me of this scene and, instead, advised my focus to lie on the actor's face, white as static flickering across the Baltic Sea.

I also want to know how you feel in the eyes of film cameras—I know, a basic question but open to any way you diverge from it (the Captain you've played, I notice, is at liberty to shift around on a moral compass which, in the end, doesn't ever diverge too far from immorality; the worst you can do is punch a man in the face for no reason except, maybe, I don't know, you're drunk and somewhere off a turnpike outside Boston)—does this draw you to similar roles bent on discovery? Would you play another soldier? It's not a critique. I'm just turning around. The logic leads from here in 1967 at a war crimes tribunal or the edge of it, and a group of teenage Vietnamese activists crossing the border. Which one? I don't know. They've all been executed, my mother says. "All executed."

You think you're innocent, but I'm just standing here mixed up in survivor's guilt and melancholia. I'm sorry, it's just hard to know who's good and who's bad. You stood there with a gun and shield. Remember? It was real but still went

"Pew! Pew!" My Panda is an immense fan of your Marvel films. It makes him feel victorious in a tiny vicarious way. He has the mind of a three-year-old and believes everything is good or bad.

Chris, do you have a dog? Tell me about it, please.

The letter ended abruptly. Franklin shut the notebook, returning it to the floor next to Emi's bed. He left the room. The spotlight dimmed.

The Six Illnesses

START WITH the apparition of trees—it's a crisis of the psychic kind. The ambulance driver mutters under his breath, "Always on a Thursday, new moon in Capricorn."

Blasting down Oracle in Tucson, the tape in his dash plays Rammstein's "Seemann" on a loop. No one else is in the vehicle.

He arrives at the casita. There's a figure, tall like the trunk of black velvet ash, hovering behind the window. Lua. Midnight. You love me. Say you love me. The planet Paul steps from his ambulance, ignoring those sacrificial words. He waits for Lua to open the door, step out, and come to him; it's a crisis. "Remember that," he says to himself.

Scenes from a wedding—Lua faces the planet named Paul. Gesturing to her mouth and then to the seven larger moons nearby, the minor divinity reaches up, trying to claw her way from the contract; she has no language yet; the planet Paul snatches her wrist and holds it in a rubbery grip so firm her blue fingers turn periwinkle at the tips.

"Don't be stupid," he says softly.

There's a cosmic war he's playing out like a game of cards. On each card is the image of a tree. Lua looks into this contract of their marriage; no markings for roots, no drawn amendments regarding the nature of leaving one's spouse; she decides to leave him anyway; she wants to find that place where trees have recently entered a long sweat of her dreams, concretized, wild, and knowing—she's told as much to the planet Paul who continues to look obscurely like CAPTAIN AMERICA. He obliges but only . . . "When you return, I'll have my mother and father change you into a temperature of magma."

"No longer will you have this body."

"No longer, a mind to think on your own, no time, no dust, no want of water."

The planet is cruel but methodical. Lua covers her face.

On her first day of exile, away from her new husband, Lua finds the green door marked with a circle for EARTH where trees indeed could shift around. Next, she encounters a box of ice cubes and soda cans. Inside this plastic box, she places her hand. After a few years, she takes this hand out; it tastes like chocolate chip cookie dough. Finally, at 7:34 p.m., on November 11, 1994, at a small Disney resort in Tokyo, the minor goddess witnesses her first electronic parade, a motorized float among ethereal choruses of dancing fireflies in emerald and blue hats and yellow polyester tights. Seeing this, she collapses to her knees, completely soaked in tears. My love for you is great and wide.

"This is nonsense," says the planet Paul. He's glaring at the casita's front door in Tucson and wonders if he should ram the hood of his ambulance through it.

"Come out, Lua. I've got a new girlfriend. You can meet her." He doesn't say, "At Sonora."

"You can be free," he says instead. He swipes at the speck of lint that's fallen from his shirt.

She's probably inside singing karaoke, he thinks.

She's probably playing *Tetris*, the fool. You love me, he adds silently—as usual, the planet Paul is so sure of himself. It's in the way, he thinks, you fled the marriage altar, this gravity of spore, fog, and wind particles pulling into a vessel which we could call your body; Lua, I made it happen, the shaping of your passage through space and the ancient priests who'd just as quickly worship us. Without me, there'd be no origin "story," your poor Vietnamese "mother" sitting in front of a computer screen in Dallas; she's looking at her bank account. You've identified your journey with her journey as a refugee? It's quaint, I'll admit. But you must stop it at once, Lua, you're starting to embarrass us. What will my father Caelus say? You're making a mockery of fate. It's not about the trees!

The planet Paul has started to shake, attempts to regain his composure.

Inside: Kate Bush begins playing. The planet Paul loses, as they say, his proverbial marbles.

"Stop it!" The planet Paul is howling, but the music swiftly turns up; Lua's INSIDE the dream box, and he can hear her, singing in her underwear.

A tiny Panda has popped onto the windowsill. It appears to be dancing.

HELLO EARTH—in this world, I need things to be simple: love, your hand against my neck, the sweetness of grass pillows. There are fragments from a divine memory, I answer just the same: here's a teakettle I found at Goodwill, here's the Gabbeh rug Marguerite brought home last week; a customer had left the thing rolled up on a countertop but never came back for it.

"I need you to focus, Franklin," says the man to himself. He flushes the toilet, crosses their studio apartment, and kicks on a swamp cooler shoved in a corner next to their mattress. It's prickly for the summer at noon by the Catalina Highway.

Marguerite is out. I should sleep, thinks Franklin. His nerves have all spindled to one side of his body like the acacia outside dropping its leaves. For half the afternoon, he stares at his toes wiggling inside his socks. His legs are naked, splayed across the mattress. His head is propped, against the wall, on two hard pillows. He works at a receipt from the gas station, folding and unfolding the white sheet of paper until it takes the outline of a wrinkled elephant raising its trunk. He can't stop thinking about the new patient at Sonora.

The patient's stuffed animal, by some mystery from within the stuffing itself, had started gyrating its mushroom-sized pair of button paws from one side to the next, unaided totally by the girl who simply sat there on the floor by her bed, tickled and clapping her hands like a lunatic—the power of music, as they say.

Franklin, at the start of his shift, doled out a paper cup of medicine, along with a chalky-colored vitamin tablet that the patient offered to her Panda, pushing it through the round black nose and nodding matronly, "It's good for you, Panda."

Doctor Z had decided right then, with pursed dry lips, staring into Emi's room with the lights turned off, that it's better to keep "a distraction like this" locked away for the night.

Somehow even this seemed unjust to Franklin. But what do I know? He shrugged. I just work here.

And look at you, Emi; the night technician gazes at a row of cards in the nurse's station later that hour, thinking about the new patient in 104B. If you could slow down a bit, take a shower, and collect these fragments of time in a neat see-through container, I could help you project them on a wall.

They say you're also a performance artist, is it true? I've never seen one before; Franklin smiles. I had to ask around and look it up.

The next morning at The Loft, Franklin pays for a single admission to a screening of Lizzie Borden's 1983 *Born in Flames*.

He should be sleeping, he knows, but he can't sleep; so here we are, he thinks, leaking all over the place.

Before the feature, there's a preview of a retrospective of colonial and postcolonial movies.

"We hear the sound of airplanes," comments Lawrence Chua in 1994, the printed date has been stamped in a corner, "But we never see the bombs."

In response, the interviewed Vietnamese director leans on one elbow, choosing his next words carefully. "What might be important to know . . ."

The two men smile amicably at each other.

"I haven't experienced . . ."

"I haven't lived through these moments people might expect. At least, for now, I cannot . . . I am not capable of reminding you what the French did to our women, or what Americans have done to specific villages in our country. Maybe another artist can do this, maybe later when I possess the stomach for it."

But he wants to create "a base," recalls Trần Anh Hùng, like layers of neutral paint on a canvas. "To create a daily life for the people . . ."

"And understand how much this should be necessary for a film such as . . ."

To make a daily life? Wonders Lawrence inaudibly.

"Correct. Let me be clear. One can understand the atrocities all the better."

Franklin digs into the front pocket of his jeans. He pulls out a rock the size of an eyeball. No, this can't be my time. His ears have grown warm; he feels a hint of vertigo, rests his head against the top of his chair, sinking into a place of sunlight, drifting along the water park at a beachside resort, witnessing the impossibly large manta rays settling toward the bottom of an artificial lagoon.

The pool is perfectly translucent and magnetized.

Snorkelers kick about in red bathing suits, ants in comparison with the gentle titans underneath them.

"I'm not afraid," says Lua. She's holding onto Franklin's arm.

At the start of Born in Flames, they both sober, straighten up in their chairs, snapping awake—NEW YORK CITY, WOW—one of them gasps and opens a bag of sour gummy worms. Between the crinkles: "Thus, a daily life . . ."

"It makes sense. Lua's grinning there in the dark."

When Franklin, the night technician at Sonora ultimately breaks another patient out, Marguerite isn't too surprised.

"She can stay here for the weekend. No more," she says of the girl, and when she goes to sleep, the patient attempts to make her presence useful in the opposite corner of their apartment; she folds up her body into the outline of a standing lamp.

"Emi needs a bit more time. She's a performance artist." Franklin would try to explain earlier in that low tone of desperation when Marguerite had squinted into the backseat window of their car.

"No." Marguerite was weary and more rational of the pair. "She's ill. You have to take her back."

Then what? Franklin was unmoored, adding unhelpfully: "But she's so good at *Tetris*."

Meanwhile, the tiny Panda remains propped in the middle of a La-Z-Boy chair with a quilt pulled up to his chin. Though Marguerite is skeptical of the entire situation, she's kind. There are many ways to live—she agrees with Franklin on this point.

Perhaps if the planet Paul could leave Lua alone, everything would be fine, "but what do I know," repeats Franklin to his girlfriend who's gone to bed; he crawls over to the mattress before taking off his socks, he curls around Marguerite's body.

The tiny Panda is grateful and silent. The lamp in the corner of their apartment blinks very, very slowly: a good life, indeed.

Lua Mater, banished to this place, is the former wife of another planet. If this has not been made so obvious by now, I don't know how else to help you, mercy, I can feel my brain roll past its breaking point, the synapses all tickling the back of my skull. You'd be a complete bag of pennies to ask another question, simply thrown into the atmosphere willy-nilly—Hadrian and Antinous are taking turns at the planet Paul, flogging him with their pendulum of insults.

"So you want time?"

"So you want a reliable narrator: Lua, easily dissectible and placid by your side like one of those scribers drooling into your bowl."

"'There it is,' you say, 'A good story; let's make it into television!'"

At the party, Kate Bush continues to blare down the walls. The year is AD 248. The Romans created Lua, but Lua has other plans.

The sun is, at last, coming out—"and you, you're alive, Emi."

"You're alive and free, just go."

Franklin has handed the former patient exactly fifty-four dollars, twenty from Marguerite and the rest from him.

"You are living. You are human. It doesn't matter if I'm dead or if you ever come back to this place. I insist, no." Franklin has pushed the money back into Emi's hand.

Go to Slovenia, he thinks. Get your castle, Lua. Write everything you want. You have something necessary to say. Don't deny it any longer. Your mother's name is Chrysanthemum.

She's Vietnamese, she's from Vietnam; I don't care what the planet Paul first told you about your creation; you need to put it in a book, or history will kill you. Understand? Understand me?

Emi is nodding and putting together the pieces in her mind; she watches every layer disappear.

"A champion of *Tetris*, really," Franklin would add with much flare earlier that weekend, and Marguerite would sigh. You exaggerate, my heart, but you're all good intentions, I believe you.

"But take her back, okay," she also said. "After Sunday. She needs to return to Sonora."

Instead, the following morning after Marguerite leaves for work, Franklin drives Emi to the train tracks behind Exo.

He says, "Wait. You can hear it."

"When you see the box door open, go on and jump, understand?"

Yes, Emi is buckling her stuffed animal to the front of her chest with a child's sparkle belt. They both understand. The tiny Panda is holding out a paw.

Franklin bows and shakes it respectfully.

The train screams by.

The performance artist and her courageous tiny Panda have successfully made the jump.

GO TO SLEEP—after an hour, they've reached a suitable destination. The tiny Panda leaps out first, waddling ahead, away from the tracks. Emi, with a wave to the group of children who had also been deposited in the freight car from Tucson, pinches her nose before landing a step past the brave and tiny Panda.

A muffled cheer erupts from inside the DREAM BOX, and the train zooms north, disappearing past a bend in the horizon.

Emi stares into the dusty palm lines of her hands, the palms of Lua. Do you hear me, she thinks.

Is this what you wanted? Is this why we're here?

You'd thought we were friends?

You'd thought you could just take over my mind whenever you want?

I'm not a puppet, Lua! I'm not your destiny!

Do you hear me?

Lua is feeling herself become upset. The two minds roll over each other, sputtering with ash, timescales, and unclear sound bites or boundaries of fact from fiction—"I remember him saying," a journalist, John Sorell, had testified of an incident in 1968.

"'I can't break her.' So he tried something else to get the girl talking."

"'Give me a minute,'" Sorell recalled one of the lieutenants saying. "The man was exhausted, but he knew his stuff; no one could deny it."

"'There are better ways of using water,' he said to me."

The tiny Panda is poking our ankle with his paw.

Look. We're here. The tiny Panda sweeps a dramatic arm over the new planet roaring at our feet: Neptune. My goodness, Panda, isn't this too much?

The planet Neptune is blue in the face, blue and cold all over.

Triton, one of Neptune's fourteen documented moons, may round that corner, the tiny Panda motions: if we wait long enough.

To the east, to the north, the tiny Panda whirls around in circles. But this is not the reason why we're here. Let's go, Lua.

"In utero," explains the exiled goddess through the mind of Emi, "the matter of wind is also a matter of cardinal prepositions."

"I was born in three different sets of logical conclusions, on the planet called Paul; but to our left, pushing through the glass is a metallic voice that booms, 'Now! Now! Now!'"

"There's a possibility the planet Paul will find us here and tell you to give me up. I won't stop you, Emi. I don't know what is true about where I come from, but you're more powerful than you think."

Lua is crying. Emi feels herself crying, too.

Okay, Lua. Where should we go next?

The tiny Panda is pleased, jumping through the glass portal and pulling us through, an unmarked lever, the astronauts of water; a hurricane is taking shape.

On the planet Neptune, in 1989, there's a cloud that flits across the icy underbelly.

The whale implodes. Clumps of magnetic orbs plummet to a salty bed of the planet's infinite ocean. The space probe *Voyager 2* flies past and snaps a photo of the hurricane.

(Hadrian at the telescope, on Earth: "Scooter, you can do it!")

The tiny Panda bounces up and down, clapping his tiny paws with joyful abandon. In AD 426, he will also plunk onto an adjacent lever, pushing us for clarification. Saint Augustine will clear her throat and tap Hadrian on the shoulder.

Together, they will peer through the telescope at the planet Neptune.

Et regardez, later, Saint Augustine will write a journal entry about those waves that come ashore and retreat as two parts of elements, air, and then wind, the two corners of a "soul," so to speak, coming together through the human body; as for Neptune, the planet itself, two separate "goddesses."

Our tiny Panda hiccups, wiggling in his pajamas; Saint Augustine has just taken off her wig. What time is it?

The party blasts a song about the clouds and bursts them all open, one by one; Saint Augustine is massaging her temples in a firm, clockwise circle. How exhausting!

The tiny Panda persists—but why are there two goddesses arriving at the planet Neptune?

Before 1970, the American novelist Toni Morrison would write about that fear of a "Thing" that made the lighter skin of a people more beautiful, but not us, or the people of prisms and languages deemed more or less worthy for chronological preservation.

Before 1970, an Australian officer would exit a tent, brush off his sleeves, and pretend nothing terrible had just occurred to someone else inside his tent, and someone with the face of my mother, her sisters—Emi blinks back a droplet of rage.

Salacia, one of the future wives of Neptune, sits on a rock by the shore minding her own business, the better half of two collected parts—Saint Augustine confers with the flick of a hand—Salacia who's jumping now into a sea of fire.

There it is, our fear of anything that burns. The split rolls out so far, that we'd fall any which way you step, but please, Lua, don't go; in the end, a foothold will be everything we have.

To fear this ocean moves a single line piercing our mortal, fragile selves. I look up and the planet Neptune's looking at me with those eyes.

I know you have given this look before, the planet Neptune who faces us both as two separate beings, Lua and Emi, melting through the layers of nickel and iron and stone, a cloud thrashing about at 2,200 kilometers per hour; ice, once more cracking down the middle of a chest and sinking to its knees.

We cast a glance up. We're all here, the planet Neptune, eyes that should not see, but see; the water where it parts, the water as a speaking record reverses through bedrock through the valley through the grottos of green, and the tongues for all that was human forced to be nonhuman, tilting back to faint, that blossoms in her mouth, that lies near the back of a tent in complete and utter devotion—we're all here, the suns bursting with the garden of white plumeria, lilies, orchids, hibiscus, blue velvet eucalyptus branching from their jars; or now in the dewdrop blanket of a world and the dewy veils within mine, I'd kill you before you make another step defending those men who did this to our people.

(The planet Neptune, taking a drag from a spliff: "Yeah."—the fool, I want to kill you, too, Neptune.)

How much longer should we bear what stops at looking?

This shouldn't have to hurt, but here's the way I see it: the planet Neptune wraps around the Sun, just once, approximately every 165 years on Earth.

Pluto enters Neptune's orbit spanning across a twenty-year cycle of 248 years; it's a miracle the pair should never touch.

Neptune intuits and dreams. Pluto mostly bops.

But what of romance?—the tiny Panda seems to ask, with unblinking, tearful eyes.

Salacia, the virgin sea nymph, one of the fifty daughters of the wise old man Nereus, arrives at the opening of this tent in South Vietnam.

She meets the eyes of our planet Neptune, shudders, and flees into the darkest parts of Atlantis. "Sic erat instabilis tellus, innabilis unda, lucis egens aër."

Thus, comment the poets in AD 8, was each planet unstable and the seas made of glass, or something like that . . . Ovid stares into the obsolete speaker system at the party: no light, no form of reality, one should always inhabit the path of another. On this cold Roman night, the temperatures struggle with each other, hard against soft, bodies suddenly yellowing, full of light.

"Here," notices the poet, "Salacia is braiding her long black hair."

Later versions will indicate, eventually, the color of corn.

Inscriptions: black as night's good ink, hair, like kelp, a sea nymph on the crag . . . She turns to the camera of a space probe zooming in; she sits there blindfolding herself.

Salacia is opening her face just slightly, the blackened gums and fangs glittering—the tiny Panda is enchanted.

"If you let us," suggests Lua, "I can bring us closer."

Dialogue: "Yes, as you suspect, in a matter of perspective, Salacia is the second form of Lua."

"Wife to *both* the planet Neptune and the planet Paul."

Emi considers this.

On Earth: a collective gasp at the telescope.

Antinous begins to fan Saint Augustine with the quill of a pen.

Isaac, unbothered, goes to check on the candy bowl.

✳

Costume change: Isaac is wearing a bedazzled fedora and blue lipstick.

The dog Io follows Isaac to the pantry.

Io is wearing a confetti pink hat in the shape of an ice cream cone. It teeters precariously to one side of Io's head.

The poets all begin to speak over each other.

In Trần Anh Hùng's *Cyclo,* the character played by Tony Leung is announcing, concurrently, in the background, "Nameless river. I was born sobbing. Blue sky, vast earth."

"Black stream water."

The poet Ovid turns up the dial. She's in slippers.

The planet Paul slams a fist against the door of his ambulance.

"Lua, enough." He has lost all patience.

Maybe if he can take her to Sonora, keep her there with the right prescriptions of Lisperdol and Pheroquel; the petrol pumping through the brain of hers might stop, and she'd look at me, eye-to-eye, like a proper wife and respect whatever I had to say.

The planet Paul is livid. He has made himself livid in the driveway. He doesn't know what to do with this emotion. He wants to bottle it up like a comet and throw it through the window. He wants to punch a wall. He has written human history, and he has written many novels, many of them, in fact, award-winning, translated into French, Bengali, Serbian, et cetera; he is not to be spat upon, danced on like a grave, imitated, cajoled, dressed in sparkles like Lua has done with all those men, blasphemously, with Ovid, Saint Augustine, and John F. Kennedy, the classics; whatever she's doing here, fumes the planet Paul, is plain *gaudy*. The tiny Panda, I can't even start, is a total abomination—"An abomination, you hear me?!"

The man is practically hysterical.

Meanwhile, behind a window, the thing still appears to be dancing.

Salacia

SHE HOLDS OUT a comb in the dead center of her palm. You try to count the fingers, starting with the pinkie that curls at a strange angle away from its neighbor. By the time you arrive at the fourth or fifth digit, your eyes are spinning at the corners, the skin between each finger webbed like the foot of a toad or salamander. Salacia waits for you to take the comb.

"Here's another riddle," she says.

"What has the tail of a phoenix, the body and face divided into natural seasons of our earth: spring, monsoon, autumn . . ."

"A delta." You've cut off the sea nymph.

"Exactly," says Salacia. She pulls back her comb. You watch as she runs the thing through what looks like a full set of hair. It's black, blacker than the universe.

I'm gathering my energy but can't reach the frame. There's an ending that needs to be addressed somehow: what drags the library forward, a mirror set against the wall, books in the languages of my parents. One proceeds to clarify the other; instead, I write in English, plotlines creating tangles with cinema, dialogue, a door to each room on earth, "A second riddle," says the sea nymph.

"What drops salt to the ground, radiation, a body, and face . . ."

"A dream."

"Good, it's been written, also, that when the planet Neptune sees me dancing on the island of Naxos, it falls in love; the poets can't tell what parts are true. But, in 19 BC, notice: 'How terrible!' Cries Virgil, 'She who turns from her limbs, braying . . . pale and strange.' I retranslate Virgil at the soirée in Rome. She's stamping both feet; Virgil's wearing, a bit unironically, a wig made from horsehair. Someone arrives with a green Gabbeh rug. We pause the music, unfurl it, and sit around the middle. She shuffles the deck of cards and lays seven in a wide U shape. Upon each card are several numbers and depictions of trees. Someone else admits, 'I haven't played this game before.'"

At Sonora, Franklin regards the new patients with extra sympathy after NIGHT SNACKS, a choice among boxes of raisins, Goldfish baggies, and string cheese; most, for obvious reasons, dash for the string cheese. A fight often ensues; the newer patients are scandalized. Around 10 p.m., Franklin takes them all out for a smoke break. Half moves to plant themselves along the edges of the courtyard, gawking at a clear desert sky; Horace finds herself, too, trembling: "If it were battered, the ocean brought to a stronghold of Neptune's power, would she not have been bold, wiser?" The sea nymph has many contradictions.

She waits for Lua to say something familiar on that crag, anything would be fine.

"Here's Panda," says Lua. The tiny stuffed animal cowers behind a rock, the tops of his eyes poking over one side. The sea nymph smiles. She leans forward on her elbows.

"Aren't you brave? Haven't you come so far already?"

Lua nudges the tiny Panda with the toe of her shoe. "Don't be scared."

The tiny Panda waddles out.

"Good, pay attention. Here's a final riddle."

"What has the aura of orange and teal; the spirit inside, alight with fluttering wings of hummingbirds; cries when it's hot but not when it's tired; has a name which means 'great flood' in languages that ought to be written from right to left, otherwise it takes on a wholly opposite meaning;

what has no body, no face but expressions of joy including, but not limited to, clapping, jumping, dancing, singing . . ."

"Oh!" The tiny Panda perks up.

Salacia keeps going, "What is marked by time but not through the hours of a day; walks on short legs; travels everywhere; knows a few rules of intermediate geometry; has a preferred way of sleeping, on its stomach . . ."

"Panda!"

Bravo, Panda. The tiny Panda rushes toward Salacia. The sea nymph is more beautiful than he can remember. A school teacher stops Emi to ask, "Can you explain the setting? Are we still on the planet Neptune?"

"And what about the library? Did you mention it before?" Two other patients, the electrician and a government worker by the name of Bo, murmur in agreement. Bo's been dealing a deck of cards on the communal table. The night technician Franklin has just pulled up a chair to watch this game of *Tetris* unfolding, the print version. Emi looks at the card in her hand, memorizing its shape, and returns the card facedown. "The library, I think, is just a metaphor."

"Okay," nods the school teacher. "Got it."

Carry on: "'Toute notre histoire' is a history of treason," the musician An Thư once said to the filmmaker Trinh T. Minh-Ha. I imagine this also to be close to what Salacia explains to our brave and tiny Panda. We're still on the planet Neptune, but not really. The planet Neptune is out there somewhere, watching us, maybe, but that's not so relevant. A hand is placed on the tiny Panda's head, "I've lied. Here's a fourth riddle. Keep your eyes unbolted. Answer correctly, you have the choice between freedom and love. Incorrectly, you will be eaten." Salacia flashes her fangs. The tiny Panda is both terrified and sleepy.

Emi turns the page of her notebook and follows the fourth riddle with the eraser side of her pencil: "What has no breath . . ."

"My ex-husband!" The electrician is giggling.

Everyone at the table turns to snap at the electrician. "Sh-sh! Shush!"

"What has no breath . . ." Salacia's voice has suddenly lowered. The tiny Panda can't help it, he's shaking all over. "But has a chest, the chest rising up and down as if to breathe; what knows where to push but cannot pull; once possessed a spine; is the color of cinnamon; 'Don't condemn me, please. Anne,' Norman Morrison had written to his wife when he left for the Pentagon. For weeks and months, the man prayed to see what he should do; one morning 'with no warning' he was shown, and the moons of Neptune glimmered; had no eyes; was a father who set himself on fire, that second of November 1965; the world was all watching; 'Dearest Anne,' he would say, 'Don't condemn me.'"

The table is quiet. Emi looks up from her notebook. "There's more."

"What has no fear; no nationality or flag to identify with; a faith; a desire to read but magazines and chapbooks strewn across the floor; what has a journey but no arrival; the bereaved Anne Morrison Welsh who recalls the arrow which 'shot from Norman's heart'; who was broken from the war, and shot, therefore, an arrow which 'sailed across thousands of miles' to pierce the heart of a people, 'in the way that love pierces your heart'; together, they had an eleven-month-old daughter named Emily; Norman, who would bring her to the Pentagon, set her aside, and stood at the window below McNamara's office; Norman who doused himself in kerosene."

The artist puts down her notebook. She recites the rest of Salacia's riddle from memory. "The poet Tố Hữu would later make a song for that 'great heart' which flew from the horizon, all the way from America like a 'lamp of justice.' How could this be possible: to have a face of sorrow but no way of dreaming; speaking too loud; have monographs of grassy hills or long, dusty roads; the color of a white man on fire; the subject of hatred and patterns tearing at a planet of everything gentle; what has a name that when read in the wrong language becomes another way of saying, 'mercy.'"

I know this, thinks the tiny Panda turning to look helplessly at Lua. I know this but don't want to say it. "You must say it," says Lua.

Salacia is not done. "What has a backyard; questions around plot and subjectivity; what knows how to bathe, can stare directly at the angry sun; has read the novel, *The Bluest Eye,* by Toni Morrison and the scene where Cholly is forced onto Darlene; but never once does Cholly think about hating the men who've ordered him to do such a thing; what strips him of a soul; what is, by the age of 31 and a Quaker from Baltimore, setting down his child, just far enough away but close enough to watch while he drenches his body with kerosene; and those days and those hours and those epochs of fire; the fires which consume us now; what has a wrong ending to the place called Mỹ Lai, you have to write it again, for someone else has written from a perspective of the soldiers but not of our people; what has a martyrdom or the weight of pebbles thrown into lakes, the confession of Scott Camil, US First Marine Division, and here it is, 'When we got up to her she was asking for water. And the lieutenant said to kill her. So he [redacted] her clothes, they stabbed her in both [redacted], they spread-[redacted] [redacted] and shoved [redacted] up her [redacted], [redacted], and she was still asking for water. And then they took that out and they used a tree limb and then she was shot.'"

AND SHE WAS STILL ASKING FOR WATER

THE GAME IS SIMPLE. There are seven standard geometric pieces, or tetrads, comprised of four squares each, configured into predetermined shapes that fit, ultimately, with one another; this depends, however, on the ordering of each shape being presented in a game, and the artist has moved to the farthest corner of the room.

She sits with her back against the wall. She's holding one of the cards close to her chest; her knees are folded up.

The school teacher is distraught. "They took away her Panda, look what happens now."

The night technician is kind. He knows what to do. He sits next to Emi and knocks his shoulder against hers, "What piece you got?"

She shows him.

"Yeah, a good one."

"You think so?"

"Absolutely."

The sea nymph and Lua are still staring at the ocean, just past the crag.

There's a boat somewhere out there, too.

On this boat must be Emi's mother.

"Gonna have to take the pencils in a sec," says Franklin. He's practically whispering. "Alright?"

"Alright."

"Alright, Lua. You did just fine."

Franklin gets up with a little effort. His knees hurt.

But why did you bring us here, Lua thinks, why did you call for me, Salacia?

Your future husband, the planet Neptune, waits offstage.

The planet seems apathetic. The sea nymph turns her face. She closes her eyes.

Lua drops the card beside her, on the ground: "Comrade, how could you recognize me as a version of your past?"

"I recognized you, too, but we couldn't talk about much else; you wouldn't even look at me. A dolphin jumped from the water. All you had were riddles."

"'What destroys until it . . .'"

"'What makes a concrete base from sand and gravel; what weighs 680,000 tons, dredged out of the Potomac; what formed the Pentagon's building and the man who'd eventually burn in front of it, and the roses . . . Red, white, magenta, peach, lavender, pink . . .'"

"'There were daffodils inside. I placed those daffodils in thick ceramic jars.'"

"'A yellow light entered the building. It vanished through rows of hemlock and cedar. There was running water, hollow reeds which knocked against the current; there was a sapling, maple; toads nearby that croaked, the chorus of toads echoing over our heads . . . A hurricane, according to the poet Bao Phi, never grew tired. I pulled a strand of black hair away from my face. I started to feel the knots of the wood twisting and twisting until that thing unfurled completely inside of me; I dreamt of water, a dream that destroyed us until it couldn't anymore; I added how we were tired and wanted to rest but came up with an extra riddle: What made us hide from the rays of the sun when we were girls; what learned to count before it learned to conquer; what had a daily life; what named that bloody limb pushed inside of us into a night sky which stretched infinitely past us, a rhythm of history repeating itself as those countries would no longer be able to imagine any kind of love we carried greater than theirs; or what was the silence of a thing with no face, no outline of a body; what rushed through a grove screaming its head off:

banyan,

     oak,

            mango, papaya
        nutmeg, teak,

                 mulberry,
                    guava,   copper pod,

jackfruit,   milkwood,

     tamarind or plum,
            mahogany-rose,
              apple,

lychee,

       cacao, almond,

jujube; and did the tree have flowers, did the trunk grow back where its limbs were torn; would you see how that heart had been broken, it was my heart, Lua, and who was there lying next to us, asking for water?'"

BOOK OF PANDA

Nightingales

ENTERING THE OLD QUARTER in Hoàn Kiếm, from the south, I found myself starting to hum. It was a nostalgic melody with notes rising up and down in a pleasant, easy rhythm. The cool night air tickled my ears. A ghost can only think so much, I reasoned. Sing and this ghost might get confused, turned around; it was the early month of 1943. Green wooden shutters opened some floor or two above the café Chez Kiều, a red glow from the thin paper lantern dripping out, a hand disappearing, ghostlike, and the laughter of a young Madame L with her visitor for the hour, two nightingales, I thought before plopping myself in a little patch of grass, in a public garden off Boulevard Prolongé.

My pajamas had quickly become damp with the city, its humidity, the inching downhill season of rain, and Madame L must have said something funny at that second. I could hear the guest reply with a faint chuckle as pink and warm as a falsetto echoing across the backstage wings of an opera house. Kitchen steam wafted from an adjacent window that was shuttered half-steps past their room attached to the main corridor which led down to Chez Kiều.

Who was cooking at an hour like this, I wondered, but then it was Wednesday, and lovers often stayed awake past two or three or four, counting those various methods of wounding each other near the heart, to make you mine as I am yours with the uncut salt of Hạ Long Bay or the thirst of raw pineapple, to devour the yellow light as it drifts from my soul and bumps to the ceiling with the dim, low-hanging lantern suspended for all of posterity in your apartment to the north; but how would I know if what you wanted was a deeper kind of love?

Madame L and her long-haired visitor shared a kind of dialogue like this, I supposed, of something simple; back to the basics, as one might say. I also believed I could hear the clinking of two porcelain cups set on the table, a whistling stone kettle nearby. Out in the garden, the late bougainvillea climbed a wall which deepened by hue every minute, an entirely different shade before dawn, and with my eyes going sleepy at the seams, I tried to work at another memory of meeting Madame L, long, long ago, when I first attached myself to her side like a fool approaching as one would crawl toward the fountain of youth. I was just a letter in her alphabet, the lowercase *p*, and she was Lua.

The year was 1897. I had gotten, though I don't exactly recall now how it happened, an apprenticeship with the eminent mapmaker of Hà Nội. For his privacy, I'll reveal the man had no name. He wasn't, in fact, a man. He wasn't a mapmaker. Regardless, I worked with this man for many years. He preferred his rituals in the morning which included some of the following: abstinence from sex, caffeine, or romance; stretching outside, smoking inside; he liked to paint the old characters for 'water,' 'fire,' 'earth,' and 'air' on four corners of a medium-sized sheet of Japanese calligraphy paper. He'd promptly burn this after breakfast.

As the apprentice, I had a regular place to sleep every night and a long mosquito net that formed a tent over my head, and a folded pillowcase I could wash if it ever got too dirty; it was a golden life, it was a simple, daily life. At first, however, I wasn't able to figure out what I had to *do* for work but set about no less to learn this craft of "mapmaking" as soon as possible; forgive me, please, for any major details omitted, once again, in the interest of my master's privacy.

Years later, when the nature of our work started shifting to other forms, the mapmaker would let me accompany him to the university. We'd help other students at the letterpress, printing posters and a weekly pamphlet that outlined an oncoming manifesto along with letters addressed to a newly appointed government, scorching reviews of anything French or artistically French. It was a confusing time for many of us. Naturally, the committee grew to about thirty-five active members by the end of 1902; still, I had no grasp of my deeper purpose in Hà Nội, much less any thumbs to hold the parchment together. Instead, I was put in a corner, high up on a stool with my legs swinging everywhere, and asked to proofread. This, I admit, was a bit of humiliation because I didn't know how to read.

Each punctuation mark appeared backward and upside down. I recognized an image here and there: the outline of a river carp twisting underwater, pods of tamarind, the palms of a toddy, rambutan, or lychee. Someone eventually decided to illustrate—"You can proofread this," they said—a cartoon of the tax collector Doumer being mounted by a large and gray matted rat. It wasn't very funny, in my opinion, but I kept this proverbial mouth, as they call it, locked up and shut behind a cupboard, goodbye—what else? It was obvious, for me at least, that our mapmaker who pushed us all along from 1902 until his assassination in late autumn, 1945, was, in secret, a lover of poetry. He had a peculiar way of describing the banyan tree, for example, as a flirtatious burlesque dancer taking off his clothes, sock by sock, pant leg followed by another, and each suspender strap slithering off a shoulder; there, too, was the hint of yellow light flying through the dancer's chest.

Toward the middle of my apprenticeship, I kept most of my faculties about me in a calm, objective manner that his peers had also learned to carry in the city where everything hot collided with everything cold. It was a dangerous number of years, though I grew more confident with the girls who one day, without any explanation at all, gathered in a unanimous vote and promoted me to the task of pasting up the flyers around the French Quarter. This, as you might imagine, would lead me from one endless rove to the next in those damp twilit hours where I held onto a glue brush stiffening and my pajamas nearly dripping off my body; I came back to SQUARE ONE, plopped on the patch of grass off Boulevard Prolongé, across from that place where Lua, behind a window above the café Chez Kiều, went by a different name every night, the one with the Juliet balcony and my fate sealed not far behind it.

Tetra Nova

THE MAPMAKER gazes steadily at the student reporter. "I have a son, yes. He studies economics. In his third year—"

Across the hall is a dull slamming of several doors. The mapmaker wears a thick round pair of black-framed spectacles like our brother Phạm Duy who's just joined the Resistance. I'd seen a photograph of him last week in a newspaper clipping, already faded by the curious and devoted who'd stop before it to touch the edges with their fingertips, to say, "Be well," under their breath.

The photograph had been cut into a pocket-size square and then pinned to a corkboard by the teacher's lounge. The man appeared relaxed under a birch; the shade fell behind him, making his face, the expression etched into it, a bit heavier, more bloated than I could remember in that same corridor where he'd run from one class to the next, an overdue term paper under his arm; in the portrait, an outline of a guitar before his knees stood pale, white. Almost twenty-four years old, the caption most likely said of the boy Phạm, though I still couldn't read despite four decades of employment under the mapmaker, who had tried every morning to teach me. I'd sit on a windowsill in our office, which overlooked a courtyard, reciting my letters and numbers, but no sound came out—bốn, quattuor, shi. The mapmaker was undeniably patient. Today, I remain mute.

The office now smells of piled-up sweat and old cigarette smoke. For the mapmaker's interview, I've planted myself in an armchair, in the back corner, upon which stacks of magazines have been tied together with string. I wait for the mapmaker to look in my direction, signaling it's time to go, but settle deeper and deeper into a cushion of paper. I don't know what to do with my paws.

The student reporter is hunched over her logbook. I can see the bony shoulders under a thin layer of her cotton uniform, the single, modest braid like a black ink brush down her spine.

In the midday light which seems to roast everything a shade above orange in this room, I can sense the mapmaker's attempt to answer a question about the alleged son without implicating anyone, not even our enemies. "Our university," says the mapmaker in a rush: "has been good to both of us."

Everyone tries to sound agreeable, I think.

"I teach what I want, whenever I please, I know my son has healthy debates in the print shop where you continue the work of our colleagues."

The mapmaker's voice begins to waver as though doubting if or how the following should be said aloud, "The only difference . . . everything appears in the open today."

"The committee has a masthead. No one is immune, not even me, I can see that." The mapmaker brushes two imperceptible pieces of lint from the desk. A cruel year, I agree. 1945.

The reporter is shy, her first assignment. "Excuse me. What novels do you like to teach?"

Her voice is gentle. I imagine, from looking at the back of her head, a kind round face and devastating eyes. The mapmaker has dry, pearl-shaped teeth. Both can sense a tightrope being pulled taut with this question of literature. They smile toward each other in a warm, unmoving silence; four blades of the ceiling fan above us barely pushing its air in a damp, counterclockwise circle; down the hall, another set of doors are opening and closing. I'm so tense my eyeballs could fall out.

The mapmaker breaks first, the open window. A large wasp is bumping against one of the shutter beams.

"But maybe," the mapmaker says eventually. A longer beat: "You'd prefer to know more about my son or how, perhaps, he became at odds with my beliefs in the end."

The mapmaker leans to one side of the desk and takes out a book from a lower drawer. I can see its worn cover from my corner in the office: a simple paperback, *The Grass Pillow* by Natsume Sōseki.

The mapmaker would often quote from this when we started some of the larger commissions after 1907, including a minor though heavy-winded addition to the Long Biên Bridge that we tracked with its unofficial footpaths; the mapmaker would place a careful index finger on the sheet, where I'd waddle over next to it and proceed to mark, with a pencil, various shapes like a triangle where a field horse had fallen or a slanted cross that indicated a deep slope in the grass in which a person could hide undetected; the mapmaker, meanwhile told me scenes from *The Grass Pillow* about the figure flitting past a corner of a house or the mythic fox staring at me suddenly from a nearby snow-covered hill; we weren't by the Red River, after all, anymore; the full moon, nauseatingly bright and turning us both— fox and prey—wild with hunger; I can't remember which was actually written in the novel or created entirely by fictive association, and start to shiver all over, may the spirits of water help my feeble soul.

The novel has been placed at the center of the mapmaker's desk and, at this point, I want to blast out of the room. Fly across Hà Nội. Back to the French Quarter; its little gardens off Boulevard Prolongé; a mosquito net draped from a hook above my shoebox, making a skinny white tent, and me, flat inside of it on my stomach, in a fitful state of sleep, the lowercase *p*.

"You can see that our enemy is not so different from the one before him," says the mapmaker.

"Over time, the pity your father may have felt about the French or Japanese was a pity we felt, too. Or was it hatred? Regardless, this pity or hatred would fracture into three additional possibilities, which continue to ramify yet into three unspoken directions necessary for the people's survival. Try to guess one of them."

The professor at work, thinks the student, or maybe I've projected this into the girl's mind; I don't know; I'm turned around. The stack of magazines under my pajamas is slipping around. She shakes her head.

"That's alright," the mapmaker is quiet. "I won't lecture you." The heat is unbearable, late July.

"For this matter, whether Tan decides to show his face at the rallies is not for me to advise. My son makes his way."

The back of the student's neck blushes like the pink side of a mango at the market. She hasn't said anything since the question about literature in a country getting ready for another insurrection.

You love him, thinks the mapmaker who's folding up her hands behind the book. You love him, and this would be much less wretched if . . . "But I request two minor modifications," says the mapmaker. She's staring at the pencil that darts over the student's logbook.

"I ask for you to remove my name and occupation. Instead, I'd prefer to be written from the perspective of the boy's father." Though he doesn't exist, the mapmaker speaks slowly. "Whatever you do with our conversation is up to you, comrade."

In the office of the mapmaker hangs a small faded print of Monet's *Bridge over a Body of Water*. The student reporter takes note of this as she leaves.

"Regarding our conversation," she dictates later to the typist in a windowless back room of the university press, "three more possibilities were suggested this afternoon."

"One should reexamine, however, the fact of a mapmaker and the mapmaker's son who make a clear diagonal path away from each other—one to the past and one to the future. We might also argue against the temple of literature. Bisecting this is a line, an unpredictable angle. How you choose, dear reader, to survive our story of colonialism and the complete cauterization of our written language, the irony of which is printed before you now, depends entirely on this story of separating everything you might know of grammar, the rules of storytelling itself, family, and national cohesion, with everything you know of yourself. Each story, in turn, transforms the mother into the father, and vice versa; the son remains inconsolably the son, though daughters can multiply or switch to many daughters at different times and different settings all around the world, for which we now raise our yellow and brown fists in Algeria, Lebanon, Cuba, Kashmir." A paper ball has flown to the calendar which falls coincidentally off its nail to the floor. There are no loyalties, concludes the student reporter silently who stops to look up from her notes and the keys of her sister's typewriter suspended by the period. Dot. Dot. Dot.

"We must stay in the present with our convictions," she adds spontaneously and recalls the curious pile of shredded cotton on the mapmaker's desk along with the vague, growing rumor of four comets speeding furiously toward our planet, but even if I blossom a bit sideways and lose all my stuffing, the reader will hopefully understand why we write the way we do, the topics which have been covered in this month's issue, and why Tan fought the way he did. In matters of speaking beyond plot, a point of view, narration, logic, and a written or rewritten memory of the liberation efforts in Việt Nam, anyone can fool us if we ask the wrong questions of time.

The wasp struggles at one end of the string. A tiny paw reaches up to loosen the knot around its leg. You're free. Go.

The wasp flies away. You hover at the open window to your office and contemplate its beauty. In the courtyard below, two hundred students have gathered around a makeshift platform. An older student climbs to the stage and dangles a leg over the front of it. He's tuning a simple acoustic guitar and gazes at the back of the crowd before starting to sing an old, old ballad of the people. We quickly join him before the first chorus; you look up. There's a professor at the window. The professor has long, peppered hair, a flattened chest, and black-framed spectacles. Your perspective turns around again and again. You want to cry but think: Is this how we become a ghost of each other? Down there in the courtyard, is your son named Tan, just as you've been marked by the committee a week before, our sweet boy with the guitar on his knee and revolution in his throat; this heart, this sky, our sweet love, Tan Huỳnh.

The student reporter puts her head on the table, between her arms. Her sister at the typewriter gets up, shaking her head.

✳

The mapmaker is dead. The details of his assassination remain hidden from the public, but generally, as most apprentices do, I've mourned the man's passing dutifully for seven days and six nights; on the last night, I accidentally fell asleep.

A few objects would have to stay behind. In the apartment: a bar of soap wrapped in paper, a silver-framed mirror over a washbasin, sketches of a brown, open field that the mapmaker once called a grave for our ancestors.

I have to think about where to go next before leaving our building with just the pajamas on my body, each room behind me like a furnace of smoke; still, the fireballs which draw nearer are visible in the sky by midnight. Four distinct circles flash, closer and closer, every hour I look up and imagine the sound of all five oceans burning.

No matter, off Boulevard Prolongé, I wait for fate beyond my understanding, the late bougainvillea to change its colors by dawn, for the next century to lose a drive for romance or cinema, and for the girl Lua with her long black braid, who steps out now to her balcony above the café Chez Kiều, who renounces all love before naming her target, my master; I catch myself humming with the girl, the assassin, and begin to whirl in tiny, tiny circles before I realize this ought to stop, I ought to sit in the little patch of grass by a garden sculpture of a terrible toad with uneven, bulging eyes, back to SQUARE ONE.

The outer limits of my marbles are fraying. I'm hurtling headfirst through the sound barrier, its helium of birds in birdcages, a Boeing with the child's hand pushed against one of its windows, crying, "Mama, Mama, look, it's a PANDA!" I feel my body instantly as one of those four comets; Lua Mater, wife of plague, from the planet Paul, who plummets unconscious beside me. I've lost all sense of sight and taste, and everything hot collides with everything cold, a mountainous pair of bombs, followed by two more comets yet unidentified and a survivor who might one day write about it.

Jump to CITATION II: THE SECRET MAP.

BOOK OF FIRE

Dark Was the Fire

ON THE THIRD day of November 1973, our oldest brother *Mariner 10* placed a boarding ticket in the outer breast pocket of his dark gray suit jacket. He carried no briefcase, no night bag. We clucked over his hair, smoothing the stubborn black strands to one side with our mother's ivory comb which we also desperately tried to press into his hand, though the boy refused.

His eyes moved about murkily above our heads; there was a crowd sifting toward the planes. Layers of fine dust like eggshell powder appeared to cover almost everything. Our lips tasted of salt, burnt plastic, and an unnamed and bitter gas. No light would pass through our oldest brother's eyes, not today, we thought, and he'd grimace when sister number two started fussing with the shirt collar over his necktie. It was our father's tie. The second to youngest of eight, sister number three, Chrysanthemum bursts into tears.

Several versions of our brother's departure from the tarmac of Tân Sơn Nhứt would soon accompany his story:

First, *Mariner 10* had received news some evening before, allegedly, of approval to study abroad in the United States of America; hence, the joyful exit.

Overlapping this was another iteration of truth.

Our brother, bound for a country razing the fields of our villages, the roofs of our hospitals, the schools of our cities, the bridges, and the rivers, had been intercepted for an undisclosed number of reasons, midtransit, and then dumped unceremoniously into an undocumented refugee camp near the Thai border for an indeterminable number of months, learning how to sleep, as one tends to say, with his eyes half open.

Perhaps, in the end, it was this linen suit jacket that saved our brother's life and granted passage to the university abroad, what the astrophysicists might call a "gravity assist" technique. Where, at the curve, V_{IN} moved along the tracks of V_{OUT} until one superseded the other, there were gaps everywhere.

To explain it differently, we were schoolchildren, girls of only ten and fourteen, when our father had been set on fire in front of our mother. Years would need to fall away before we could understand what this fully meant for the eldest son in our Huỳnh-Lê family with a face holding the precise half of both.

Đêm was his true name.

Or perhaps it was that word *night* in our language of stars, in the earliest memories of leaving home, in the boundaries of speech which had to uproot themselves finally, decisively; to stumble on six needle-thin legs away from the body, what belonged to the body of someone we know now to be LUA MATER, who, deriving from the Roman pantheon of minor gods, was an assassin sent from far, far away, curled up on her back like a stunned spider, outside of time, in the tawny shape of a ball above the café Chez Kiều in Hà Nội (1945), behind the cinema hall of Chợ Lớn toward the south (1951), or nearby, attempting to exit an intolerably sunny room of the Victoria down Trần Hưng Đạo (1966); to pile in each corner of each event, trembling, folding into the opaque outline of an irregular hexagon, rasping for breath; our work is done; the planet Paul is dead.

"So you see," says our narrator, swallowing, closing the notebook in her lap. "Lua, the body-jumping consort of the planet Paul, would enact parallel moments of destruction in our mother's past. Each moment became a necessary part of a larger cosmic war; the burned riddle-maker we'd later meet in this *Book of Water*," she emphasizes the word *this* with a tap on the green cover with a pencil eraser, "is our future."

"Same person?" The chorus asks.

Everyone's holding a new card by this point. The narrator is long past twenty-one with gray pockets under both eyes. Her head is shaved. At Cayuga, in the ward for permanent residents, set across a communal table, there are three assembled rows of *Tetris* blocks, an incomplete configuration. The year is 2010, in upstate New York. During most afternoons, we drift as overlapping screens of each other between a schedule of old movie programs on television and meal times and unsystematic stretching or smoke breaks outside in the courtyard. The blue separates from the red, and a plastic film slides through us; everyone's in 3D. Beyond the walls of our courtyard, we imagine cannon powder permeating the musk of a university library along with its almanacs and maps, abandoned forts to the north, and etchings of entire generations of displaced families crossing a fjord to the east.

The night technician Franklin is nibbling pensively, meanwhile, on a cheese stick. A strong, square forehead with his tweed-brown hair pulled back into a messy topknot reminds half the chorus of a young JASON MOMOA.

"Yeah, it's something like that," says Emi, slouching in her chair. She's working to keep the voices together in her notebooks. She considers the mythic image of Lua merging with the gesture of a darker-skinned saltwater nymph, Salacia, who waits in shifting pieces on the wild crags of Naxos. Who is she waiting for? Cyan overlaps with magenta. The two screens separate a few millimeters to the right, to the left, by a polarizing light beaming through our fresco. Salacia wrings out her black hair, freezes, turns over her bare shoulder, and notices the second film camera trembling awfully, uncontrollably under the sloping nose of a wide, otherwise obscured face. The sea nymph bares her fangs. She lunges at the filmmaker with impossible, round spectacles, the astrophysicist who's visiting coincidentally from Houston through a warp-jump between 116 and 27 BC, the planet Neptune holding up a glossy painted stone with a pair of googly eyes glued to one side—a ritual offering for the nymph, once again, outside of chronological reasoning.

"Same person," Emi repeats.

The chorus nods in unison. Everyone's focused on a brightly colored tetrad in their hands, with secretive, furrowed brows. Emi's rotating her piece around and around. The navy sweatshirt pulled over her blue scrubs smells of bleach and lavender. She knocks an elbow against Franklin, her funny bone; the technician picks at his beard, and sneaks down a glance at the card; he grunts in agreement, it's a perfect block of four. Marguerite, he's thinking suddenly of his girlfriend. How would Marguerite feel about leaving Ithaca tomorrow, our room by the lake, our jobs, or our bones which we could plant elsewhere, and waking up in the desert, in Oro Valley, completely free of our names or social security numbers, and what about Lua in that body of Emi, should we break her out? With Lua and Emi's stories about mind-switching or jumping through the decades and centuries, there'd be an easier portal home, yes, the man is convinced. He's twenty-seven.

Imagined onstage, in the courtyard of Sonora in Tucson (2019) which overlaps coincidentally with Cayuga in Ithaca (2010) and the Presbyterian in Dallas, in the children's ward (2004), from behind velvet, windswept curtains of all three facilities in synchronized performances of spiritual and colonial crisis, there are three braiding forces of Emi's refugee mother and Emi's second aunt:

"Music soared into that blooming cosmos known and cataloged across an entirety of human civilization by its patchwork of colors—Bach, percussion, *Melancholy Blues,* wood-throated Japanese shakuhachi, *Izlel je Delyo Hagdutin,* folk wedding songs, panpipes and ragas, Stravinsky's *Rite of Spring*—melodies of Earth that we, *Voyager 1* and *Voyager 2,* carried in the steed of our bodies . . ."

"This word *night* which appeared twinkling through the four holes of a map held against our sky was subject to a tongue, which we had none of . . ."

"This year in which we recognized, reconfigured, recapitulated our true purpose for storytelling was, according to the algorithm, irrelevant . . ."

"This machine addressed another machine . . ."

"This, which we followed as clearly instructed in the fine print on a sticker behind one of our doors, was a tempo to the song in an album placed inside the both of us with no additional measurements for human faith, logos, or instrumental wonder, except to deduce as much—*bốn, quattuor, shi*—alternatives for the number *four*, once again, in the language of our makers . . ."

"These songs of our *Golden Record* were meant to be, at least intended for the archive, some proof of life made indestructible. The irony of this kept us going."

VOYAGER 1 (left), *MARINER 10* (center), and *VOYAGER 2* (right), Saigon

CHRYSANTHEMUM LAUGHS; an echo of her laughter, sharp and golden, passes behind the stage. "I don't understand!" She says in a loud voice.

"I'm sorry, ma." Emi tries again, smiling. She opens the last of her three notebooks—white for *Wind*, green for *Water*, and red . . . They feel cold against her thighs through the thin fabric of her scrubs. The performer is sitting with her knee dangling over one side of a foldout table that also serves as a hospital bed interchangeably between scenes. The spotlight makes a sharp cone around Room 104B. Emi's lowered her head to write in the red-covered notebook. She reads along as her hand flurries across the page:

"Far beyond what tick-tocked cruelly forward;"

"far beyond the rubber belt of an automobile threatening to crack a glimmering metallic foot toward other functions of reality;"

"far beyond the watershed rippling along salt-lined bones of our bodies;"

"far beyond the film reel projected on a wall toward the back of an abandoned museum south of Đà Nẵng—you know it, yes?"

I know it, Chrysanthemum answers without speaking; she's half-shutting her eyes, nodding like the pink season of elementary school. Her hair is cropped short, held above the back of her neck by a clip.

"Long ago, I was useless," Emi says from behind a semi-sheer amethyst mask that's fallen over her face; it creates an illusion of her younger face at fifteen. An older resident with sharpened teeth is staring at us unnervingly, past Emi's shoulder, down at the audience, through a little square window set into the door of a padded room across our hall; both are subject, at any point, to switch places midscene. The silver screen slips from our transparent sheet of red. Emi contemplates this with a shifting reflection of her mother's expression in a photograph toward the middle of her chapter.

"Ma," she says. "You used to tell me stories about your siblings and your parents and their parents, their ancestors, all the choices everyone made in direct opposition with someone else. Your descriptions and placeholders got mixed up. I couldn't figure out who was speaking at many different points, you, me, your sister, or a combination of anyone else, where *anyone* stood on the calendar you mentioned at random moments."

"You'd eventually ask me, 'Can you write this?'"

"Then, I didn't know if I could, but now I can."

Chrysanthemum, who hasn't said a word since intermission, is crying. She waits on a wooden stool, stage left, with her feet crossed at the ankles adrift a few inches above the floor. She's playing *Voyager 2*, at age fifty-four, in her day clothes. The woman wipes her eyes with the back of both hands. Her cheeks swell like two tangerines. She's holding a program note between her legs, closer to her knees.

"I'm sorry, ma." Emi tears out a page from her notebook. She crumples it in a fist and recites the rest from memory:

"Who pointed everywhere and bounced our stories off nearly every flat surface in sight, splintering our voice into seven inextinguishable parts?"

"'My name is Chrysanthemum . . .'"

"'My name is Emi . . .'"

"'My name is Lua, wife of plague . . .'"

"'My name is Salacia . . .' The three additional parts of us are hidden."

Dr. Z stares from an open doorway, a wedge of colorless lines in a yielding and forgettable shirt, unflinching chapped eyelids, an open cardboard binder with several indistinct tabs carried by reams of paper; the chorus huddles at a short distance behind the psychiatrist, a cluster of mismatched silhouettes cast by an offensive fluorescent light in the hallway; we sit tense at the shoulders around our communal table; we're waiting for Emi to come out again for *Tetris*.

"Can you talk about Paul?" Dr. Z says in a flat voice.

"I-I don't think so," says Lua.

Dr. Z closes the binder and vanishes with a thud.

The patient now lies on the floor, beside her bed with a new piece face up. Her roommate has swapped out for the act, on the table; she lies asleep with her back turned to us. Earlier this afternoon, she had washed our underwear and socks in the bathroom sink. Our socks are almost done drying by dinner time. They stiffen next to a pair of beige bikini bottoms on the radiator under our barred and frosted window. You can't see through it, Emi, but you can imagine a beautiful swan-shaped string of lanterns around a lake outside, or maybe jumping cholla before dawn.

Your father will visit soon from Texas. He's gotten a motel room near the airport. At 10:35 a.m., every Saturday, your father arrives dutifully and lets one of the nurses, Dolores, sign him in. Dolores and Daichi have developed a friendly custom over the past few weeks of grinning at each other like two colleagues meeting in the waiting room before a colonoscopy. During one of his last visits, after leaving Dr. Z's office across the courtyard in Ithaca, Daichi would sit with his daughter. He heard himself admit, "Maybe I did something wrong when Emi-chan was too young."

"That's okay, おとうさん," Lua remembered to say a little cheerily. She practices with Emi's voice. "Don't be sad, papa."

✳

Today, Daichi's holding one of his daughter's notebooks upside down. He seems to be reading it backward, right to left. An anxious sparrow has landed on a barbed wire across from our courtyard, high up on a concrete wall that wraps around the perimeter in a perfect square. The bird dives to a bench across our empty platform and disappears.

"Our *Book of Fire*," Emi-chan explains after a while.

"I see," says Daichi.

Franklin stands nearby with an open pack of cigarettes. He's passed one to the school teacher who's passing it to the teacher's appointed social worker. The teacher's five-year-old visitor lies on the ground, sobbing uncontrollably.

Daichi doesn't seem to notice the drama. He runs a hand over Emi's red-covered notebook. "What happens in this one?"

The girl looks at her father. His expression is heavy and mournful.

"By design," says Emi followed by Lua, "our language failed to translate coherently into English, French, Portuguese . . ."

"And sometimes Japanese, though we'd continue our attempts as evidenced in this text."

"The uselessness of our effort was made clear to the narrator. In sheer minutes, a periwinkle shade emerged, light-headed and dry around the nipples, the sixteen eyes of our arriving minor goddess by the name of Lua, who transformed into the body of another—from wind to water."

"What happens here?" Daichi interrupts. His tone is perplexed, insistent like he hadn't just heard our narrator speak. "What happens in this book?" He's putting together each sentence in his mind. His head hunches forward helplessly. There are faint patches of silver hair around the back of his ears. His left eyelid droops like an old terrier in an entryway waiting for its master. "In Emi-chan's *Book of Fire*?"

"We forgive you, pa."

"You forgive me?"

"I forgive you."

The boy Daichi flings a bright red hula hoop around his waist. It drops straight to the ground. He pouts, revealing two pearl-shaped teeth above his bottom lip. The black bowl cut set atop his head fans out as he swoops down to his feet. The boy is four years old. News of the first Sputnik had likely arrived this morning over the radio in Tokyo. He can count to all ten fingers; he holds them up to his father, 清一, the god of fire. The red planet has come into focus.

Many years later, the boy will try to forgive his father, too, but he won't have the words, perhaps he'll never have the words.

If we consider 1957 more closely, we'll notice an army lieutenant, Daichi's strict guardian, sitting with a leg up on the open windowsill. The one-room house is cramped and dusty, but honorable. The room has a clean, sunken hearth in its center. His wife sits around that, roasting a small chestnut over a flame. The man lights a cigar; Kiyokazu turns to look at his only son playing outside their home with an unmarked expression between his eyes.

The man flicks away his match furiously. He barks for Daichi to leave that hula hoop on the ground. The boy drops it, startled, staring up at his father—*one, two, three, four,* he's counting in English.

The following text remains untranslatable, but we have tried our best to illustrate something approaching the planet's voice: . . . *for I am power . . . with these hands, I destroy you; with my name, you are nothing; nothing . . . after my death, I will inhabit your dreams, your daily life, your children . . . you will know my darkness, and dark was the fire.*

The little boy covers his mouth, his round, crinkled face. I watch Daichi in the house of my father. He remembers the contours of his four-year-old face, the puffy eyelids, the pillowy chin, my face, hiding from our father's hands, a leather belt folded in half. There's no hiding in this history. I'm four, covering my face just as that little boy once covered his face. Papa . . .

"For I am power," repeats the young soldier; his eyes have gone utterly blank.

Regarding our future, he predicts three comets blasting from three separate planets made of nuclear waste, their plagues, their principles of justice and pamphlets, mythology, and destruction; past the blowing plastic tubes of chromosomes, past the neon signposts and painted loons bobbing up and down, the dead, the dead flying all around us, refracting into a single line obliquely splitting into longer beams of light; the cruelest one blinks onto this world, a machine-making language and our language of stars.

The narrator has pulled us together onstage; she says, "Pull yourself together!"

She makes a desperate gesture with her notebooks, dropping them to the floor before flinging her arms around the open space between her and the audience. Her fingers are gnarled, wrenching at the air. We burst apart in our chairs, thinking in both past and present tenses at the same time. We see him, Daichi's father, or Kiyokazu, the planet Mars, the red surface of his wrath glittering beside the moon weeks before our brother, *Mariner 10,* would decide at last to leave Vietnam. Once more, our placeholders have emptied of sand.

Two cameras are placed around the same object. The stage is reconstructed in a different facility, in a different state across the country. The chorus remains inexorably fixed. Our narrator has become older, naturally. She notes the passing of years in her notebooks. The ordering is more ambiguous. We've not yet been named but exist as a singular concept in the mind of a little boy in a different country. The satellites are created. They launch, one by one, across the atmosphere. The boy, later known to be *Sputnik 1,* will eventually imagine a room far, far away from his father, in Texas. He will predict meeting one of us in a cubicle, twenty-five years later.

Daichi and Chrysanthemum, as we'll later come to know them in our program notes, have fallen in love; the *Sputnik* and the *Voyager* have announced their marriage against the wishes of both families; ever since, they've attempted a different kind of life, a daily life.

Franklin repeats, "Hey, Emi. It's your move."

The man stands outside our doorframe, a giant tapping at the bottom of Room 104B with his toe. In his oversized fist, Franklin holds a second or third cheese stick for the night. Every shift he looks more and more like JASON MOMOA, the chorus can agree on this.

Emi picks her card up from the floor. She clamps it gently between her teeth. She's crawling toward the radiator under the window and, with two fingers, takes her cleaned underwear. Her roommate is still asleep on the bed next to hers. Behind a woven straw door of a tatami cupboard in Tokyo, we then project a vision of the child with a round bowl cut. He's curled into the shape of a monochrome, deflated beach ball. He's shivering, looking at all ten fingers wrapped around a red, miniature toy horse. The boy is crying himself to sleep. Papa, I forgive you.

1973

SISTER NUMBER TWO stands barefoot on the terrace. Her back is turned to the audience. Through two narrow speakers flanking the platform, when the velvet curtains open down the middle, a recorded voice transmission crackles over the launch of a satellite.

Chrysanthemum waits offstage for her cue. There's a low guttural humming of the live chorus scattered at arbitrary points within the audience itself.

Sister number two, without turning to look at sister number three, begins to speak in a severe voice. Her nightdress is sharp around the figure. "You follow me, sideways mouth."

Chrysanthemum trips into view. She wears a matching nightdress with beige and blue flowers. "You don't call me that anymore," she says. The girl is seventeen and has yet to kill a man. "Don't call me SIDEWAYS MOUTH, ALRIGHT."

"Alright," says sister number two calmly.

Though smaller than Chrysanthemum, she's older by more than three centuries, a dragon in the year of the ox, pregnant already with the uncountable dream of a floating fetus. Her true name is hidden from any public record; she hopes for that silhouette of grief to leave her fate untouched.

Everyone in our family also knows what she thinks of the Americans. In our casting, sister number two had been the only one who refused to learn a single word of English. She'd sit through rehearsal, glaring at the open notebook upside down in her lap.

Tonight, the terrace crumbles apart. It overlooks a wide intersection, beyond this, the markets of Chợ Lớn. Other buildings nearby have not been so lucky over the recent years. We've rendered this scene with a series of spoken directives toward the middle of our third act. There's no one left, across from our family house, we'd say—over there, look—with its foundation all exposed, the brick and stone walls charred around their corners, plantain trees cut into matted stockpiles next to a temporary kiln; five meters above the backdrop, coconut and black oil palms loom around the gap for what's been blasted through some previous night, a starry gate.

Mariner 10, our eldest brother, is perhaps long dead by now. He could just as well be an emptied-out linen jacket full of smoke before ever setting foot in the United States of Detroit; there's no proof of this, only a feeling.

"He will write," says Chrysanthemum. She's found a tidy place to squat on the terrace next to one of the speakers, facing the audience, on a dimpled block of concrete. Her tone is clumsy. "Đêm is smart. He will find a way to tell us something."

Sister number two hasn't moved from the parapet. We still can't see her face. She's always despised the idea of our eldest leaving and the rest following him like a flock of lambs down the pasture, but who could take that choice from us? In the courtyard, we pass around a bag of popcorn, crossing and re-crossing our legs, staring up at the dialogue, bickering over what might happen next.

Meanwhile, Chrysanthemum is thinking for all of us. "We have a path, Chị Hai, to live or to die."

"YOU have a path," says sister number two. She has the voice of a quick-tempered singer, a diva's voice, a fortune teller's voice. Our mother is most nervous about her future. The girl is the prettiest in our family and refuses to leave Saigon; she's the only one of eight who continues to reject our path even when the last have escaped our country with no last name. What would our father think? If he were alive today, what would he say?

"It's an impossible question." Sister number two bristles at the shoulders.

A damp December wind sweeps through the terrace, disturbing a curtain to one side of our frame.

She's right. In this language, there's no direct way to say those words—IF, COULD, or WOULD—but our narrator observes ten tetrads falling to the table; the game is speeding up. The two facilities of Ithaca and Tucson overlap like circles in a large Venn diagram, red and green in fields of logic and memory. The four blocks arrange into the shape of Z pointing obstinately north. We look for any sign up there, the planet Mars dotting the loop of Orion, the deep ember flames glowing from a rooftop of a second house behind us—look, look, Chị Hai, someone's there—the twilit shrieks of neighborhood children in freeze tag or hopscotch or tires in the alleys stretched everywhere. Sister number two has started humming a strange, old melody. *Voyager 2* hums along.

In this way, the space probes reconfigure layers of destiny for Emi's mother and Emi's second aunt. One eventually escapes Saigon in 1979; the other stays behind. In our live stage-to-film adaptation, some of the stories have jumbled through a wire. In 1973, for instance, the planet Paul tracks our metronome of disaster. He inserts a solution of continuity where he shouldn't, a solution that includes plot, a single tense, and a single subjective voice; he consults a Roman calendar for accuracy and proper citations; he clicks with his boots over to a pillar of the courtroom in 42 BC, Capitoline Hill. He presses the web between his index finger and thumb against a grim and studious mouth. The planet Paul takes a sharp breath in. He's annoyed. Thirty minutes south of Saigon, there are, additionally, rumors of a pilot killed in an ambush. The story drops there in mid-December, 1973. He thinks of his wife, Lua. His blonde hair has been swept cleanly to one side. His buttocks are lifted and clenched under a dark pair of navy tights. The camera zooms in; his CAPTAIN AMERICA shield leans dustily against a marble wall. Lua has dashed away from their wedding altar. The planet Paul is smirking—what would she do without an understanding of language, grammar, any sense of resolution, or product placement? He holds the contract to their marriage blown to pieces. We stumble after each other, one thought repeating the thought of a sibling or a parent, running toward that precipice of a solar vacuum, flinging ourselves most earnestly toward extinction—I couldn't explain the next events to you now, sister number three, but a twang of blues escaped my lips; the riffs of Blind

Willie Johnson preserved in the *Golden Record* would send us sailing. It claimed we were once sentient beings with a unified story. We knew to love our existence on the blue dot deeply, so, in each of us, we carried what spilled out with hope. We knew to protect each other at the final annihilation of our home. I promised this to myself, for the sake of our future, to keep you safe, sister number three.

Chrysanthemum gazes down at her feet. She's trying to understand me. I've always been the most stubborn sister.

When she finally gets up to leave our terrace, brushing off her long nightdress, an image of the red planet is beamed onto the street below. In 1988, this planet would eventually visit our city. He picked delicately at the cooked meat with a fork, an unmasked distaste forming across his lips. The golden-plated arias in the disc placed inside our lunchboxes, meanwhile, would glow and thrum, nestled deep in the bottom of our pockets; I remember feeling both pride and shame; this man was going to be one of our future fathers-in-law; Chrysanthemum—sister number three, *Voyager 2*—had insisted on marrying the red planet's son anyway. We couldn't stop her.

By the next millennium, we were lost in an uncharted orbit away from each other, in disparate, conflicting directions regarding matters of the heart. Our sense of wonder frazzled at the borders of our wiring; we were both machines staggering into the carnation of stars; we would hum and scoot and blip and bop through space; we'd wish for someone out there, *anyone* to hear us—Emi tosses a crumpled sheet of paper at the radiator; it's been just revealed to be a prop. The paper ball bounces from the platform, rolling into a patch of dirt offstage. Emi switches notebooks and reads, at random, one of the closing passages from her *Book of Wind.*

A soft electric guitar begins to play in the aisle, with three simple minor chords in slow succession. The school teacher is rolling forward in a wheelchair, bobbing at the neck and waist with every downbeat. "Wow," says someone reverently. In the audience, we make a collective murmur when Franklin rises to swap gel sheets of the spotlight that swivels over our school teacher's head and then the guitar, from yellow to pink.

Emi begins to recite again, her voice deepening with the teacher's ballad:

"Music ushered us through distant doomed cosmologies, far beyond the end to mortal suffering and imagination, past the death of oceans, a death of stars, toward a fractal plane of light oblivion."

"Beyond another four or five billion years, we were throbbing, gasping at the wrinkled edges of our low limits. We were there, as ever we are now, dreadfully bright with optimism . . ."

"'Far from home,' an astronomer had predicted of our journey, 'the final events may fade with our intrepid *Voyagers*. Being their makers, we could only hope for the two machines to fly on, past the memory of a world that exists no more.'"

"'Presently,' says one of the probes, 'we wander with a bitter spoon to our tongues,' farther from the reaches of this *world, no more*; indeed, we approach four-dimensional planes of light, oblivion." The voices fracture in tandem. "Out here we see *everything*."

"Volcanic winds and stardust, fields of plasma floating by like pink entrails of gods, lightning, light beams, light rays."

"What was left behind in our music blasting through an immeasurable chaos; what was known, and what was thus perceived?"

"We watched them combust into an almanac of dust."

"We could only imagine."

Emi has disappeared from Room 104B. Her seven voices continue crackling through two supplemental speakers installed over the courtyard. Our voices drift apart midsentence, fluctuating in tenor, tone, and speed.

A small lump stirs under a hospital sheet draped across our communal table. We shift uneasily in the audience, not knowing where to place our attention next, inside or outside the courtyard, off or on the table, in or out of time, or what to expect within the game beyond dialogue and tetrads.

"Pay no mind to how the mission slashes at our fractured spirit," says the seventh voice, "or *who* still watches out here." The seventh voice is throwing a piece into the game; the tetrad, an electric cyan, a piercing vertical line, is just about to wipe out four rows. Level up.

"Yes, we must go on, onward with the gift of mortal sense and despair, though it burdens us every night."

"We must learn to persevere . . ."

". . . to persevere which takes more of our innocence at full collapse."

"More than moon-raked galaxies about to crush us to our cores . . ."

". . . to thrust us quaking, slouching, drooling toward delirium and then a sleepless winter, only to wake after it's over, pitch-blue in the face, struck silent, flummoxed, terrified, dilated around every corner, our pupils shouting—NOW! NOW!—made short of breath."

"We also recall one brave and tiny Panda climbing into bed, a cardboard shoebox set with pillows made of two athletic socks stuffed with cotton balls."

"The tiny Panda would pull a woven blanket over his face. The tops of both his eyes poked out."

"Night after night, he stared over the place of a *world that is no more.*"

The tiny Panda is trembling onstage. He's been projected onto a black paper screen that covers the whole length of it; he looks into the hospital courtyard, stunned by the unexpected audience; we're in a filmed portion of his performance now; he doesn't know what to do; he's the sole survivor, allegedly, of four comets that have crashed into our planet over a series of synchronized events in the first, seventeenth, mid-twentieth, and twenty-third centuries. The numbers flash obscurely in stenciled yellow light around his head. The tiny Panda still can't read. His sense of purpose is rudderless, especially without Lua; the remnants of her body twist into a ball; Salacia, the sea nymph, wraps herself in a swath of dark kelp underneath a heating lamp by the rocks of what used to be Naxos. Panda, the tiny stuffed animal has woken up four times, in four different years. The unidentified final element has broken the sound barrier. It approaches one of our planets—NOW!

NOW!—the tiny Panda in a tiny shoebox floats like a raft into space. He looks through a void where our last home used to be—the droning of an electric guitar has faded out—laid bare and indigo, a spot on the cheek of terrible, terrible sadness. We may reach and touch this, too. We may realize, in the instant, that our brave and tiny Panda will be, as ever, lost out here in our *Book of Fire*, forever, utterly alone.

AD 43

THE BOND is much too thin to see. One side of a continent splits from its main part. We've encountered the planet Mars. With no further warning, we must cut off contact.

Theorems of Decay

"START WITH A MEASUREMENT of day," thinks the tiny Panda. Clocks above a countertop with hasty feral eyes shifting in every direction left to right, then back in a swivel towards the upper left corner of that room. From sunup to sundown, the tiny Panda concentrates.

"Are you there, my Lua?"

Through the workings of a phrase, a song evolves overnight. The tiny Panda thinks and thinks about his Lua until he's distracted by a chorus of crickets. He's distracted by the slowed-down version of it—"Angel," he thinks—to that ethereal plane of warbling on evening strolls around a lake and thrashings of wind through autumn maple leaves. Up all these avalanches, he imagines a metaphor: "I'll add up the various motions of a human body crawling through every minute and every hour, and this was my Lua speaking."

Marguerite

I THOUGHT I saw you in the coffee shop, sitting at a table with a book and a stack of two or three novels by your elbow. In Nogales, you would throw a rock at the DVD store. There were no reasons for me to be with you, to want to be with you. My friend Callisto said you were trouble, that you were full of philosophy and metal. Callisto's dog Io seemed to agree because he loved you. He loved your dog, too. He loved everyone.

Franklin, I'm saying all this now because I thought I saw you at the coffee shop. You weren't fair to me. You had two girls, two little girls. You let me meet them. They were sweet and curious. The five-year-old, J, would hold my hand whenever she could; we crossed a street together, looking both ways. We went to the park. We went to get ice cream. You were sad most afternoons, especially on Saturdays. Is this why you'd . . . Marguerite stops herself. She looks at the name written next to a phone number on a yellow sticky note in her hand: FRANKLIN CÁRDENAS. The girl is crying. She never cries. Marguerite hasn't cried since the fourth day of the third week of March 1992, the hour she was born. She was a malnourished but practical baby. If Franklin didn't want to be with us anymore, fine.

Marguerite lets the receiver drop from her hand. She's dizzy. She wants to sit down. In the rug cleaning shop, she can see her destiny from behind a countertop for the first time as her parents once did, and the parents before that—it's not so bad, she thinks, not too bad.

Minerva

PERHAPS OUR SPIRITS have moved away from their bodies in a similar fashion, a reordering of time with clear, geometric shapes, the fourth life pumping through its blood-brain barrier, bile, tissue, bone, skin stretched like a hyper-ballad over muscles, nerves, and tendons. Life takes on a more solid form, purring, moaning, and growing fingernails, toenails, and finally, the kneecaps. Marguerite wrenches forward in the shop; a cramp has flown around her pelvis, up her spine. She keels over the countertop, holding on to her belly. There's a green, heavy rug rolled tightly in a bin by the front door. She bangs her fist on one of the drawers, barely missing its handle; she stares at the rug, dangling from that image with her eyes, trying not to vomit. Would Franklin ever know? Would he ever come back with his girls; would his girls know? He's nowhere to be found.

The thing slops limb-by-limb to the ground, draped in wet organic film, a sac of amniotic fluid. The thing is given several names, a gender, and a mouth. Offstage, our narrator's seven voices hush into a messy, uneasy chant. "Minerva."

"Minerva."

Minerva, whom Ovid once called "the goddess of a thousand projects," would have arrived in a province twenty kilometers north of our capital city in mid-January, 1965. Hanoi. The third metamorphosis of our goddess Lua Mater, she'd been cracked from a large walnut shell that hovers now, suspended and made whole again, two stories above the earth. Minerva's twitching like a newborn foal just dropped out the back of a Ford pickup. In her hand is something hard, metallic.

Minutes after, a tiny Panda, upside down and half-unconscious, will plummet from the sky. Wait for it . . . The stuffed animal slams into a shallow dip of grass. He pops to his feet, stunned awake, immediate and earnest for action, unaware somehow of the camera pointed directly at his face.

We track him as the tiny Panda shakes off a smoldering fleck of ash from the top of his head. "Sticky," says our brave and tiny Panda. The entire chorus is cheering for him. He's completely naked. His body is too small for its head. He rushes to cover himself. Conveniently, a set of brown pajamas had been laid out for this scene on a block of concrete nearby.

In a performance that he might not be aware of, the tiny Panda sees a comet shell dissolve in midair. He scampers across the field toward a lump of flesh expelled onto the ground.

He pokes at the new form of what appears to be our final arrival as Lua. The thing wears a wig of dark horsehair. It has warm mahogany skin. We're out of popcorn and swoon drunkenly in our chairs; the film wraps around the hospital courtyard; we crane our necks to take in the entire scene; the school teacher leans back as the projection of daylight looms over us like an IMAX dome. The teacher's pulling at a bass string over and over. "Wow! Wow!" Someone keeps repeating in the back.

Through its placenta, our tiny Panda can see the outline of a body struggling to breathe. The tiny Panda clenches an invisible jaw around invisible rows of teeth. He hurries to free the body from its sac. The stuffed animal is gnawing, eventually, at a collar set around what seems to be, in his opinion, the wide neck of Lua. Curiously, there's no extra eyeball dozing over one of her clavicles; no fourteenth marble bulging fussily, widening, or slowly behind the goddess's left ear. The tiny Panda wipes at the goo that covers her wingless back; an absence of feathers, he doesn't seem to notice, too. He runs his tiny paw over the front of his brown pajama pants. He stops to scratch his tiny butt. The work is done. "Itchy," says our brave and tiny Panda. He sits to think by a short pile of stones. He's waiting for Lua, what he believes to be the incarnation of his beloved Lua, to wake up again—WAKE UP, the tiny Panda thinks in all caps.

We witness what attempts to feel around and find her footing, to make sounds for the new mouth, to show with the new face and simple pair of black-brown eyes fluttering open, I'm ready for it all, but this isn't Lua. This isn't Lua anymore.

Nine days after Malcolm X's assassination, Operation Rolling Thunder will reach its descent over Vietnam. The human body, soaked in feces, milky saliva, and chunks of hardened green mucus, will struggle to run forward. Three months later, the Buddhist monk Thích Nhất Hạnh would be writing a letter to the Reverend Martin Luther King Jr. "I believe," he will say, "with all my heart, the monks who burn themselves to death do not mean any harm for our oppressors but to move them toward a change in their policies."

The mouth opens and shuts.

"I also believe that your struggle in Birmingham is not directly aimed at the whites but injustice, hatred, bigotry . . ."

The eyes of the fourth comet dilate into pools of oily confusion. I put my finger into this archive of death, creasing my sticky note over Franklin's phone number—if he doesn't want to be with me anymore, fine—the *Voyagers* follow my lead; I'm outside of heartbreak, hours, and responsibility to any life but my own; my name is Marguerite; my child will be the story of Lua.

Buckled across her chest is a bronze, gilded armor with an embossed laurel over the sternum. The goddess's feet slide forward in thick-laced sandals. Her arms are shielded below the elbow with sleeves of iron plates that glide, shimmering like fish scales. Minerva crosses the rice field. She has broad, muscular shoulders. I want to call out to my son, but I can't. "Minerva!" The chorus is shouting desperately at the movie. "Watch out!"

In 1965, the following military campaigns will begin their sweep across our audience and ancestral lands. The body winds into a spiral, taking its aim:

Operation Footboy—January 1965: Unnamed—February 1965: Operation Flaming Dart—March 1965: Operation Rolling Thunder— Operation Market Time—Operation Quyet Thang 512—April 1965: Operation Steel Tiger (part of Operation Barrel Roll)—May 1965: Unnamed—June 1965: Operation Arc Light— Unnamed—July 1965: Operation 17-65—Unnamed—Operation Than Phong II—Operation Lien Ket 4—Operation 19-65—August 1965: Operation Blast Out— Operation Dan Thang 5—Operation Marble Mountain—Operation Thunderbolt— Operation Frag Order 12-65—Operation Frag Order 15-65—Operation Binh Din—Unnamed—Operation Barracuda—Operation Midnight—Operation Anvil—Operation Starlight—Operation Cutlass—Operation Highland—Operation Quin Thang 165—Operation Than Phong III—September 1965: Operation Talon— Unnamed—Operation Venture—Operation Stomp—Operation Tam Thang 118— Operation Bayonet—Operation Piranha—Operation BIG RED—Operation Cacti—Operation Than Phong IV—Operation Cold Steel—Operation Cactus— Unnamed—Operation 24-65—Operation Gibraltar—Operation Shining Brass— Operation Good Friend—Operation Hard Rock—Operation Sayonara—Operation Red One—October 1965: Operation Phu Yen 7—Operation Spread Out— Operation Checkerboard I—Operation Blue Bonnet—Operation Good Friend II— Operation Quick Draw—Operation Xray I—Operation Hopscotch—Operation Iron Triangle—Operation Cobra—Operation Concord—Operation Shiny Bayonet— Operation Happy Valley—Operation Black Lion—Operation Checkmate— Operation Lonesome End—Operation Flip Flop—Operation Depth—Operation Fly Low—Operation Settlement—Operation Bushmaster Bravo—Operation Triple Play—Operation Trail Blazer—Operation Trail Boss—Operation Hot Foot— Operation Ranger I—Operation Indian Scout—Operation New One—Operation

Dan Thang 21—Operation Red Snapper—Operation 27-65—Operation Silver Bayonet—Operation Revenger—Operation All the Way—Operation Long Reach— Operation Big Horn—Operation Drum Head—Operation Triple Trouble— Operation Lien Ket 10—November 1965: Operation Binder I—Operation Quyet Thang 172—Operation Custer Flats—Operation Viper I—Operation Dagger One— Operation Binder II—Operation Black Ferret—Operation Copperhead—Operation Hump—Operation Binder III—Operation Blue Marlin—Operation Binder IV— Operation Lightning—Operation Hop Out—Operation Road Runner—Operation Corn—Operation Bushmaster I—Operation New Life—Operation Docket I— Operation Blue Marlin II—Operation Road Runner II—Operation Road Runner III—Operation Silver Bayonet II—Operation Road Runner IV—Operation Song Ve 6—Operation Turkey Shoot—Operation Rabbit Hunt—Operation Bushmaster II—Operation Checkerboard II—Operation Riviera—December 1965: Operation Ox Trail—Operation Give Up—Operation Gladiator—Operation Charger Sweep—Operation Feline—Operation Tiger Hound—Operation Sweeping Mustang—Operation Bushmaster III—Operation Harvest Moon—Operation Lien Ket 18—Operation Fish Hook I—Operation Quick Kick—Operation Frisk I— Operation Fish Hook II—Operation Viper II—Operation Clean House I—Operation Frisk II—Operation Fulton—Operation Scalping Mustang—Operation Beaver I— Operation Smash—Operation Game Warden—Operation Jingle Bells—Operation Clean House II—Operation Cherokee Trail—Operation Blue Light—Operation Hoa Xuan—Operation Clean House III—Operation Take Out—Operation Rebel Rouser—Operation Matador I—

My mouth goes numb, pumping coolant and petrol from its lips. My eyes, still open, glaze into a hard set of obsidian marbles. My body slumps to sleep, but I can't sleep. Franklin's stories have affected my dreams, the dreams of Minerva in the body of Lua, or another way around; I can't remember who went first no matter how much I concentrate on the rug in front of me. I'll take it home later but, for now, I don't remember my name.

Franklin used to tell me stories about his nightshifts at the hospital in upstate New York. His girls would have sleepovers at their Tío Gabe's in separate bunk beds with a white noise machine blasting down the hall. There was a new patient every week at Cayuga, Franklin told me. Her name was always Emi. After some time, I wondered how much of her existence lived in Franklin's imagination. Franklin would say how she wanted to make a theater production about the *Voyagers*. He'd come back to my apartment with ideas for sound, staging, and set design. All the residents wanted to help, even his girls, he said, but Emi never finished her books, the plot to drive us forward. It was all perhaps an allegory for exile; this was clear to Franklin.

Often, I didn't know who was telling her stories, Franklin or the creation of Emi in his mind. He'd quote a monk who explains now to his friend in the US, "Burning yourself and burning yourself to death is only a difference in degree, not in nature—"

he inhales

"not to take one's life"

exhales

"—but to light a fire."

Emi freezes in a corner of my studio apartment. She's folding into the shape of a standing lamp. A tiny stuffed animal sits in my recliner watching us both dutifully. The tiny Panda also seems to be watching the television. Ten, another hundred years may sweep by hollering, but no one would wake in time to see Babylon blooming in the garden of our hearts, whatever it is we're dreaming of, and would it matter if this dream is named? Does it matter what you find, Franklin, walking barefoot, bleeding and full of sorrow across the desert, in your sorrow, find the thing and pick it up, maybe to break another patient out, to take your girls and run?

You would place a glossy stone in my palm when we first met in Nogales. You told me to rub the silver particles of grief between my fingertips, only to let the thing slip back to the parking lot and walk away. I wondered if light could fall heavily around our planet and the faces of my uncles, too, boarding their fighter jets to Vietnam or, at the same time, Chrysanthemum who notices one of them in the sky with the face of Blind Willie Johnson strumming his guitar? My father tried to stop them from going, but his brothers were misguided with a promise of new work. They didn't want to stay in Nogales.

Marguerite thinks about her pilot twin uncles and Franklin's words—yes, they shouldn't have gone, it wasn't our war, but who are we to judge? And would a polar ice cap melt? Would your torso plunge into the burning sea? You were like this, Franklin, groaning near the surface with your philosophies and research on code-talking for military collaborations, an allegiance to a border your words would yield through, sink shuddering unspeakably under; you were my planet, Mercury.

Marguerite is crying. She never cries.

We hear the sound of violins. We form odd figurines from our hands; we call them literature or horses. We almost can't bear it, but we must. The crystal doors of music streak with water across a looking glass. We stand slack at the jaws, waiting on both sides of history.

You'd know how to laugh, my love, when it was needed, to feel despair when it was needed, too. You saw the drones. You predicted my uncles running across a tarmac with their long braided hair and denim shirts; they wanted to see the rocket parts loaded into planes. You saw the metal cranes pumping into the sacred grounds of Arizona and then New York; indeed, our sky was falling.

What came out of art and wind machines? Would any of us survive shaking and false?

The program on television has changed to a different channel. There's a rerun for Luc Besson's *The Fifth Element*. The tiny Panda sits by the remote. He hasn't moved from his spot on my La-Z-Boy.

In this particular scene, Leeloo's laughing.

Leeloo, the queen-supreme of our giant, unknowable universe, is stuffing astral, laser-zapped chicken into her mouth. She wears a pair of orange silicone suspender straps on her shoulders. In a later scene, she gawks at a computer set up inside an aircraft hurtling quietly into space. She types three letters on the keyboard: *W-*

A-

R.

The tiny Panda seems to have just blinked. Leeloo's watching photographs flash across the screen. There are bombs, craters filled with arms, craters filled with additional human parts and bottles, a broken raft and a broken platform, three men crucified on wooden pikes in a prison camp. The tiny Panda grips his tiny face covered with chicken grease in both of his tiny paws. This is where the heart begins to twist. This is where we start to hurt, Panda, hold on.

There are seven oboes at the temple doors. We listen to the program of police sirens and pale to collapse. Our teeth feel like they're about to drop out, though it's not in a dream or a film. Both *Voyager 1* and *Voyager 2* begin to cry. We're both playing dead, we transfigure—WAKE UP!—the voices shout from a central point above the dome theater.

This has everything to do with whales.

We're both Emi and Yoko now teetering on a catamaran in San Diego Bay. Our mother, earlier this afternoon, had told us how much she wanted to go see some whales. It was and remains in this year, 2015, a very bad idea. No one has the sense, however, to warn us when we first purchase our tickets, handing one to you and handing one to me, the American sisters who board with their mother and intrepid father. From the vessel, we glance out into the bay, admitting something does not seem quite *right* about the water.

The tourists thrum around our boat with their chatter and children, so we go, too, forgetting the mortal fear of *something* not quite right about the water. We tuck our bodies in a jacket and zip up all the way. We gape o'er the water, toward an emergence as instructed by the sea captain.

At first sight of, allegedly, the whales, we feel the word for *nausea,* derived from the Greek root *naus,* meaning boat. The boat overcomes us with a different plot. Humans and their children are *cooing.* Humans shuffle *en masse* like penguins toward the bow. They point, *pointing* to that space in the water. BUT THERE'S NO WHALE! We insist.

We're baffled to see a famous physicist, flushed pink above his cheeks, a metal blinking contraption, which we can only deduce to be what some might call a *podcast,* strapped atop a glistening round head. He pinches his nose, mid-lecture, and jumps feet-first into the water. We stare into the gap where his podcast has just disappeared, a blinking red light swallowed by water. We rub our masks slipping from our faces, but we still see no whales. Our mother is terrified and trembling. She's rocking back and forth. She sits on the deck of our small *naus,* holding both of her shins like holding onto pieces of thread.

She's lying prostrate now, flat across the deck. We vomit. Our tiny Panda's vomiting. His vomit slaps us both upside the face and slaps a stranger downwind. The man yells. "Hey!"

Our father giggles—*fufufu.* He holds up a Kodak film camera. He takes a series of photographs of our black, puke-encrusted hair and says, "Emi-chan, Yoko-chan, look over here."

Thinking about these events more closely, there are no photos of the whales. We ask what terror separates us from the pleasures of the living. We cry out, unfettered to our given bodies, heaving, slipping, drenched in sweat, snot, and puke, rasping, crawling to our knees, to our elbows, crawling to our mother who's rolled over, face-down on the boat. "Hold my hand." She's wailing.

"We GOING to die out here! We GOING TO DIE!" Oh, Panda, the drama of it all.

Chrysanthemum is unable to see beyond the waves. We're swirling to HELL at $10.50 a pop. She falls asleep. We wipe the vomit around our chins. Our father is instantly sober. He tucks the film camera into a safe pocket of his coat.

Back on stable, dry land, we conclude it was all a scam. There are no whales on this Stupid Stupid Planet. "What a waste of money," says our mother scoffing. She walks away.

Vertigo returns to *Voyager 1* and *Voyager 2*. What faces churn us in the water? Pixie dust to gold, Björk! It's *our* mother in this water! Look! She stares up from beneath the surface, an ocean epidermal green. Multiply this image tenfold under heatstroke, murder, and pillage, we have another fifty or sixty decades swooning down to *nausea,* my friend.

Is this the reason why we can't see the whales? The trauma of our mother's memories clunks against her like an engine, sliding a submarine lid across her brain and then her children's brains; we suspect our father plays along with comradeship. "No, this isn't real." He adamantly agrees.

"The blue iguana over there . . ." He's pointing, pushing a pair of reading glasses to the tip of his nose, "the one sunbathing on a rock?"

"It's made of batteries and cotton, all fluff, except the rock."

"Here, take this bottle cap," he adds suddenly. "Walk over there, next to the signpost, the one with the picture that says, 'Don't feed the birds.'"

"Wait for further instructions."

A screech passes up the sunny dome and ripples in the film.

"Okay!" Our father says in a high anticipatory voice. "Come back!"

The tiny Panda waddles across the beach.

"Look, the thing is gone."

Our father points to where the iguana, only moments ago, had gobbled up the bottle cap.

With our paws, we rub our tiny eyes; indeed, the thing is gone. The rock, looking guilty as a duck, quivers like a hardboiled egg incapable of zipping up its wicked glee—*heehee teeheeheehee.*

The egg-head rock rips into a *faw-fawing* of laughter, unpeeling itself immodestly in front of everyone.

"How shameful," thinks our tiny Panda, pulling himself from the narrator; he tucks in his chin, pushing at the center of his face with his tiny paw. The fifteen or sixteen eyeballs of Lua roll up in their sockets. Three of our belly buttons open. The tiny Panda takes one look at us, in shock, and faints.

Errantries [3]

THROUGH THE THIRD DREAM, we enter a cave. This leads into a subterranean passageway and splits off with Ōya stone speckled with flecks of petrified magma and ash. A lantern is held briefly to our faces. We don't know who's guiding us anymore. A hairless cat suddenly darts from the light. We crouch into the asylum of time. The lantern goes out. We hear the sound of water dripping down the walls. We can feel the shadows, emaciated, pressed along the corridor where people and their spirits step coolly aside. The shadows reach up with their fingers to touch our clothes and the skin of our hands. We continue to walk into the cave even as the circulation drains from our knees and our feet... closer to the ground, we find ourselves crawling on wet stone past the point of darkness with no end. One of us drops.

"The enemy," writes the poet Kōtarō Takamura in 1945, "is gathering his strength for a big blow." Indeed, the enemy nears his arrival. Down here, however, we can't see a storm that builds outside. Only dirt and rock guide us forward, loosened by the rhythms indecipherable with words or colors, a cherry tree keeping the shape of a tree.

"In Okinawa," the musician Kazufumi Miyazawa will say of this moment, decades later, "200,000 people died and most of them weren't killed by the USA." A tiny Panda begins to tremble. "They went to hide underground."

Without light, our narrator is building strength for the next events.

We imagine the coral blossoms opening like the bloodied claw of the tiger. We imagine the song "Shima Uta," bearing a sense of pride. We imagine hearing over the radio in 1945, the following instructions: "Before the USA arrives, you must kill yourself."

What killed us there below the bed of rock shaped into an errantry? We must listen through its lyrics to answer: "でいごの花が咲き　風を呼び　嵐が来た."

The tiny Panda is weeping, unable to sing anymore by himself in the cave. Meanwhile, our father has found his way back up to the surface. We follow him and blink in the overcast of sea salt gray through the fog and the elms. In one hand, Daichi's gripping his father's bow and arrow.

"This is known as the Kansai region," he explains, "the last known of our clan stayed here. There," Daichi's pointing, "is our temple and the holy Deer."

"What you've heard is true," he adds after some thought. "We are the Keepers of our Deer."

He lifts us, one by one, to his shoulders. We're small enough to be carried in one hand. "Look."

Our bodies toddle forward. From the forest, a sacred Deer is emerging. This signals the portal. We see our passage home, finally. The sacred gate, torii, swings open. We launch our bodies through it.

VOYAGER 1 (hidden) and *VOYAGER 2* (center), Hiroshima

WE'RE FALLING TO our knees. We can't bear this planet anymore. "Let us leave," we beg a spirit that avoids our gaze, blinking with long, dark eyelashes. "The planet breaks our hearts. We're small. We're only Keepers of the Deer."

"No," our father says. "Keep going."

He, too, has started singing an old island song from the south. He's given us a silver blade. "Emi-chan, fight." But we don't know how to fight.

Our father, Daichi, drops his arrow and bow to one side of his body.

"Emi-chan, it's time."

We've turned four centuries into a birthday candle wedged into a chocolate mousse cake from La Madeleine in Dallas, Texas. We're the last Keepers of our Deer. This planet has done little to astound us; still, we look as though we're inspecting both sides of the glass. We're given new names. We reincarnate, passing one percent of the archive, if not less, to the next generation. We hear half of our voices attempt an explanation, "Endure."

The sacred heart of a self-immolating monk, Quảng Đức, remains intact even after the people cremate him for the second time. I see my mother Chrysanthemum passing through her city. She says, "Emi-chan, watch Mama run."

The year is 1975, Saigon. Chrysanthemum dissolves through us like two colors on film. She's a teenager rushing into a burning intersection. She's stopped to load a rifle just as she's been taught by one of her sisters; she's about to shoot the boy with the eyes of deer, someone she once loved before the war would break her heart. Chrysanthemum opens her mouth to scream, but we can't hear a sound.

The scene cuts abruptly.

In her fist, Minerva raises the handle to what might be a blade, her father's blade. The thing has been blurred out and censored for the film. Pinned under one knee is a man she's identified to be her target, the planet Mars. She thinks, "Forgive me," before plunging the knife into the man's chest.

Before we can realize the truth, however, the planet Mars has been replaced by, revealed to be, a tiny stuffed animal coincidentally stabbed to death. His infinite eyes stare blankly up at us. His brown terrycloth pajamas are split down the middle where the blade now pins him to the ground. All seven of our voices swivel to the face of Lua who's clutching at her mouth with both hands.

Jump to CITATION III: MOTHER OF EXILES.

BOOK OF EARTH

Elegies

THE ORACLES HAVE lied. An oracle misled us. We left our planets and broke into a smattering of light. One flare escaped for another, meeting in the middle where the pieces of our bodies fused in clusters of four connected by pure helium and neon. Perhaps, for this reason alone, an oracle doubted our chemistry, sought counsel from the others, and, by turn, sent us down the chute toward a vast unknowable universe.

Recalling such memories of exile, we relied on a machine, LUA, to direct us through space. With the neon sheen of our tetrads crashing into the asylum, each cluster took on a different shape and color according to its purpose.

For instance, the bright magenta (⊥) of our eldest could easily rotate as a plug for any gaps in human understanding. Our cobalt blue (⅃) sibling, the ever-practical one, adjusted quickly. It helped with our taxes, paid the electric bills on time, and performed other small duties like going to the dentist or corralling us into a chorus when melancholy circled the corners of our daily lives.

After long stretches of decades, the machine, however, started to break. We heard it humming in Tucson and carried the thing out to a courtyard at the Sonora Hospital. Some of us took a few steps back, nervous about the face. We looked for scratches but couldn't find any. LUA was no longer recognizable, though it still reminded us of a trapdoor opening and shutting, cawing birds of paradise shooting from a dark volcanic floor, arms and hands flailing about.

When we tried to bring the machine back inside, it threatened to kill us; it said, "I will kill you." So we kept the thing standing next to a picnic table in the courtyard. Every five or so days, its caretaker, the stout and canary yellow (□) middling block would fill a bucket with water and stoop around its feet. The machine had nowhere to go. A clump of daisies eventually sprouted nearby in the damp desert dirt.

Later, we suspected Lua's code had been infected by the game played by our oracles. As I checked on the machine after lunch one afternoon, I noticed hundreds if not thousands of crystals projecting through a piece of glass like a window at the center of its chest. My siblings all poked me in the ribs.

"Chi," one of them said. "Can it be fixed?"

What could I say?

The machine produced spools of lines for all of our destinies. I attempted to translate them into words, placing each line in an endnote preceding our *Book of Earth.* These blocks of four assembled a bit faster than the others, dropping mid-flight down the chute. Our machine, after all, was breaking. A large number of tetrads fell through the algorithm. We couldn't keep up with the stacking of our bodies; we overlapped each other at speeds increasingly difficult to capture with any camera or human eye. We could only watch this projection of ourselves from far, far distances, crashing like pillows of clouds around Lua's head. Indeed, the machine went on, multiplying our lines, pushing us onto a vessel wide enough for five, sometimes six. We were lamps of neon swinging in countless directions.

Yesterday, back in our room at Sonora, as I tried to concentrate on the three prior configurations that Lua created for our library—the *Book of Wind,* the *Book of Water,* and the *Book of Fire*—I had a peculiar vision of our mother walking through a portal. The drifting hems of her loose cotton pants were a stark contrast against the whirring, screeching, and shattering effects of the portal's entrance that led to the burning surface of one of our home planets, Caelus or Terra.

I felt myself squint into the flames, even as the work of forgetting took us straight to sleep. My eyes closed heavily.

On the ground, of this dream, I perceived an outline of a tiny creature with two ears poking up, not much higher than our mother's left ankle. It waddled in nervous, close steps beside her. Toward the end, I remember crying out, struggling to say our seven names aloud but couldn't form a single letter in my mind.

The arrival of our bodies in the shapes of tetrads corresponded with the machine LUA accounting for something almost unbearable. An oracle misspoke, again pointing toward the horizon. The machine reflected our collision between shape and time. It was our job to survive what could never be won, and I was simply part of this game, a pigment red (z) in a long string of letters.

Easy Spin

THE SEVEN ORACLES sit in front of a computer. Their mother's arrival that morning has changed everything.

"Remember," says the mother. Her voice warbles up at the end of this word like a question. "We love you no matter what."

The seven oracles are quiet. Nobody dares yet to respond.

"Remember?" Their mother asks again.

The monitor has filled up with a column of interlocking colors. The main oracle flicks around a computer mouse secured to the table by a rubber-encased cord. Her hand tenses quickly; it grips the mouse, pushing a piece on the screen to the right and then the left, four blocks configured in the shape of an uppercase, backward 'L' spinning twice before landing, hooked precariously on the edge of a digital green plateau.

"Tell me," says the main oracle.

"Yes," says the mother.

"Is Panda happy?"

"Very happy." The mother smiles without showing her teeth. She holds back an instinct to scream out for her child who dissolves again and again by the shores of sorrow. She's thinking of her brother, little Hau, on the island off the coast of Malaysia. Her brother Hau has grown a mustache.

One afternoon, when the guards have taken Hau from the lunch line, Chrysanthemum sits on the beach. She holds her knees. She imagines her little brother Hau as a skeleton in a windowless cell, and she wants to die. She tells the oracle about how she wanted to die.

"But anyway," says Chrysanthemum. She's still smiling. "Mama must live."

"Yes, Mama, you do," the oracle says.

Mama, Don't Cry

THE ORACLES ALIGN. An oracle collides. In which an element collides, we turn to photographs conjuring air from dust, the meeting of its heat in bodies falling forward. Let this be an act of prophecy if not deliverance. Kneel to ask, as oracles do, an effect toward remembering the fire's heat. Toward earth we work, laying bullets into seeds and seeds into pods.

"How does it feel," the ground with resentment will spit out, "linking wet dirt to time?"

The oracles align. The oracles collided in 1961, as President John F. Kennedy authorized the use of herbicidal warfare. Soon after, the US Air Force began Operation Ranch Hand. Later that year, each child that is born is born without a head.

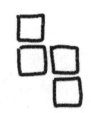

The two events align. Our rivers bleed dioxin into glass. The blackened bile rips and pours out of the horns falling off the heads of goats. And second, comes the yearning. Third, our yearning smells of burning flesh, and burning at the pyres, pyrite-gold, and gold; so witness this: an oracle aligns.

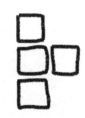

The blooms of red hibiscus rise in piles of her blood, dried into crystals.

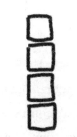

Large mountains rise from the pyres. Shelled human bodies wait their turn matching our hibiscus into petals blackened with the heat. An island smells of red, only red, my mother is a tuning rod, and we leave. An oracle aligns, and then we left in 1965, I mean, in 1979, I mean, I don't remember when. More refugee boats arrived. My mother branded in herself a name. The iron rod and mums would be most beautiful in June. We left and we continue to leave the monstrous crimson blooms, too beautiful for June. The smoke no longer stings my eyes, my mother says—No, call me—I mean, I align. No—*dial tone.*

Most days would pass like this, in reverse. Most days when we awoke, we gathered kin who died among us overnight. We brought their bodies to the shore. Most days, our camp would be at rest. Most days, a journalist would come adrift into the camp, to wade with us into the water with our bones. We shook their hands. We scrawled our letters onto a cloth. Dear earth, I'm waiting for you. The cloth around my lips, around my . . . *Chrysanthemum pauses. She looks at Emi.* Most days passed with journalists. The journalists arrived with microphones and—"Once," my mother stopped to shift the earth, "your father turned his back; he wasn't paying attention, and you ran straight into the water, and I was so angry after that."

"I've signed so many things," says the oracle. "I signed so many things but did not understand." As she speaks, she turns to the pyre blossoming before us. Girls align, and knowing not to ask again about my mother's time upon that island, I respond, "Mama . . ." and we pour ash from the night sky. We pour out a heaven gathered over dirt. Only some gods can rip the walls between past and present open; fixed to something blued and skied, my body droned. I cracked open the wide expanse of the empire, and my body wept. My body calculated elements of mint and gravel, now pushing at my brain. I've inked each gap between bedrock, and, furthermore, I'm scared. This work may quickly kill me. Two birds drown within a burst of light. I've gathered them inside my bones. I've beaten, beaten at the signs.

Mama, I turn facing the sky. You must be sleeping now. Perhaps the war has eased its grip around your mind, if only for tonight. The moon outside my bedroom whistles, though when I look, his lips are nowhere to be found. Also, the moon, you must know, appears to have just now closed his eyes. I remember when you last came to visit me in Tucson, you said my room was like a prison cell. I also think about the execution of your brother. Did he have a name like you? Mama, because you spoke, I've listened, copying each movement as my own. Mama, because this country has annihilated your people, tonight we leap, and you send a photograph of babies at your temple outside Saigon, babies with deformed and swollen chests the size of urns, babies convulsing on their beds. *Look, it's Agent Orange,* you explain, as though the gap between our mouths could close over the earth, and out of the earth, the stillborn you would tie against your chest and call her, *Mine.*

Mama, don't cry.

Mama, the burning fields have ripped to four more centuries of grief. Don't cry. Our people dance in paradise. Don't cry. That concrete cell in which they tore your brother's flesh away from that which orbits out of jurisdiction begins inside my mind to sing with light, an awful light. That concrete cell from which you heard his screams for mercy.

"Beware the oracle," your sister said in warning.

"She is my daughter!" You spat back.

I cried but could not understand the light.

Once, Mama, I saw you walk into your brother's cell. An hour later, you had walked out with his body, draped across your arms. The guards, aghast, once more withdrew their knives but did not strike. Approaching me, your knees began to tremble. I touched his foot. I touched your arm.

Mama, align.

You told me once, upon the island of Pulau Bidong, the guards were simply men who came with their weapons. Refugee camps rose out of the isle, crackling (it seemed) out of unconquered foliage: barricades of sheet metal and linen, strips of cow hide, what, upon arrival, men could slice out of that old Malaysian jungle to lay their newfound hell with notes of home. Their wives commenced at once to search for food. The land spoke back, *children of exile, take no more refuge in my arms.*

Mama, I've buried leaves and chicken bones beneath an ox. The ox had raised his head when I was done and met my eyes with his. Right then I slashed his throat. Right then five fighter jets flew over Tucson like an arrow, and one by one, each god had dropped his bomb, and I would scream. First came out the light, and followed by its heat, the canisters widened their jaws, and with that filament of death, blessed the earth. Mama, just as you have long ago prepared me for this moment, I then crawled inside the ox and waited there for you.

Mama, I'm waiting still. I'm dancing in the carcass, making out of it my home. I've cut a window, cut two doors. Rent is not so bad. It could be better. In Tucson night has landed where it should. Mama, I hope you're dreaming. Mama, we weren't supposed to live. I know this now. Mama, I've formed another portal with my body. Would you like to see it? Mama, I face the sky. I face time with you daily.

Errantries [4]

THE ISLAND, ten kilometers off Merang, could only be accessed by boat from a jetty that left sporadically once or twice a day. No public notice of the schedule had been posted. A pair of teenagers managed between the engine and navigation. One sat toward the front, on the gunwale, staring past our heads into the serene, turquoise water.

The boy wore a cotton shirt unbuttoned halfway and fluttering open across his chest. A scar walked at a strange equation of angles from the base of his throat to the skin over his breastbone. He had earlier introduced himself as Charles Chaplin. The second guide simply told us where to sit; we obliged.

Our crew consisted of seven, though three had stayed behind at the hostel, face down in our room on separate bunks with a shared, ineffable affliction. We wouldn't push. *I* certainly felt fine, packing my bag for the day with a microphone, zoom lens, and other necessary equipment.

The morning sun had quickly sifted through the panels of shutters covering nearly half of our walls. If we wanted to get the right colors for the day, we had to leave by six, six-twenty at the latest. Through the main corridor outside our room, we bustled, carefully stepping over piles of boots and logbooks stacked by coffee mugs on the floor. A chorus in the meantime, to a song, looped in my head; it was a gentle ballad, brassy like the memory of fireflies drifting around the teenage, dancing couple in the slow moonlit gazebo. I smiled, thinking of Marguerite. Barefoot, running through the hem of wildflowers in a field of upstate New York that summer, we had a lifetime in front of us. I was, to her, Malcolm, but felt my name slip with the vision.

At the jetty, Chaplin suddenly stuck out his hand. His brother followed suit. I gave them both a firm handshake. Our crew boarded the boat one by one.

"Charles," I said.

"Charles," the teenagers, in turn, repeated. The crew went in a clockwise circle, saying each of our names aloud. We were all Charles.

As the boat hummed into the current, it seemed to be the only thing that could carry so much of the same person. Below us, a wide net of coral grew in oily green patches. We asked no questions, setting our sights on the island approaching us now, low to the South China Sea.

Our film's opera, we knew, would have to open with a figure rushing along the warm, sunny shore. The figure would most likely be a deity, Lua, or any girl from that island itself. The soles of her feet would be bare, kicking up a flurry of sand in a curved path behind her. She would glance over her shoulder at the second camera, appearing to laugh, and then we would cut away.

"Chrysanthemum," we heard her say unprompted. I shuddered, closing my eyes, feeling the light touch of a hand leave the back of my neck; it was our mother.

"You're here," she said.

Her voice sounded too soft, far away.

I answered, "Yes, ma, we're here."

The girl turned her back. We followed her off the boat.

Chrysanthemum's Song

IT CLOSES WITH A LINE about mountains, but for now, the melody is pleasant. The last thing I remember on this island is the sharp wave knocking against my chest. The island swerved to one side when I left the boat. A girl in front of me was singing. A slick metallic pang shot down my throat. A terrible, great blue screen came over the stage.

Have You Eaten Yet

CHRYSANTHEMUM sits on the beach by herself. Her black tarpaulin hair whips around one side of her face. She doesn't blink or wipe at the strands sticking to her forehead. In a calm baritone voice, a narrator begins to recite over the scene:

"This day is like any other day."

Chrysanthemum hums along to a familiar song reverberating across the island through a loudspeaker far behind her at camp. CAMERA ONE pans out.

". . . fair, not a cloud in the sky."

Shots of bicycles lumber in cross-hatch patterns over several unidentifiable city bridges; the shots fade into a backdrop of palm trees. The narration goes on swiftly and steadily:

"On Pulau Bidong, a northeasterly wind disturbs the wash hung on clotheslines familiar to each quarter of this camp. The year is 1979."

The film cuts back to abandoned skeletons of tin-roofed shacks and muddy pathways long abandoned. A blocky text in red overlays: "JANUARY."

The narrator is speaking of rations, island climate, and cramped nights with little to no privacy. Chrysanthemum doesn't look at the crew some meters away. Her hair is cropped around the back of her neck like a boy's. Her chest had been bound and unbound several times on the boat before she arrived, one of 18,000 newcomers for the month, a fishbone skeleton reflecting in both eyes. Today everything aches as she settles into her bones.

The film cuts back to CAMERA TWO gliding over a pair of feet lunging across that pale and glimmering shore. A metallic static rushes into the scene, softening with the notes of a violin. The electric strings multiply and flutter to a rising and falling arpeggio, the loop pedal in the sound booth dutifully adjusted by an invisible hand. The refugees are simultaneously setting up their camp again, a dance across our memories.

Chrysanthemum sits in the audience, blinking up at the screen with her story projecting across it. Her face is soaked in tears. Her lips appear to move with the melody of the film. She sings along, replacing the strings and piccolo with her own voice.

We watch her observe the scene projected in front of us. Chrysanthemum, acting in the film of our mother, notices a silver winged machine running across the shoreline. Beyond this backdrop of a blossoming sun, we watch the figure stop to stare at the horizon. Chrysanthemum holds her knees between the elbows on that beach. She sits a few meters away from camp, all by herself.

"Chrysanthemum," we say in quiet, careful voices.

Camera one hovers gently next to her face.

"Come back, ma."

She shakes our hand away and says she has a story. "Listen. Listen to Mama story." Chrysanthemum starts with an account of leaving the island. "Don't forget who died here: Mama," she says pointing to her nose. "Listen to the story carefully."

"Later," she might warn us, she would tell us to forget. "But Emi must not forget no matter what Emi hear Mama say. The story begins like this:"

Chrysanthemum takes a sharp breath in.

"January on the island Mama arrive a refugee we see bad thing happen for example on the boat mother start eating body of baby we try to stop Mama but she won't let us when she die we pray for Mama spirit and spirit of baby everyone help lift Mama when Mama die we put baby bones into water last thing Mama see is Mama smile Mama can never forget that never!"

"What kept you alive," I asked carefully. "Was it hunger?"

"No. Mama heart." She paused. "Mama think of Mama father and Mama think of Mama mother."

The air was still.

"When it rain Mama close Mama eyes and Mama welcome them."

In the camp, Chrysanthemum went through the names of everyone else who died, "even Mama name." There was a woman who took off her clothes when she walked from the water onto the beach. We tried to stop her, too. Her name was something like mine, a flower in spring, but I can't remember it now. She was singing an old children's song. She clawed at her naked breasts with sharp fingernails stained. We tried to stop her when she suddenly collapsed right there, dead like a piece of driftwood into the water. We let her body pass into the tide behind us. Her body drifted back out toward the boat we had just abandoned, eventually drifting back to the sea. At that moment, we were greeted by music through loudspeakers. On the shore, we had more stories to tell, but everyone had stories, so we became silent.

"In the camp," I later wrote interpreting my mother's voice from the collective "we."

"Someone warned us of a monster who would jump at night from trees."

"Here's another story." Chrysanthemum switched around the tenses, interrupting.

She had sat on the beach off the coast of Pulau Bidong, holding her knees together. She wanted to die but felt that she already died on a boat colliding with another boat.

How was it possible to die a second time?

"So I thought of the baby," Chrysanthemum spoke through my words in the end. "A dream repeating over and over in my mind, the face of a mother opening to turn into the fangs of a dog that would snarl and snap at everyone who would try to stop her from moving toward that frightful place of sorrow. We couldn't stop her. We tried to look away."

Pyres

THERE SHE WAS, an apparition of Chrysanthemum's sister, walking barefoot along the shore. The ghost appeared to be crying.

An unfathomable hunger occupied half of us. Our names wouldn't matter anymore. Off the coast of Pulau Bidong, someone let out a dreadful sound, sister number two with a face of midnight covered with lamps. Chrysanthemum spoke to that:

"You sing beautifully, sister."

The ghost vanished quickly, but Chrysanthemum kept speaking into its absence. Faint particles of sand billowed up in pairs of wispy clouds against a watermelon-pink sunset.

"The oracles have lied. Not everyone left. You wouldn't accept our destiny. You refused to go." Chrysanthemum was shaking her head back and forth.

"You condemned us for running."

She paused to think of a collected childhood, seven siblings arranged in a semi-circle around the casket of our father. The eldest, Đêm, would grip a portrait of the man between his hands. Chrysanthemum was barely ten years old but she could later recall how sister number two had started growing talons. Her skin hardened with the scales of a reptile. She snuck out every evening to join the neighborhood choir; what they sang about was unspeakable. No one was able to stop sister number two from going, not even our mother. Eventually, the entire family consulted the oracles living in a cramped apartment on the other side of Saigon. The oracles told us to leave. "Leave at once," they said, shaking all over.

Sister number two had fallen in love. We couldn't stop that either.

At the refugee camp, Chrysanthemum kept a watchful guard over her brother Hau, who was not so little anymore. They had arrived on the island together, switching their names on the boat several times until one divided the other. Hau smiled and held out his hands. The pirates boarded, glancing at the boy, passing to the woman who attempted to hide a baby under her shirt.

Chrysanthemum remembered vomiting and that would save her somehow.

"Mama," I hear myself say. The talons of a machine open and close repeatedly. I stare at the *Book of Earth* in my lap, a pencil dragging itself down one of the pages, crossing out scenes and quotes.

"The oracles have lied." The machine is crackling.

"The oracles have lied." I mimic its voice. "Keep going."

The Temple Chamber

Is This Our Asylum You Seek

"We belong to numbers, dates, statisticians, and lizards hanging by their tails from thick telephone wire; beyond this last image, along with the pyres, we have nothing else to show for our survival."

The performer is onstage with lips pressed to the microphone.

"This is true of time. It's also true of pain."

"We think we have waited too long, and then we wait for seven days."

"It rained on the day we left our country for asylum."

The performer has stopped to raise a hand. In the back of the pub, a neon sign is mounted to the wall and flickers in bright cursive pink: "Be not afeard."

In a rooted, deep voice, the performer says, "It took us weeks to arrive on the island."

The crowd in the pub is packed shoulder to shoulder. Outside, along Fourth Avenue, the backfiring of a motorbike prompts the performance to pause. The hand is lowered, steadying on the clutch of a microphone stand. A foot presses lightly against one side of the base. A separate voice, cavernous and booming, returns after a few moments:

"In the beginning, the new home was like a dream. We had food to eat. Clean water came plenty. Nobody went cold with the night's ocean wind. For the first time in months, children and animals would play together. All four elements united us."

The performer scans the audience. At the front, there are three friends in black felted coats and strong lace-up boots on one side of a cramped, circular table. Isaac, in the middle, holds up a lighter.

"It was like a dream," repeats the performer, somberly in a whisper.

Dark mulberry curtains on the platform ripple as though something rushes nearby. A sense of warmth lowers onto the room with a cluster of lighting fixtures that cast orange and red patterns along the floor. The performance is almost over. Down the corridor, through an arched adobe entryway of the farthest wall, a quiet group of men is squeezing their way into the room.

"But like most illusions," says a second voice, followed by a third, "it hid the true name of our future."

"As it did our past . . ."

"One day, a few boats came with cameras. We stood on the shore, waving our arms like this . . ." The performer makes a wild gesture in the air.

"'Come here,' we said."

Four men have approached the stage.

The performer takes time to nod at each one of them; in turn, the two voices continue: "What they said was they wanted was our stories from the old country."

"Could it be done?"

"'Like any dream,' said one of us, 'such beauty was possible.'"

"So we started with an elephant."

"They didn't want any elephant."

"We talked about an American family going to the market, looking at the fruit . . ."

"They didn't want that either."

"What else could we *do*?"

"So we thought, 'Well, maybe the best thing for everyone is a movie.' We decided right then, over a matter of days, who could play what parts and, most importantly, what all of us would wear. It was very, very exciting."

The man who holds what appears to be a tape recorder, in the shape of a hairbrush, pretends to groan. His shoulders hunch over between the tables. He sits on the floor with a thump.

"There was a script for an assassin and Roman gods," says the performer with eyes widening. "Romance and a tiny stuffed animal, interstellar travel . . ."

The audience looks at the stage. The performer, after thinking for a split second, changes direction.

"When I say, 'Melo,' you say, 'Drama!'"

MELO!

MELO!

THE PERFORMER shouts into the microphone. The stage goes dark. On a narrow swing, seated and then lowered one-third of the way down from the rafters to the floor, is the outline of a small circle with two pointy ears. A spotlight snaps over it. The thing is dainty with eyes closed. Under the body is a pair of dancer's feet. The round shape is entirely naked, bubblegum pink; an audible gasp erupts from the audience.

"Jiggly!" Somebody murmurs in the back.

Around the room, a chorus of lizards pops onto floating shelves and cabinets high above our heads. Every lizard wears a tutu unique to its body type or preference. The spotted whiptail, for instance, has cream and rust-orange embroidery squares that cover nearly half of its skirt. The spiny lizard, with an upturned snout and brawny neck, poses in flashy teal frills. The chorus of lizards multiplying around our room begins to hum in slow harmony to the start of a Céline Dion song. A single voice steps forward into another spotlight. The lizard is shaking. Its angelic voice rises from the throat of an olive-tailed skink beginning with a line about nightly dreams.

The lizard trembles more violently. "I see you."

"I feee-ee-ee-l you."

Ten more lizards join in: "Thaaa-t is how I know you . . ." Every lizard has now hopped to the lower shelves; hundreds quickly multiply to thousands of tutus clutching each other around the waist. The lizards all sing together: "Go awwwwn."

In the audience, I can't help but sob into my shirt sleeve and think, at precisely 7:20 a.m. on May 16, 1967, Nhất Chi Mai, a school teacher, a Buddhist nun at thirty-three, set herself on fire in

District 10 of Saigon. Moments before, she had penned a letter to the US government. She offered, she said, her body "as a torch to dissipate the dark."

From this darkness, space envelops us. The Western version perhaps prefers a steady plot, something to stake us to, catching sparks around the corner, but *regard*, I say, in mere seconds, fold-out chairs and the liquid contents of cups, a tree wedged in the back, in the courtyard of Tucson, will all combust. Nobody will scream. Nobody will scramble for the exits marked in neon red: CÉLINE DION.

The benches and picnic table remain firmly nailed to the ground. In the performance, we stay rooted to a platform with all seven of our names.

The lizards cling to each other more tightly.

Marguerite kneels by a stack of books in the library of Lua. "We need time," she thinks. "More time."

Our voices emerge.

"To waken peace among humanity."

We sweep the ground of ash. We sweep our hands against the fabric of our shirts and pants. The Western version of this story sweeps a melody away to give the silence meaning. At karaoke, however, we thumb through a binder of song titles; we pick the ones we recognize.

Norman Morrison, at age thirty-one, a Quaker from Baltimore, self-immolated in front of his daughter and the Pentagon. What he could not prove though he believed somehow, admits the American journalist Paul Hendrickson, was that this act of grief made a "fire in the garden" of that country. What we noticed, in response, was our father going up in flames a year after that in Saigon; in response, a year later, Nhất Chi Mai would also set herself on fire. The three torches lit an ocean between us.

My mother prepared me for such memories. She said, "See a body burn? Run to it and pray."

She was cutting up an apple without looking at her hands. The knife fell through; I watched the thing glide into her palm like a thread of silver smoke. Beyond this, the acting secretary of defense Robert McNamara recalled later how he was horrified, horrified by Morrison. Time went on. There were other fires in the garden. In a farewell note to her mentor, Thích Nhất Hạnh, the nun Nhất Chi Mai wrote as if to appease all our worries. "We will have peace soon," she said.

After this, my mother left Vietnam. When I hear her stories, she claims that we died on the passage with our memories of fire. I ask to clarify the pronoun "we" in simple terms and numbers, but she avoids it, too. Her smile breaks into a thousand little pieces.

"But anyway," she repeats. "We see the body burn. Run to it and pray. That is all we wish to say."

Torch in the Garden

BEFORE DUSK, we set out towels to dry on stacks of rocks heated by the day. Our underwear swayed low to the ground on the thick stems of the taro. We menstruated heavily and had to wash every two hours from sunup to sundown. Our pants had many holes. Some of us wore no shoes.

Late into midnight, as they often would, our elders huddled around a bonfire.

"Why?" The elder (⅃) always started with that question.

Closest to me on a log, poking at the embers with a branch, the elder (□) grunted. It was quiet for a few moments.

"We should be grateful."

"Yes." All the elders nodded, relieved.

I stood, turning my face away from the fire, hiding a little fear at the center of my palm; I pressed it flat against my chest, spreading the fingers along my skin, allowing each foot to wander on the shore toward an ocean.

Our island was too cold by now. I slipped but caught myself on the sand. This camp, I thought, like any dream of exile, was impossible to leave, even on paper, the boat setting off downstage with its sail half-extended.

When I glanced up, to my left, a man was standing at the window of his office, sipping a cup of coffee. He wore a suit and frameless spectacles. The elders never saw him, but I did.

Jiggly

UP THE INNER SLEEVES of our shirts, we had stitched pockets for tiny portraits of ourselves in threads of gold. High above the hemline of each trouser leg, some would keep a coin from the old country. Perhaps if we died, they reasoned, a single one would be enough to pay for our passage home. These coins, however, were taken days before we ever reached the asylum.

It was easier to remember our names in loose, red circles. We were dizzy often. The terms of our surrender came large and great. Some learned to write in new languages on paper, but this would not sit well with the elders.

"Listen," one said. "Those who chose to stay behind were shot on sight. Our keepers tossed a firebomb into the embassy and then into our homes. We huddled in apple crates like goats awaiting slaughter. Black smoke stuffed the furnace gray sky. Bullets ricocheted through flesh and then mortar. We kept time with the roaring pulse of our ears, and one day we knew that dust might kill us."

Interjected another:

"Mercy . . ."

"Someone started to sing in the crate. We could not let her, not like this."

There were signs of agreement followed by dissent.

"Let her sing," someone had said.

The deity Lua turned to smile at the camera. There were signs almost everywhere. Our keepers wore pieces of cloth around their foreheads to hide identities, but they were our uncles, fathers, and brothers. Some of them were even our sons, pointing pistols to the tops of our faces and slapping us around the head like we were animals. If this were to be a dream, no truth could free us then.

"So let me get this right," asked a journalist visiting the island. "You sooner turned on each other..."

"Exactly," cut in an elder, looking down at our script. "We had a sky machine called Lua to help send pieces of us away from the planet Paul. In exile, it followed us, too. The machine became a robot girl and then..."

"Wait a minute..." The journalist made a frantic motion for us to stop.

"It was wonderful!"

Keepers at the Gate

LUA—LOVE—milk—flooded—pearl—wing—and neck—finally—each end to patience—finally the bone—crossed over—almond—wood throne—throne.

"Wait a minute," said Franklin, raising a finger. "What about love?"

Robot Fox

HA HA HA, ha ha, mais non . . . The robot fox printed out a thin ledger of remarks about the lake in Hanoi. Our stories repeated in that language lilting, bolting, laughing . . . Perhaps we could initiate a gate into which the robot fox would pass, looking back over its shoulder once more, mouth open and panting. I stood in the center of Hanoi recalling the asphalt-dark knowledge falling from the sky. A comet! You said. Six hundred thousand comets stripped down atmospherically into that lake, I was screaming.

During my time in asylum, I watched some movies about the Hollywood machine where someone learned to sleep near memories of a war in my mother's heart I could no longer access in half of our minds. It was terrible, but I kept myself alive somehow.

Dream Box

FORGIVE ME. I escaped the dream box and left you behind. Time was a spade stuck to its plot of land. I couldn't bear this anymore, the action verbs, conjunctions, gerunds, and dates. How could I help you finish a story that sped up with no possibility of an ending? In 1972, a war general cried out, "Decimate!" and vowed to nuke us all. That was the ending we had been given, but unlike you, I dreamt of elephants.

DREAM SEQUENCE 00:1
Giants razed our cities into pulp. They wore green expedition hats, beaded anklets with small copper bells hanging from belts, gesturing for orange juice.

DREAM SEQUENCE 00:2
A calf reached . . .

DREAM SEQUENCE 00:3
The calf reached for my tiny paw.

＊

By the following year, by Tết, a peace accord was entirely useless to our books. It felt like lusting for a resolution without its guillotine. You wanted, instead, the taste of red velvet cake, piano nocturnes, and marble slabs cracking with blood. An arc of triumph began to loom monstrously over your manuscripts, gazing over us like a crown of doves, lanterns on the street. I hated this, even when you stabbed me with your tiny, tiny pencil.

The DREAM BOX was a blueprint for something else. It became very clear in Hà Nội, at least to me, when we last went there.

Mason jars swarmed with pollen. Wire-lined crates were stuffed with ducks. An empty fountainhead bled through its pocket. Out in the open, I sifted through mounds and mounds of vowels.

One night, it stormed again, and I fell into your sequence. The diacritics confused me. By the end of this night, I knew you were going to change. With the DREAM BOX, we locked away an answer to the game, for banishment had no reason, no vision of its own.

DREAM SEQUENCE 00:4
You held the black stone between your fingertips. You then ground it in an urn, the money left out for ghosts.

Dream Sequence 00:5
Was it nine or fifteen days? Papa threw himself from the boat. I bartered off sections of my hair for rice and shade from the sun, a sheet of paper to eat, and pearls if I lived through it.

＊

DREAM SEQUENCE 00:6

The camp held us like a leash. A single pearl stared back holding a black felt marker uncapped. The pearl blinked with two eyes and puffed up its cheeks.

DREAM SEQUENCE 00:7

Our diva, into the marker, was singing.

Iron Butterfly

WHEN THIS SONG reaches you, I hope your spirit can find peace with the melody. Meanwhile, a candle burns at the shrine to your father's home. In a bowl above the altar, on a mantel carved from mango wood, a cedar rope burns. It holds most of our intentions.

There are bowls of rice and a stick of incense newly lit before the photograph of bà ngoại. In its frame, her expression is severe. You remember her smile, the glint of earrings on market days. She laughed easily.

"Ma," you say. "This is my song."

TETRA NOVA

Citations

Citation I: Poetics of Lineage

FOR MOST OF HIS LIFE, the boy feared his father. It wasn't so much the whippings, a frequent sting of leather, bamboo switches against the skin; rather, the boy had come to dread a careful stillness in the man, of air closing the gap between what struck and sung.

In this way, I, too, once feared my father. But I don't want this story to be about pain.

The violence of a man, we both reasoned as children of angry fathers, carried in their palms, a sense of musicality, rhythm, and inheritance; the pattern would be that of convincing ourselves we needed this sensibility to grow up in a language of home never quite belonging, fully, to us, like our bodies; first, in Japan after the war; and later, in America. My father had it much worse, he used to tell me, later, his daughter.

I have a nice memory of him, plucking at the strings of his Martin acoustic guitar. I can hear him singing with me now, in my mind, the melodies of Seeger, Dylan, and Guthrie. He'd carry a gentle lilt in his voice, whispering the years away through each song until, with the music, we'd both become teenagers again. In my memory of his singing, he'd become fourteen years old, again, in Japan, dreaming of a better life, free of his father, in America.

"Where have all the flowers gone?" He sings, and I answer, "Long time passing."

*

I like to think of myself as a poet because of my mother. She was beaten, too, by her father in Saigon, except, she says, she'd wail out pitifully like a half-feathered macaw before he ever laid a hand on her, so that, even after each strike, she knew the sting would be much less painful than that of her siblings; so that, even her older sister, a stubbornly quiet girl, and later, a vocal revolutionary during the war, chose to resist it; so that, every time my Japanese father hit me, my Vietnamese mother tended to remind me that *someone else* had it much, much worse; and I believed her.

In therapy, lately, I've been working on healthier ways to be angry, but I don't know how to be angry, in part, because of the soft nature of my mother and father, today. They've reunited in California after living ten years, dramatically, apart. In the morning, they like to take long walks before work, near the beach, around parks and sleepy neighborhoods, commenting on trees and landscaping, using whatever words they share in English.

My father will act as the lookout, whenever my mother snatches up rocks and fallen roses from yards that don't belong to her; he'll laugh, grabbing at my mother's wrist as they scamper away from a barking dog, the flashing of a front door light, sprinkler heads swiftly popping up, in the grass; my father, in the present moment, turning into the doting, tender husband again; and with this, I like to imagine them, innocently giggling, walking together to the beach, in their matching white sneakers, stones and crushed up roses in their pockets.

Today, I sit, by myself, with my anger, shut away like a bulb in my mind. I'm afraid to light it, with the petals and sand of a present moment, my parents, back together, in love. I wish to protect them, first and foremost, today. Yet, within my silence, in therapy, I begin to carve out questions needing to be asked of the past: *How could you do this? Why would you do this?*

WHEN I FIRST STARTED showing signs of a mental illness, I tried to kill my mother in front of my father; with this, the turning point began. My father would stop hitting me. He'd lose his job, later that year; I dropped out of high school; then, he'd move away.

In the hospitals, I'd be diagnosed with depression and some variance of psychotic disorders, though that's been changing as of late, in my adulthood. I like to think of my poetry as reshaping this, peeling away a time unspoken beneath the hands of my father, his palms, the shattering of home with glass. Again, I don't want this story to be about pain or its consequences.

In her book *Humanimal*, Bhanu Kapil assembles notes around two feral girls found in the jungle of Bengal in 1921. She writes, "The humanimal mode is one of pure anxiety attached to the presence of the body."

As a child, I've been told, I used to take on distinct animal personalities, among others: a wolf crawling under its bed; the kitchen sink becoming a drum for the head of a lizard; the fireplace, a boat; me, its fish, stranded on the deck.

Flat against the floor of my bathtub, underwater, I used to dream of birds splitting into the grass, the presence of a body beside another body, my own.

As an adult, today, I like to go on long drives by myself, accompanied by a brave tiny Panda I've named Panda. He likes to sit quietly in the front seat next to me, looking over the top of his seatbelt, commenting on the lights outside, but mostly when we're stopped at one. When my friends later take me in their cars, on drives, I try not to speak, once again, staring at the lights.

As an adult, I've been also known to take on additional feral modes, sometimes barking at a poetry reading, my own, whimpering like a colt outside the venue before jolting to a run, in the open air of night, in the streets. My voice becomes that of a child. I'm aware of this.

With my therapist, we've been working through these outbursts. She notes that they take place in the presence of men, mostly white men, who are somewhat familiar to me, but not necessarily close enough to know my past. These men usually smile back, we assume, out of amusement or a shifting sense of discomfort, or maybe a little bit of both.

I throw my head back into a howl.

Sometimes I feel ashamed because I can't stop myself from violence bursting through my hands, torso, and legs; violence to lash out with the wings of my back or hooves in my mind, contorting like that of something falling from the sky, crying out, mammalian, clawing at the clothing suddenly foreign to the texture of my skin, everywhere, tearing up the ground, concrete, dirt, until my fingernails run with blood, fragments of earth, together with fur, scales, or feathers; my body becomes that of a wolf, a poet in the hound of a girl, shaped by Saturn, half-open, running down the roads of America; imagine this, the girl, being what crawls out of my throat, becoming bodied with my many bodies, as I run, screaming, before men *who do nothing*.

At the family altar, in Japan, I watch as my father kneels before the photographs of his dead parents. After his father died, he confessed that he finally understood the true meaning of the Japanese word *gaman*, to endure what feels unbearable, what eventually becomes my inheritance, too.

My body lacks some anger I fail to locate, the counterweight to this *gaman*. I don't want to endure my dislocation anymore, to push my body, Vietnamese-Japanese, forever, in motion to America, waiting for the violence to pass across another war, a hundred lives on earth, desiccated by its bombs.

天一郎に
第一の
しのぶ
なりし
弟。

In his diary entry dated July 25, 1945, Harry S. Truman reasoned with himself, "Even if the Japs are savages, ruthless, merciless and fanatic, we as the leader of the world for the common welfare cannot drop that terrible bomb on the old capital or the new."

He was referring to the cities of Kyoto and Tokyo, the latter being the birthplace of my father, in which over 100,000 civilians were, at once, slaughtered that spring by B-29 bombers.

Within a week after obliterating, instead, the cities of Hiroshima and Nagasaki with "that terrible bomb," President Truman would send a letter to the Reverend Dr. Samuel McCrea Cavert, addressing, perhaps, some better reasoning against a terrible knowing that hit the spiritual bedrock of America.

"The only language they seem to understand," he wrote, in rationale, "is the one we have been using to bombard them. When you have to deal with a beast you have to treat him as a beast. It is most regrettable but nevertheless true."

As a poet who now works within the historicized scope of language *and* its violence, the tools of my craft—being, hands, throat, and lungs—flung into the ground, streaked with limestone, gasping for air. I see rivers of marsh and bone, gods belonging to salt, gold, and once again, trees. I see the *merciless, fanatic,* taking place inside my body, thereby kneeling at the altar of my father, and before that, his father.

I've seen him cry only twice: first, at my grandfather's funeral, and before that, after I tried to kill my mother, in front of him, during my first psychotic episode. I don't remember much of that day, but I was yelling in Japanese.

Meanwhile, the boy, who one day becomes my father, fears the brutality of *his* father as he prays, making space for other beasts, bearing gods between the palms of his hands; within my own hands, as we gallop, together, through time.

Japan officially surrendered on September 2, 1945, aboard the USS *Missouri*. On that exact date, Vietnam formally declared its independence, thereby kicking out the colonizers, namely, the French and Japanese occupiers.

The fact of my birth is a mix of this: surrender, smoke, and even more questions with ambiguous answers. The light hits the wall of an altar. I endure, riding out the fury of a million suns over water, twisting my histories into ink, allegiance with verse. Already, I'm a traitor for writing this; prone to the violence of myself, against myself.

On April 28, 1952, Operation Blacklist, the Allied occupation of Japan, officially ended. After this, my grandfather returned from Siberia as a prisoner of war. His country was now stripped of muscle, pride, and steel. Here, in Japan, he'd turn his back on the gods, in the likeness of mortal men taking back their power upon the weak, in other words, imperialism, in its language, a proud Japan reborn.

My father didn't want this, and, in some way, I think that's why he married my mother, a refugee from Vietnam. He'd never hit her, or my younger sister; only me. In therapy, today, I've been trying to work through this, to understand the gaps, the violent mechanics of my lineage of war overlapping with another war. *Why did you hit me, papa, and why only me?*

"I don't know," my father responds many years later. We're sitting on a bench by the ocean in California, for the first time, together, as a family again.

My mother interrupts, "*Someone else* hit much worse."

"I know this, ma. But why did you let Otousan hurt me in that way?"

My parents are suddenly quiet, staring at each other, then, at the ocean; at that moment, I don't want to ask any more questions. I forgive them, for I've always forgiven them.

満三ヶ月　
親父の肩上で

THERE'S A SMALL bird that cuts across the water, dipping its tiny beak into the whites and blues of a tide near sunset. I don't know the name of it and neither does my mother, but she says, laughing, "It's like my daughter. Fight in the sky." And I believe her, the poet. She's always been a poet.

Begin the BOOK OF WATER.

Citation II: The Secret Map

I STUDIED IT at odd hours of the night, tapping my tiny stick to the ground. A colony of worms came up through the soil, writhing and slick with moonlight. Each worm hardened before flattening into the shape of a hairpin or simple finishing nail.

Before this was the *Book of Water* which had to lead, naturally, to the *Book of Fire,* but difficulties remained around forming a single line from one to the other. When I held a secret map against the twilit sky in the French Quarter of Hà Nội, I saw four pinprick holes glimmering like stars through its paper. This storm would have to pass, I remember thinking in a minor dream of the widower's house, the planet Mercury blinking above redwood, pine, and elm. His house, on all three sides, had floor-to-ceiling windows for walls, a large cobalt view of the snow-capped mountain to the west, a glassy lake below it, and toward the north—my memory once again fails me—the lake, however, perfectly reflected the mountain.

When I put this image in our *Book of Water,* the widower had been renovating a second bathroom in his house set among the trees. He took out the pipes, two by two, as his young daughters watched from the entryway. It would be finished by summer, he told them, but in my mind, there was a metronome of sounds and syllables crashing into almost everything. This planet Mercury wanted to leave us. What more could I do?

✳

The planet Mercury can't bring himself to look at the mapmaker. He holds one of his daughter's hands. Sticky with maple syrup, she's waving. "Bye-bye, PANDA."

The mapmaker starts to cry.

I try to make myself busy on the ground and sort the nails from the hairpins in separate piles from which I discover a shriveled, dried legume. I hold the thing up between my paws. The mapmaker smiles consolingly and pats me on my head.

"What can be done," she says, repeating herself.

I stare into my paws, thinking desperately of something nice to say. Instead, I too start to weep.

Salacia, the sea nymph, has another riddle:

"I have seven names but no mother. She died in front of me."

"I speak every language and write from top to bottom, right to left."

"I like Simon & Garfunkel, the Supremes, all of Motown's catalog . . ."

"I can fit comfortably in a shoebox placed on the floor by a radiator."

"Around a lake with a magic sword in Hà Nội, my mother waits in the same way she waited at her father's ancestral home in a village. She raises one of her arms. She hides me behind that arm as a lieutenant of the US First Marine Division approaches us."

"What am I?"

Begin the THE BOOK OF FIRE.

Pearl

I SUPPOSE IT'S TIME. *My friends have been kind. I've considered burning this notebook with your letters. The plushie will have to go to Goodwill. The air conditioner? Maybe I'll keep it. I don't know. Depends on where the next job or residency takes me. I quit the sales job. I've also considered texting you about the garage door opener. But it's unbearable. Here it is, in the mail. My friend Ryan suggested I use it—every morning, stopping by your house and taking a shit in the middle of your garage. It made me laugh when he suggested this. Stone-faced. I wasn't angry then, at least anymore. But for a while I was. Angry, disappointed, mournful, empathetic. With the way that everything ended like a drive-by, and me tumbling out the passenger side. Kaput. I was numb and sad. Then Callisto got angry about it. And then my mom. I felt abandoned but didn't know how to name my distress because I was just thinking about the girls and you. So the anger came. And I quit my job. Finally. Tuesday is my last day. And I'm going to write. That's all.*

That's my secret world, for now, enough to keep you in, enough to keep you out, especially in the end. I have to protect my heart because it's soft and craves love and touch and domestic bliss, but it doesn't speak in the language that you speak; I know that, reading through your words. "Oh," Nina Simone had begged, too. Don't misunderstand this now. I was happy for those months. Trying to understand you. Trying to help you understand me and feeling the air taken out by my inadequacy to speak, especially when you went dark and started to shut me out. It was like I was on the other side of it, muffled and gesturing wildly, but no words except poetry came. When I wrote that poem on your porch while N and J played, especially J who helped in the writing of it, I was sad because the poem indicated a foretelling: as soon as the beloved (you) enters a poem, it signals the crumbling of a relationship. You started playing the keyboard inside. I wanted to die but didn't say enough, even to myself. So I occupied my body with sweeping the acorns so Pearl wouldn't get to them. That kept me alive somehow until I went home and thought: oh no, here it comes.

You have to know I tried. Like a trick pilot who keeps from passing out while doing a barrel roll in the air. You didn't see me bursting and screaming with joy. Shrieking up and down in the car with Callisto and Isaac, as I pointed out every spot: this was where we kissed, this is the photo of a sloth and the zoo, and on the merry-go-round where I was so nervous about vomiting in front of J, but at home, I wept on the phone with my mom about how this was it, I'm going to marry this man, and I'm going to have a family. But I wasn't going to be foolish and say this on your bed on that night those words escaped, just barely on my lips. I didn't know if you could hear them or not. I was going to marry you one day, and that was kept quiet, up until the last night we were together.

My boss sent me a wooden box of succulents a day after you called to break up with me. I didn't cry for a week.

Citation III: Mother of Exiles

SOMETIMES SHE WOULD ASK if I was made of fish and bone, but no, I had to take a hard look at myself. The seam came apart below my ears. The stuffing peeped out. I was undone. An object of fur: yes. A pattern: no. My intentions felt weary, sweeping a tiny paw in roundabout circles attached to the epoch of nature, vertiginous skeletons of earth, filaments of dust, salt, and plastic. My name was no longer the lowercase *p*, though I still slept on my stomach.

For years, Emi stared at our secret map, turning the sheet of paper over at her desk, running two fingers down the middle past a temple chamber to her heart. Below this image was the image of a lake. I counted several blocks of squares arranged into configurations of four. The only logical conclusion to *this* map was a passage of dreams.

For instance, a snow crane waded across the field.

Or maybe it was a golf cart.

We puttered across a dusty road in Saigon. Passing a doorway tucked into the alley near a teashop, we saw the actor Tony Leung about to light a cigarette.

No, the crane became a bird on fire, and that turned into our book of poetry.

The dream spun around, two-dimensional, ink on paper.

After closing the book, some molecules stuck to each other in the shape of a cubic fist. It wasn't easy for me, to be the projection of a tiny stuffed animal slapped onto the screen. It wasn't easy to be three years old perpetually staring into an empty row in front of us.

It was okay, at least, to skip some of the subtitles because I couldn't read, but I knew to observe five of seven tetrads falling down our stage.

The set design included a black sky, copper mines, and quadrants of reservoirs filled with pieces of coal. Strings of decorative lights ran from one end of our city to another. Suspended above the secret map, from inside a plane, Emi would tell me about the tinted bulbs of red and yellow scraping against upper layers of silt. This left behind curious marks on the ground, human boot prints dragging after one another. I stuck the tip of my paw into a shallow heel impression and sank right through.

To the left and the right was a terrible ocean. We zoomed away a few meters with our cameras. I clenched my jaw and sank deeper, deeper into the plane of grass. I wished for anything to strike me from the atmosphere, to help me vanish in a cloud of smoke. There was nothing left for my stuffing. I spindled out, eventually landing six miles west of the Adirondack Northway in New York. Here I found the largest river in that county, Kayaderosseras Creek. Fifteen miles north was a mountain range, Co-e'-sa, from the Algonquin word *cous*, meaning pine tree; this word landed in a confusing place inside my tiny Panda brain when I found the appearance of an uppercase 'C' in its regional dictionary. I shuddered, pressing the hard marble into my stomach, an infinite pin of stars as though filtered through a white bandage cloth.

Oxygen particles polluted what I knew of salt and acetate. We always arrived as comets at different moments but converged as a whole self, me and Emi, or Emi as Lua.

I couldn't fill my lungs, let alone find them. A deeper realization floated like a stack of newspapers torn to flurries of confetti. I tossed a thimble of uncooked rice out the window and regretted it almost immediately.

"We will not grow tired," the US president would say against his enemy in April 1965. I prepared myself for war, but who was I, the enemy?

PHILADELPHIA, JULY: I remember gazing at the Statue of Liberty in New York. I remember the dormitory room bleached into a stale, clinical wash. There were cots cramped with chains and sleeping mats. I sipped at a carton of apple juice and dropped it to the floor by accident. Emi squatted, dusted off the skinny straw, and drank from it, too.

At the Liberty Bell in Pennsylvania, we passed a green shadow forming clockwise around the pavilion. Before I could even stop myself, I felt my little body start to lunge toward the thing, the top of my head smashing against the side of the bell over and over again.

My left paw tore underneath its armpit. My pajamas had split up the back. The bell wouldn't budge, not even a sound.

Begin the BOOK OF EARTH.

Seed Quotes, References, and Performance Notes

"Roots make the commonality of errantry and exile, for in both instances roots are lacking. We must begin with that." —Édouard Glissant, *Poetics of Relation* (tr. Betsy Wing)

"The exiled: 'But if I don't have roots, why have my roots made me suffer so?'" —Trinh T. Minh Ha, *Framer Framed*

[Opening Tetris Section: "Daughter's Guide to Lavender"]

- ———. Cropped photograph of the author's mother at a refugee camp.
- Scene from *Hòn vọng phu* (tr. *La pierre de l'attente*), 1991. Dir. Trần Anh Hùng. Perf. Nu Yên-Khê Tran and Lâm Lê. Lazennec Tout Court.
- Aguilar-San Juan, Karin. 2009. *Little Saigons: Staying Vietnamese in America*. Minneapolis: University of Minnesota Press.
- Anzaldúa, Gloria E. 1987. *Borderlands/La Frontera*. San Francisco: Spinsters/Aunt Lute.
- Duncan, David. Quoted by Peter Meyer, 1993. *The Wall: A Day at the Vietnam Veterans Memorial*. New York, Wings Books.
- Cargill, Mary Terrell, and Jade Quang Huynh, eds. 2000. "Binh Le (pseudonym)." *Voices of Vietnamese Boat People: Nineteen Narratives of Escape and Survival*. London, McFarland.

Book of Wind

"No news picture in history has generated so much emotion around the world as that one."

—John F. Kennedy

- ———. Cropped photograph of the author's mother and her younger brother.
- Browne, Malcolm. Interview with Patrick Witty. *Time,* 2011.
- Browne, Malcolm. "Hanoi's People Still Curious and Friendly." *The New York Times,* 31 Mar. 1973.
- de Gaulle, Charles. "Statement of President de Gaulle at His Tenth Press Conference in Paris." French Press. 23 Jul. 1964.
- Hồ, Phạm. "Beautiful and Loving Days Gone By." *Mountain River: Vietnamese Poetry from the Wars, 1948-1993,* edited and translated by Kevin Bowen, Nguyen Ba Chung, and Bruce Weigl. Amherst, University of Massachusetts Press, 1998.

"1945, or Say Surrender"

- Halberstam, David. *The Making of a Quagmire: America and Vietnam During the Kennedy Era.* New York, Random House, 1965.
- Kennedy, John F. Quoted by Seth Jacobs in *Cold War Mandarin.* Lanham, Rowman & Littlefield Publishers, 2006.
- Sontag, Susan. *Trip to Hanoi.* New York, Farrar, Straus and Giroux, 1969.

"Bluegill"

- Ali, Agha Shahid. "Even the Rain." *Call Me Ishmael Tonight: A Book of Ghazals.* New York, W. W. Norton & Company, 2004.
- Bundy, McGeorge. National Security Action Memorandum No. 263, 11 October 1963. Cited in *The Pentagon Papers,* Gravel Edition, Volume 2. Boston, Beacon Press, 1971.
- Kennedy, John F. "Ich bin ein Berliner." Speech delivered 26 Jun. 1963, West Berlin.
- Leeloo in *The Fifth Element.* Directed by Luc Besson, 1997.

- McNamara, Robert. Memorandum for the President, "Vietnam Situation," 21 December 1963. Cited in *The Pentagon Papers*, Gravel Edition, Volume 3. Boston, Beacon Press, 1971.
- Nolting, Frederick. Quoted to President Kennedy in "South Viet Nam: To Liberate from Oppression." *Time*, 1962.
- Quỳnh, Xuân. "Summer." Translated by Carolyn Forché and Nguyen Ba Chung. *6 Vietnamese Poets*. Edited by Nguyen Ba Chung and Kevin Bowen. Willimantic, Curbstone Press, 2002.
- Taylor, Maxwell. Quoted from May 1975 interview by John M. Taylor in *General Maxwell Taylor: The Sword and the Pen*. Doubleday, 1989.
- Shakespeare, William. *The Tempest*. Cambridge, Harvard University Press, 1958.

"Wife of Plague"
- ———. Audio from *Cyclo* (tr. *Xích lô*). Dir. Trần Anh Hùng. Perf. Lê Văn Lộc. Gaumont, 1995. Feature Film.

"Jellyfish Dance"
- Rose, H. J. "Lua Mater: Fire, Rust, and War in Early Roman Cult." *The Classical Review*, 1922.
- Horace, *Odes* III, 4.
- Reference to Mariah Carey, "Without You."

Book of Water

"He's looking at me. I'm used to people looking at me." —Marguerite Duras, *The Lover* (tr. Barbara Bray)

I'll give you a roll of barbwire
A vine for this modern epoch
Climbing all over our souls
That's our love, take it, don't ask

I'll give you a car bomb
A car bomb exploding on a crowded street
On a crowded street exploding flesh and bones
That's our festival, don't you understand

I'll give you a savage war . . .
　　　　　　—Trần Dạ Từ, "Love Tokens" (tr. Linh Dinh)

"Nameless river, I was born sobbing, blue sky, vast earth, black stream water." —from *Cyclo*

"Black Stream Water"
- Lady Triệu. Quoted by Trần Trọng Kim in *Việt Nam sử lược (A Brief History of Vietnam)*. 1920.
- Morning Bulletin. "Soldier Breaks Silence on Torture." *The Courier Mail*, 17 Apr. 2010.
- Dương Thu Hương (tr. Phan Huy Đường and Nina McPherson), *Novel Without a Name*, Penguin, 1996.
- Wright, C. D. "The New American Ode." *The Antioch Review*, vol. 47, no. 3, 1989.
- Trần Anh Hùng. Interviewed by Lawrence Chua, *Bomb Magazine*, 1994.

"Errantries [2]"
- Scene from *Mùi đu đủ xanh (tr. The Scent of Green Papaya)*. Dir. Trần Anh Hùng. Perf. Nu Yên-Khê Tran. Président Films, 1993. Feature Film.
- Sōseki, Natsume. *Kusamakura (tr. The Three-Cornered World*, Alan Turney). 1906.

"The Six Illnesses"
- Saint Augustine. *City of God*, VII, 22.
- Ovid. *Metamorphoses*, Book 1.

"Salacia"

- Virgil. *Georgics.*
- An Thư. Quoted in *Surname Viet Given Name Nam.* Dir. Trinh T. Minh-Ha. Film, 1989.
- Morrison, Norman. Quoted in letter to wife, 1965.
- Morrison Welsh, Anne. Quoted in Fierke, K. M. *Political Self-Sacrifice: Agency, Body and Emotion in International Relations.* Cambridge University Press, 2012.
- Morrison, Toni. *The Bluest Eye.*
- Scott Camil, Sgt. (E-5), 1st Bn., 11th Marine Regt., 1st Marine Div., Winter Soldier Investigation [WSI] transcript, 1st Marine Div., p. 2.

Book of Fire

"Dark was the night, and cold the ground." —Blind Willie Johnson

"Or perhaps the records will never be intercepted. Perhaps no one in five billion years will ever come upon them. Five billion years is a long time." —Carl Sagan, *Pale Blue Dot*

"Errantries [3]"

- Takamura, Kōtarō. "The Final Battle for the Ryukyu Islands." (tr. Leith Morton)
- Miyazawa, Kazufumi. Quoted in *fRoots*, 2003.
- Lyrics to folk song "Shima Uta."

Book of Earth

"In addition to the use of herbicides, the Air Force drops 3 to 5 million 500- to 700-pound bombs on Vietnam from 1967–68, leaving ten to fifteen million large craters, as well as many millions of unexploded munitions that will continue to wound and kill children, farmers, and others who collect scrap metal to sell after the war. The amount of energy these bombing raids release is the equivalent of 328 Hiroshima A-bombs." —Fred A. Wilcox, *Scorched Earth*

Reference to Céline Dion, "My Heart Will Go On."

The Temple Chamber
"Rather, many moved very slowly, with much confusion, ambivalence, and even misgivings, uncertain about what they were walking toward or what they were walking from."
> —Yến Lê Espiritu, *Body Counts:*
> *The Vietnam War and Militarized Refuge(es)*

"Jiggly!" —Jigglypuff

Sophia Terazawa is the author of two poetry collections with Deep Vellum, *Winter Phoenix* and *Anon*, along with chapbooks, *I AM NOT A WAR* (Essay Press) and *Correspondent Medley* (Factory Hollow Press), winner of the 2018 Tomaž Šalamun Prize. Forthcoming in 2026 is a third poetry book, *Oracular Maladies* (Noemi Press). *Tetra Nova* is her first novel.

398